Orland Park Public Library
14921 Ravinia Avenue
Orland Park, Illinois 60462
708-428-5100

ORLAND PARK PUBLIC LIBRARY
14921 Ravinia Avenue
Orland Park, Illinois 60462
708-428-5100

JUN   2010

OUT OF TURNS

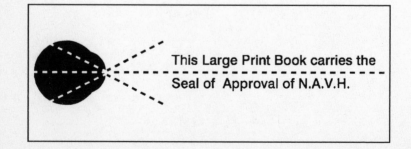

This Large Print Book carries the
Seal of Approval of N.A.V.H.

OUT OF TURNS

ANNE G. FAIGEN

THORNDIKE PRESS
A part of Gale, Cengage Learning

GALE
CENGAGE Learning·

Detroit • New York • San Francisco • New Haven, Conn • Waterville, Maine • London

ORLAND PARK PUBLIC LIBRARY

FAIGEN ANNE G.

 GALE
CENGAGE Learning

Copyright © 2009 by Anne G. Faigen.
Thorndike Press, a part of Gale, Cengage Learning.

ALL RIGHTS RESERVED

All of the characters in the book are fictitious, and any resemblance to actual persons, living or dead, is purely coincidental.
Thorndike Press® Large Print Clean Reads.
The text of this Large Print edition is unabridged.
Other aspects of the book may vary from the original edition.
Set in 16 pt. Plantin.

LIBRARY OF CONGRESS CATALOGING-IN-PUBLICATION DATA

Faigen, Anne G.
    Out of turns / by Anne G. Faigen.
        p. cm. — (Thorndike Press large print clean reads)
    ISBN-13: 978-1-4104-2631-4
    ISBN-10: 1-4104-2631-9
    1. Female friendship—Fiction. 2. Americans—Taiwan—Fiction.
    3. Missing persons—Fiction. 4. Taiwan—Fiction. 5. Large type books.
    I. Title.
    PS3556.A32325O98 2010
    813'.54—dc22   2010008039

Published in 2010 by arrangement with Thomas Bouregy & Co., Inc.

Printed in the United States of America
1 2 3 4 5 6 7 14 13 12 11 10

For Mark: my center, steadfast through
all the twists and turns

CHAPTER ONE

"Come in, please."

Like the nameplate with its precise letter-ing — ELVIRA SMITHSON, HEAD MISTRESS — the voice was smooth and well-polished. Figgy Newton tried to sound the same. Despite college and graduate school, she sometimes reverted to the Iowa farm girl, self-conscious and uneasy in the presence of authority.

Shadyhill's principal looked up from her place behind her antique desk, its pristine surface uncluttered by a computer or stacks of paper, and smiled. Dr. Smithson, like the others at the private school in suburban Philadelphia, liked the young woman stand-ing awkwardly before her. She was friendly, effective in her classroom, and popular with students.

"Please, Hazel, do sit down. If you were any stiffer, you might fracture."

Despite her fondness for the teacher, the

7

head mistress couldn't bring herself to call her Figgy as everyone else did. It may have been her preferred nickname, but to the head of the school, it seemed undignified.

"How are your classes going?"

Figgy's face lit up. "Great. This group of fifth-graders is the best yet."

"I believe you say that every new term."

But her expression changed from benign to solemn as she cleared her throat and got to the point of the meeting.

"I read your request for extra time off at the end of winter break. You said you'd be traveling out of the country and would return with new teaching ideas and materials to share with your students. Shadyhill doesn't usually grant an extension after our holiday leave, but you mentioned special circumstances. Those would be . . . ?"

Figgy took a deep breath. *Come on,* she prodded herself, *you've rehearsed this speech in your head for days, so just say it.*

"I know the school's policy, and I respect the reasons, but I'm going to Taiwan and I hoped —"

"Taiwan? Is Tessa Kalen involved in this venture?"

Here it comes, thought Figgy. Tessa, her apartment-mate and best friend, had been a successful, admired teacher at Shadyhill.

But on an impulse, she had decided to work in Asia. On short notice, she resigned her position notice, alienating the school's trustees and administrators, disappointing her students and their parents, and causing no small resentment within the faculty.

The gossips among the teachers muttered that, because she came from a moneyed Boston clan, she could abandon her responsibilities without a qualm and do whatever she pleased. Rich and spoiled, they said, forgetting Tessa's kindnesses to them and her generosity. Earlier admiration had turned sour and mean-spirited.

"I'm going at Tessa's invitation, but I've always planned to visit Asia, and this is a great opportunity. I'll return with new perspectives to share with my students and bring back lots of pictures, maps, and other materials. I can e-mail them my observations during the extra days I'm away. I'd expect the time to be deducted from my salary, of course."

Dr. Smithson regarded her. Fingers were intertwined on her desk, her knuckles pale against the raised veins and tan spots on her hands. The ticking of the old-fashioned clock on the bookshelf behind her was loud in the silence. *If only Tessa hadn't caused such a furor,* Figgy thought, *there would be*

*none of this resentment and hesitation about
my asking for extra leave.*

"I know how conscientious you are; you
don't have to convince me of your sincerity.
But I needn't remind you of our disappointment in Tessa and her cavalier disregard for
her responsibilities at Shadyhill. My concern
is that she may influence you to opt for
adventure over obligation."

"You needn't worry about that. Teaching
fifth-graders is all the adventure I can
handle."

The head mistress smiled but her heart
wasn't in it.

Before she could respond, Figgy rushed
into her prepared speech: how she would
create a new world cultures unit, share it
with other faculty, involve some of the
Asian-American parents of Shadyhill students, collaborate with the music and art
departments to bring back recordings,
museum materials, all kinds of enrich-
ment —

"Obviously, you've thought this through
and are determined to visit Tessa, so I won't
attempt to stop you. Unlike your friend, you
have a strong sense of responsibility. I shall
depend on that. Let's assume that you'll
return from holiday recess no later than
January tenth."

Elvira Smithson rose, leaned across the desk, and shook Figgy's hand.

"Have a fine trip, and do take care of yourself."

Dr. Smithson sat back down and opened a desk drawer. Figgy knew she was dismissed. Returning to her classroom, she resisted the urge to pound on doors along the corridor and shout, "I'm going to the other side of the world!" *Good thing I teach ten-year-olds,* she thought. *I often react on their level.*

The weeks before Shadyhill's winter vacation were too busy to dwell on her upcoming travels. After e-mailing Tessa the news and contacting the airline to verify her return date, Figgy called her parents. She explained that, as much as she'd like to see them, there would be no visit to Iowa until spring. They knew about her hoped-for trip to Asia and understood, but Figgy was certain they were disappointed. She was their only child, and her parents hadn't been happy when she finished school and chose to stay in the East rather than teach in Iowa.

Her college experience convinced Figgy she was happiest living in a big city. When her parents visited, she took them sightseeing in Philadelphia and, once, to Manhattan for a weekend. They gamely assured her it was all very interesting — and she knew they couldn't wait to get back home. She'd teased them about how some rogue traveling salesman must have gotten into the family gene pool, reappearing in her DNA. They were not amused. Her parents and Elvira Smithson would easily bond.

Unlike the adults, her students were excited about her trip, their enthusiasm spilling over into sporadic rowdiness. Some of it was due to the approaching break from school, but she tried to keep them focused. They studied maps of Taiwan, went online to learn about the country's history, and created posters to illustrate the stories they made up about their teacher's upcoming travels.

On the last day of school, Daisy Tang and her cousin, Emily, brought pastries filled with sweet bean paste to demonstrate the kinds of desserts Miss Newton would be eating. Their classmates grimaced when they saw the thick red filling inside the cookies, but when they tasted the pastries frowns turned to smiles. By the end of the day, Daisy and Emily had taught their classmates to say *delicious* in Mandarin.

The morning of her flight, Figgy arrived at the airport even earlier than recommended, deciding that pacing in her apartment and double-checking to be sure she hadn't forgotten anything was making her more anxious than excited. The flight schedule would take her from Philadelphia to Chicago, and then to Hong Kong. Tessa planned to meet her at the Hong Kong airport; they would stay overnight in the city and spend a day there before flying to Kaoshiung together.

"You have to see Hong Kong," she'd said in her e-mail, complete with caps and exclamation points. Figgy could hear the echoes of Tessa's voice in her head. "It's a FABULOUS city. We'll shop and eat and join the crowds on Nathan Road. Wait till you see the mix of people — like a rainbow. And the harbor at sunset, when the city lights come on! MAGICAL! I can't let you just get on the plane to Taiwan and miss all that."

At O'Hare Airport, Figgy plowed through the crowds, following the signs to the international section. At times like these she realized she was still a midwestern farm girl, intimidated by the surges of people, the confusion of signs, languages, and conversations buzzing around her. The noise of loudspeaker announcements made her head ache. *If this mild uproar gets to me,* she thought, *how will I handle the noise and melee of Asian crowds?* Forcing her doubts aside, she reminded herself that Tessa would be there to guide her. With her own chronically malfunctioning sense of direction, that was comforting to remember.

After what seemed an eternity, Figgy found the international terminal and the gate to the plane for Hong Kong. When the boarding announcement came she gratefully made her way to her window seat, then watched other passengers filing along the aisle. Most were business types, interspersed with families probably visiting relatives or traveling to holiday celebrations. There were jeans-clad young people hoisting backpacks into overhead bins, then carrying their laptops to their seats. Figgy felt like her students, released from school into a much bigger world than she ordinarily occupied.

She was so busy watching the stream of fellow passengers that she nearly missed the one who stopped at her row, checked the seat numbers, then arranged his carry-on next to hers in the bin above them. He, too, carried a laptop but, unlike the jeans crowd, wore well-tailored slacks, a black turtleneck sweater, and a tweed jacket. After removing the jacket and folding it over his carry-on, he sat down beside her.

"Getting there's half the fun, isn't it?" he

said, smiling at her before he opened the slim briefcase he carried with his laptop.

"I'm grateful to be on my way," she answered. "I wasn't sure I'd make it when I got off my earlier flight."

"Your first trip out of O'Hare?"

Figgy nodded. "And to Asia. I've never been further from home than Canada."

"Where's home?"

She liked the way he seemed genuinely interested, blue eyes alert and trained on her. His hair was lighter than hers, medium brown and neatly groomed. He probably never struggled with knots and tangles the way she did after each shampoo.

"I live near Philadelphia now, but I grew up in Iowa."

"That makes us both midwesterners. Chicago's my hometown, but I never get used to the craziness of O'Hare, no matter how many times I fly out of here. Are you vacationing in Hong Kong?"

"I'm on vacation, but I'll only be in Hong Kong for a short time. I'm visiting a friend in Taiwan."

"That's where I'm going too. I'll be working in a big industrial city in the south, called Kaoshiung."

"What a coincidence! That's where my friend is teaching English at an insurance company there."

"I guess it's true what they say about a small world." He extended his hand. "I'm Will Bowers and I work at a steel plant near the city. They have a consulting contract with my company, so I go back and forth on a regular basis. Will you stay long in Kaoshiung?"

"About two weeks. Then I go back to my students. I teach fifth grade at a small private school near Philadelphia. My name is Hazel Newton, but my friends call me Figgy."

When her seatmate smiled, she said, "It's better than Nutty, the other possibility and even worse than Hazel."

"I think you'll like Kaoshiung," he said. "The people are friendly, even without speaking English, and the place has grown from a sleepy port town to a prosperous, bustling city with skyscrapers and fancy shops."

"I'm used to bustle and fancy stores. I do a lot of browsing and window shopping when I go into Philadelphia. I was hoping for something a little more, well, storybook-Asia. Folksy."

He smiled. *Quite a nice smile,* Figgy thought.

"You can still find local markets, street

vendors, and old folks doing Tai Chi in the park. But your friend will probably take you to the posh new restaurants and department stores."

He looked down at his briefcase and laptop. "Now, if you'll excuse me, I have to get to work or I won't have answers to the questions my Chinese colleagues will be firing at me."

He smiled again and unzipped his briefcase. By the time their plane took off, Will Bowers' focus was on the stack of printouts in his lap. Figgy stared out the window and watched the land drop away beneath them.

Despite the thrumming of the aircraft transporting her to a part of the world as remote to her as the fantasy novels she liked to read, Figgy could hardly believe this trip was happening. Her life had always been so ordinary — *normal* was probably a better word — and she liked it that way. The only child of a dairy farmer and a homemaker, she'd grown up in a community where everybody visited neighbors, surrounded by several generations of relatives. Until a few years ago, after some petty thievery, doors were left unlocked and people dropped by unannounced to be fed as well as probed for the latest gossip.

When she went east to the University of

Pennsylvania, Figgy told Tessa Kalen, one of her new friends, that her upbringing was like a fifties television sitcom, with strict rules for dating. Tessa laughed at what she assumed was exaggeration, but Figgy's description was close to reality.

During the summer of her junior year, Figgy enrolled in a film class at New York University. Living in New York City and dazzled by its myriad attractions, she'd resolved to leave the Midwest and seek a teaching job near an eastern city. It was during that same summer semester that she'd also experienced her first real heartbreak.

One of her classmates, Jay Trenze, had transferred from a Rhode Island college to study film. Jay was different from any of the boys she'd dated before. Carelessly dressed in his jeans, baggy T-shirts, and sockless track shoes with trailing laces, he sat next to her on the first day of class. His running commentary on their boring instructor, done in quiet undertones that belied the sardonic criticisms, nearly made her laugh aloud.

Figgy looked away from the window when Will gently tapped her shoulder.

"Dinner's coming, so you'll want to put your tray down."

"Thanks. I hadn't noticed."

Without commenting on her obvious distraction, he asked the attendant for wine to accompany dinner, then turned to her. "May I order some for you? The momentous occasion of your first visit to Asia deserves a toast."

"That would be nice. I brought a bag full of books about Taiwan to read on this flight and I haven't opened one."

"No matter. Just keep an open mind and you'll learn as you go. I think that's the best way to experience a new place." He opened their wine and poured a glass for her and himself.

"Here's to your great adventure. *Gumbai!*" Will sipped from his glass, as did Figgy.

"What was that you said?" She was slightly disconcerted by the intensity of his gaze.

"Gumbai? It's a Chinese toast, a little like 'cheers.' You'll hear it a lot if you share any meals with the local people."

"We probably will. The person I'm visiting makes friends more easily than anyone I know. Her kindergarten students loved her, and I imagine her new colleagues feel the same."

"Anyone who can make little kids cooperate on a daily basis has my admiration."

"Do you have children?" Figgy asked.

He shook his head. "With my limited

patience, it's probably just as well."

Figgy sipped her wine between bites of the ginger chicken and rice on the tray before her.

"It's easier to be patient with children than it is with some adults," she said.

"That's probably true," Will answered. "Especially adults who behave like children having tantrums. Unfortunately, they sometimes sit across from me at conference tables."

"I guess I'm lucky to deal with childish behavior where it's appropriate. But the friend I'm visiting has traveled all over the world and knows how to connect with all kinds of people. I envy Tessa her worldliness."

Will regarded her again, then poured more wine for them both. "Sometimes that's a mixed blessing. Too much sophistication can produce a cynical world view. I envy you and your fresh approach to new experiences."

"I never thought of it that way, but thanks for the vote of confidence."

Will took a last sip of his wine, handed their dinner trays to the flight attendant, and opened his laptop. "Back to work and all that wearying world experience."

Figgy pushed the tray table back into

place and thought about reading, but turned instead to her darkening window. Jay Trenze had a world view too, she thought, as she remembered all those nights listening to him describe his plans to make movies, travel the world, and collect awards for his brilliant independent films. She soon learned his more immediate goal was charming numerous girls on campus, with seduction as his reward. When she hesitated about adding her name to his list of conquests, those long talks far into the night evaporated. It had taken a while to get over the breakup.

Despite her excitement about arriving in Hong Kong, she must have slept more deeply than she'd expected, because the next thing she experienced was a gentle tap from her seatmate.

"You'll want to see this. We're getting ready to land at Kai Tek."

Peering through her window, Figgy saw rows of lights marking the runways, but the rest was darkness.

"The runways are surrounded by water. If we were landing in daylight you'd be impressed with the pilot's skill."

"In the dark, I'm grateful for it." Her hands gripped the armrests of her seat. "This is the part of flying I don't like."

"You should plan to travel more often so that you could get used to it."

"On my salary, I'm more likely to get used to traveling by bus."

Will smiled, putting aside the newspaper with the crossword puzzle he'd finished. "That's a bit limiting, but as I recall from my college travels, you meet a lot of interesting characters."

"Hasn't happened yet. Last summer, I decided to take the bus to Ohio to visit a friend. A middle-aged guy with a supersized belly sat next to me, fell asleep as soon as the bus moved, and snored in my ear the whole trip."

After a smooth landing, the plane taxied toward the terminal. Will lifted down his carry-on and hers.

"Expect a mob scene inside. This place bustles, no matter what time of day or night."

"Good. It'll help me stay awake until I meet Tessa."

"It's a challenge finding time for sleep in Hong Kong. No matter how often I come here, the city never fails to fascinate. It's the best place there is for people-watching."

"Knowing my friend, I expect she'll be moving too fast to do much of that."

Will extended his hand.

"I have to rush to make my Taiwan connection. Have a great vacation, Figgy. Who knows — maybe we'll see each other in Kaoshiung."

Figgy returned his handshake. His fingers, surrounding hers, were warm. No harm in hoping to see him again.

"Good luck with your job, Will. I finally lucked out with a seatmate."

"Me too," he said and, with a wave, hurried off.

Resisting the fatigue dragging at her limbs, she tried to move faster, despite the crowds surging around her. Will had been right. The din of voices in a cacophony of languages was overwhelming. Adding to the mix were announcements in Cantonese, French, English, and other languages she didn't recognize. Men in turbans and dashikis and women in saris hurried past others garbed entirely in black, with the face coverings of devout Muslims. People pushed past, dodging bearded men in black frock coats and others wearing jeans and T-shirts much like hers. She saw a few travelers who looked like they'd just stepped off fashion-show runways.

Taking her place in line, Figgy waited, clutching her passport, Taiwan ticket, and her Pennsylvania driver's license, people-watching as her line crept forward.

Finally out of the restricted area, she scanned the crowd again, hoping to see Tessa in the blur of faces accompanied by the relentless roar assailing her ears. Unbidden, the memory of a childhood Sunday school class popped into her now-aching head. Mrs. Perkins, whose family lived on a farm near theirs, had intoned a Bible story about the Tower of Babel where no one understood what anyone else was saying and the tower came tumbling down. Or was that the Battle of Jericho? Figgy shook her head, trying to clear it and ignore the pain gripping her skull.

"Figgy! Figgy, over here!"

At last, she thought, peering in the direction of that welcome sound. And there was Tessa Kalen, grinning, shouting, and waving a huge bouquet of roses.

Hugs exchanged and luggage retrieved, the friends waited outside the terminal for their turn to claim a cab.

"How was the trip? I can't tell you how glad I am that you're here. Did Dr. Smithson give you a hard time about the extra vacation days? You look fantastic — not even daunted by the long flight. And who was that good-looking guy I saw you talking with before you got into line? I was standing right behind the glass panel where we wait for arrivals and saw you together. Have you already made a conquest, even before you landed?"

Each time she tried to answer a question, Tessa peppered her with three others. Figgy started laughing. Clearly her friend hadn't been changed by thousands of miles' distance from home.

"Do you speed talk like this with your students? You'll train them to be the fastest English-speakers in Taiwan."

Tessa joined in her laughter. It was always easy for her to laugh at herself. Figgy admired that. She wished she was more like her friend instead of so self-conscious.

"When . . . I . . . teach . . . I . . . am . . . careful . . . and . . . deliberate." Tessa's dragged-out monotone made them both laugh harder.

Settled in a cab, Figgy rested her head against the white doily adorning the top of the back seat. "I'm so tired, I think I'm getting spacey. How far is the hotel?"

"Not very. We'll drop off your luggage and go for a little walk. It'll make you feel better."

"Are you kidding? All I want is to be horizontal in a nice, soft bed."

"Not yet. You have to see Hong Kong at

night. It's spectacular, with the lights glowing on the harbor and the crowds. People rarely sleep in this city."

"Can I start a new trend? Later, when I'm conscious, I'll be glad you haven't changed at all, but right now you sound demented. I can't tell what day or time it is, my legs feel like Silly Putty, and you want to go for a walk?"

"Precisely. You need to stretch those calf muscles. Being out and about will help you adapt to the new time zone."

She turned to the window. "Oh, good. That's our hotel up ahead."

Tessa paid the driver, picked up both of Figgy's bags, and propelled her inside.

"You rest here in the lobby in one of those big, comfy chairs. I'll drop off your luggage and the flowers in our room, and we'll go out again. You'll see, it's exactly what you need. Are you hungry? We can get some food along the way. Now, just relax, I'll be right back."

Figgy glared at Tessa's disappearing back and slumped in the chair. Her friend was a force of nature — no point trying to fight it. From beneath drooping eyelids she could see that the hotel lobby was only slightly less frenetic than the airport. The people at the registration desk were a microcosm of the United Nations. Young children chased each other through the lobby while others peeked out from behind their mothers' skirts. Maybe Tessa wasn't exaggerating. People don't sleep in Hong Kong, even in the middle of the night.

Or was it the middle of the night? Who knew, she thought, eyelids threatening to close again.

"Okay. Up and at 'em." Tessa was back, using her let's-get-organized voice as she took Figgy's arm to hasten her separation from the chair.

Soon after they began walking, Figgy had to admit Tessa was right. She did feel better, picking up her stride as they moved through the warm, moist night air, redolent with aromas from the food stands lining the sidewalks.

"No way," Tessa said when Figgy stopped at a stand to admire crusty chunks of meat on wooden skewers, their barbecued spiciness making her stomach rumble. "You don't have the right bugs in your gut to eat street food and not get sick."

"Thanks for the mouthwatering explanation," Figgy groused. They moved on, stopping to peer into shop windows filled with pearls and diamonds, silk scarves, and leather designer bags.

"Those are the real thing," Tessa said as they studied two huge purses, their reptile skins and metal clasps shining under the display lights. "But you can buy amazing copies at stands in the Night Market. I'll show you when we get there, but let's find a place for dinner first."

"Dinner? I thought I'd be eating breakfast."

"Doesn't matter what you call it, silly. Besides, until you get used to this time zone, everything will seem a bit confusing."

"That's one of the few understatements I've ever heard from you."

"Next you'll accuse me of being inscrutable, like those detectives our parents watched in the awful, clichéd movies about China."

"You have many interesting qualities, Tessa, but I would never call you inscrutable. More like impulsive, but endearing."

"Endearing's not the word Dr. Smithson would choose. You have to fill me in on all the Shadyhill news and gossip."

"Could we eat first? I think I'm hungry. Or maybe only sleepy and jet-lagged. I guess I can't identify what I'm feeling, but let's try food."

Tessa stopped in front of a large window and peered inside. Figgy followed her gaze.

It was a restaurant, with most of the tables occupied. She watched, fascinated, as a woman wearing a necklace of gold links and a black dress that clung to her curves picked up noodles with her chopsticks, several strands at a time. She was elegant and impeccably groomed but she slurped them down exactly like Figgy's ten-year-olds, who'd be reprimanded for rude manners in the school dining room.

Tessa, meanwhile, finished studying the menu posted on the glass door, its selections described in Chinese characters.

"This looks fine. Let's go in."

Figgy tried to eat the rice and ground pork stewed in soy sauce that Tessa had ordered, but kept dropping food from her chopsticks. She'd been practicing at home, with mixed results. She looked around, but the other diners were intent on their own food and companions and paid no attention to her ineptitude.

As usual, Tessa barely touched her food, too busy asking questions. She'd only nibbled at meals when they shared an apartment, although she tolerated her housemate's cooking attempts, always willing to try her latest, often failed, kitchen experiment. Figgy sometimes muttered that it wasn't fair: Tessa could exist on junk food snacks and still look trim, while her own calibrated chocolate indulgences showed up immediately on the bathroom scale.

When she finished attempting coherent responses to Tessa's barrage of questions, Figgy declared it was her turn.

"You haven't said much in your e-mails about life outside of work. What do you do for fun?"

"Work is fun. The hours are long. I often have dinner in the company dining room, then stay afterward to tutor employees who request evening lessons. When I get home it's usually late, so I read or listen to music and go to bed."

Tessa saw the expression on Figgy's face.

"I know that doesn't sound like your friend, the party girl. But life is so different here. The people I teach, especially the guys, like to laugh and tell jokes, but they're really serious about work and learning. They want to get ahead so English fluency is important to them, especially if they have international clients. Most of them hope to head company branches in London or San Francisco. They compete for European assignments, so even the unmarried ones don't do much partying. Sometimes we all go out to a club to hear some music they like or to sing — they really love karaoke — but that's about it.

They don't go to movies or restaurants much, the way Americans do. They like bars, but mostly to discuss business over their beers."

Having eaten as much as she could manage with her chopsticks, Figgy put them down on the small dish next to her bowl and rubbed her achy wrist. She hoped using chopsticks would get easier.

"You can always ask for a fork, you know," Tessa said, rolling her eyes in a way that always amused her friend. "They have forks and knives in Kaoshiung too."

"No. I'm planning to immerse myself in the local culture."

Tessa laughed.

"Be prepared to drink lots of tea, pick up rice with your chopsticks, and memorize the Mandarin names for a dozen kinds of beer."

"Mmm. Maybe not that local. But, seriously, what do you do when you're not at Serenity Insurance?"

"A lot of the time I work on Saturdays. Everyone comes in, at least for a half day. I often stay longer with students who request extra tutoring. And sometimes on Sundays I go sightseeing with Ken."

Figgy waited while Tessa paid for their food, blinking as they reemerged on the sidewalk. The neon signs and flashing advertising lights made the outdoors brighter than the restaurant had been.

"Now we're getting to the real story. Who's Ken?"

"Kenneth Chu. We've become good friends. He takes me on outings on his motorbike, leaving his fancy car at home. That's how most people get around in Kaoshiung. The roads are so congested, cars are a nuisance. On a motorbike a driver can zip around the cars and pedestrians and get to places faster. Whole families ride them. Wait until you see Mom, Dad, and the kiddies all clinging to their bike as they cruise along the highway."

"I didn't ask for a traffic report. Tell me about your relationship with Ken."

"You've been watching too many lawyer shows. You sound like you're cross-examining a witness."

"Whatever works."

"There's no 'relationship' in the way you mean. I'll tell you about Ken on our way to Victoria Peak. It's my favorite place on the island. We won't be able to go at sundown, which is the best time to be there, because we're leaving tomorrow, but you'll get some of the same effect when we get to the top.

"After the ferry, we'll board the funicular

at the tram station. When we get to the peak, I'll explain about Ken Chu."

On the tram ride to the mountaintop, Figgy could only stare. Their car was crowded; people boarded at each stop on the way up. As they rose, neighborhoods changed from modest to elaborate. When the funicular climbed past increasingly larger homes, Tessa whispered, "Real estate here makes Manhattan apartment prices seem like bargains. Wait till you pass the mansions on Victoria Peak. A glimpse is mostly what you get because they're screened by elaborate landscaping."

Emerging from the tram station, Tessa led her lagging friend to an outlook far above Hong Kong's harbor. Figgy thought she might be half-dreaming the fairy-tale scene below. Buildings taller than any she'd ever imagined climbed skyward from the island. Reflected lights danced on the water of the harbor. In the surrounding darkness Hong Kong floated, a glittering colony in some magical fantasy.

"The perfect time to be here is at dusk," Tessa said, smiling at Figgy's open-jawed wonder. "As the sun is setting, lights begin to come on all over the island until the whole city glows in a blaze of color, with the mountains outlined in the distance.

"The first time I saw it I was a teenager, traveling with my family. Dad came to Hong Kong often on business and brought us up here to a restaurant he liked. We sat near the windows and watched the sun set and the lights come on. Even Zach, who usually inhaled food, stopped eating long enough to gape at the sight."

Tessa rarely mentioned her younger brother. Figgy turned to look at her, but her expression hadn't changed. Like Figgy, she was studying the scene below.

Zach, Figgy knew, was the youngest of the Kalen children. With two older sisters, he'd been the pampered one, his socialite mother's favorite. And when Tessa's father, a lawyer who started his own securities firm and was rarely at home, did find time for family, Zach was the one receiving most of his attention.

When he was fifteen, Zach borrowed a motorcycle from an older friend, sped around a curve near the family's home and lost control, flying through a fence and down a hillside. His life ended in a horrendous, fiery crash. Tessa was away at school when word came.

Everything changed after Zach's death, Tessa told her one rainy Saturday night when the two of them, bemoaning the lack of men in their lives, shared too much wine and told family stories.

Tessa's parents, in their grief and pain, blamed each other. Her mother accused her husband of being too involved in his work, too distant from his family. He retorted that she'd been overly indulgent with Zach, spoiling him and neglecting her daughters. They divorced a year after their son's death.

"Did you feel neglected when you were growing up?" Figgy had asked, thinking of her own parents' doting attention.

"Not really. If I did, I thought of it as freedom. As long as I was running with the 'right' crowd — the children of my parents' friends and our neighbors — my mother was fine with that. What she didn't know — or chose not to — was that a lot of those kids were experimenting with drugs and alcohol."

Figgy was silent, not sure how to respond.

"I can guess what you're thinking, Miss Wholesome Middle America. Yes, I did want to fit in with my so-called friends, like most teenagers, but I soon decided I didn't like their values, no matter how cool they pretended to be. So I dropped out of the party crowd. It was harder for Maggie."

Figgy had come to know Tessa's sister when she visited Mersdale. Maggie wasn't as pretty as Tessa and was also quieter than her sister. Figgy liked her quick sense of humor and her gentle manner.

"Our mother used to push Maggie to be more social, more 'outgoing,' as she put it. Besides the obligatory lessons we had, the tennis and golf, swimming and riding, she made Maggie go to some stupid charm school to make her more 'poised.' Maggie has more poise and style than most of my mother's shallow friends, but she gave my sister a first class case of insecurity. Luckily, with some help, she got over it."

Figgy knew that Maggie Kalen had a breakdown during her first year of college. She'd gotten counseling, transferred to another school, and was now working for an architectural firm in Florida. She was happily married to a marine biologist.

"Maggie turned out to be the best of us," Tessa had said, pouring herself more wine. "She knew what she wanted, learned to ignore my mother's interference, and found both a career and a man she loves. Who could ask for anything better?"

Figgy understood that Tessa was still searching for what would make her happy. After Zach died she transferred from Vassar to Penn, lived in Figgy's dorm and became her good friend. She told Figgy she'd decided to major in elementary education to spite her parents, who thought it was too ordinary and servile a career choice. When Figgy applied to Shadyhill, Tessa decided to do the same.

She quickly distinguished herself as a skillful and devoted teacher. Yet, outside the classroom, Tessa was restless and distracted, searching for the kind of completeness her sister had found.

After three years at Shadyhill, Tessa chose to look for other ways to satisfy her restless spirit. So here they were, on a peak above Hong Kong harbor. For Figgy, the grounded midwesterner who believed teaching was her calling, it was all like a dream. Her sleep-starved grogginess added to the sense of unreality.

"It's like a fairy tale, the land of lights," Figgy said, staring at the glitter stretching beneath them.

Tessa laughed.

"Here you are, looking at one of the most glamorous sights in the world, and you see a child's fantasy land."

"I guess it's the naiveté you needle me about." If she sounded grumpy, too bad.

A hug from Tessa assuaged her feelings.

"It's not naiveté, it's a gift of wonder. One of the things I love about you. Now, we better go to the hotel, so you'll be awake for more wonder tomorrow."

Figgy didn't notice much about their trip back. In a stupor, she fell into bed.

CHAPTER TWO

The next morning, after a shower, she felt alive again. Tessa was already up and dressed in white slacks and a navy blue shirt. In the college apartment they had shared, Tessa was always slow to awaken, making their last minute rush to classes a habitual source of stress for Figgy.

"Come on, sleepyhead," Tessa said. "I've been waiting forever for you to open those big brown eyes. We only have one day in Hong Kong, so get moving. Chop, chop."

In the hotel restaurant, when the smiling waiter arrived to take their order, Figgy had barely looked at the menu.

"Never mind, it's mostly in Cantonese." Tessa handed the menus to the server. "We'll have Congee please, big bowls. And tea."

When he left Figgy glowered at her friend.

"I was hoping for bacon and eggs. And toast. I have no idea what that was you

39

ordered."

"Didn't your parents tell you when you're in Rome, do as the Romans, or however that old bromide goes?"

"Since they never expected to be in Rome, or nearly anywhere else outside of Iowa, the subject didn't come up. What is this Congee you ordered?"

"It's like rice porridge. Asian soul food. Supposed to cure everything — fever, headaches. Ken Chu says it's great for hangovers and he should know."

"You were going to tell me about him."

Tessa poured golden fluid from the pot-bellied metal vessel their server delivered to their table. She raised her blue porcelain cup, inhaled the flower fragrance, and drank.

"My supermarket tea bags never produce a drink like this," Figgy said after tasting her tea.

"It's jasmine, my favorite."

"What about Ken Chu?"

"He's the boss's son and has most of the spoiled traits you'd expect. Very full of himself, but fun to be with. Great sense of humor, nimble mind. He was my first student at Serenity Insurance. He'd gone to college in California but he was still having trouble with some idioms and the way to string together English words. I think what he mostly learned in the States was how to party."

"Is he still honing that skill?"

"As much as he can with the limited opportunities in his hometown. It irritates his father to no end. Mr. Chu is very dignified and serious, unlike the younger guys. Most of them have a great sense of fun. They like to tell jokes, tease each other, go out for a night of beer and music when they can. Although he smiles when he's pleased, I haven't seen Mr. Chu laugh out loud in all the time I've been in Taiwan."

"So what's the deal with you and the boss' son?" Figgy, between sips of tea, kept looking in the direction the waiter had gone. Despite her late meal, in what felt like the middle of last night, she was hungry.

"No deal. We're just friends. But Ken's been great in helping me get settled in Kaoshiung. He made arrangements for my apartment at the hotel."

"You live in a hotel?"

"It's the most convenient place. I can walk to my office, there's a tiny kitchen if I want to cook, and apartments are hard to find in the part of the city where, without a car, I need to live. It's cozy and comfortable, you'll see. Oh, good, here comes our breakfast."

Figgy watched as the waiter placed steaming bowls in front of them. Their contents looked like the cereal her mother used to make her eat before she went off to school on cold mornings. Colorless and a little watery. She wondered if she could still order eggs.

"Dig in," Tessa said, spooning up some from her bowl. "This is guaranteed to fix all maladies. There's sugar on the table if you want to add that. Or some grated ginger, which is great for stomach upsets."

She tasted the Congee and tried to squelch the face she nearly made, like the expression she sometimes saw on students in the school's dining room.

"Is this what I'm going to have every morning? I wish I'd brought along some peanut butter."

"Picky, picky," Tessa said, spooning up her breakfast with apparent enjoyment. "Think of it as health food, like the stuff you kept foisting on me in our apartment."

"So this is revenge?"

"No, silly, part of your introduction to local culture. You can get eggs and toast any time in the dining room of our hotel."

"That's a relief," Figgy said, picking up her spoon and trying again. A few more attempts and she gave up, concentrating on the tea.

"Ready to go?" Tessa, who was finished, said. "We have a lot to squeeze in to our day in Hong Kong."

With Tessa guiding her through throngs of people packed together on the sidewalks, Figgy barely managed to look around.

"Stop," she said, catching sight of a gift shop through a break in the crowd. "I see miniature ceramic figures in that window. Maybe I can find some things to take home."

"There are plenty of tourist traps in Kaoshiung," Tessa said, but followed her friend, who had elbowed her way to the window.

"If I could find some little things like figurines, they'd be easy to pack."

Figgy stared at the window display.

"Oh, my! I guess I won't take any of these back to my classroom."

Tessa's hoots of laughter brought a few stares from the crowd. She and Figgy were looking at an elaborate display of erotic figures, graphically entwined. They were small, but anatomically complete.

"You could tell Dr. Smithson you were planning a show-and-tell lesson. Or, better yet, buy her a statue as a souvenir!" Tessa bent her neck to examine some of the porcelain models. "No real humans could contort their bodies that way. The artist is out of touch with reality."

"Touch is the operative word here. Maybe he hired an acrobatic team to get some ideas."

Tessa was still bending and turning to check out the display. "No one could fault him for lack of imagination. Want to go inside and see the inventory?"

Figgy grabbed her arm and pulled her back into the crowd. "Good thing we're in a foreign country. I'd be mortified if anyone I know saw me looking at those statues."

"Don't be so priggish. Everyone knows travel broadens the mind."

They were both laughing as they approached the harbor, joining the line waiting to board sight-seeing boats to the floating village at Aberdeen.

Although Tessa had taken the trip before, she was as fascinated as Figgy by the boat traffic in the harbor. Every kind of vessel, from the tiniest rowboat to the ferries transporting passengers between Kowloon and Hong Kong Island, crowded the watery space.

Of all the sights she'd seen so far, Aberdeen was the most amazing to Figgy. Tessa explained that generations of families spent their lives on the boats that were their homes, setting foot on land only for emergencies. They fished and bought necessary supplies and produce from vendors who approached their floating homes from their own boats. Tessa said the hard bargaining over prices happened on the water just as vigorously as in the street markets.

Figgy stared at women hanging clothes on lines stretched across the bows of their boats. A boy played with his dog, both of them running, surefooted, on the deck of their floating house. On one vessel she saw a toddler learning to walk, a rope tied around her waist to keep her from lurching overboard. Some of the children waved as the boat cruised past, but the adults went about their tasks, so accustomed to gawking tourists they could easily ignore them.

Looking down at the water between the closely clustered houseboats, Figgy saw a dark, murky surface, often disturbed by discarded plastic cups and bottles. Unrecognizable objects floated past as she watched.

"They eat fish taken from these waters? With all the traffic and discharges into the harbor, the boat people must cope with lots of sickness."

"You'd be surprised how healthy they

are," Tessa said. "Generations of fishing families have lived in this harbor and developed immunity to the pollution. The right bacteria in their guts, I guess, to make them an amazingly sturdy bunch. What I don't get is why they aren't sick of tourists gaping at them. But they're good at ignoring us."

As she spoke, a tiny dinghy — every space filled with baskets of cabbages, melons, and greens unfamiliar to Figgy — passed near the side of their excursion boat. A lean figure stood in the vessel, steering through marine traffic with a long pole. As the dinghy passed, Figgy stared into bright eyes surrounded by spider webs of wrinkles. When their gaze met, the boater's wrinkles deepened above a broad grin punctuated by spaces where upper and lower teeth once were, her long, gray braid swinging across one shoulder. The woman's erect carriage belied what must have been a long life on the water. Figgy waved and the produce peddler's smile lasted until she passed from view.

"My students will love hearing about a vegetable lady older than most of their grandparents, selling produce from a boat smaller than a canoe."

"Maybe it will get them to eat their carrots," Tessa said.

"Or inspire them to start a floating snack business on the lake at summer camp."

"You might want to try that yourself," Tessa said. "Probably pays more than teaching."

"I think I'll wait till my hair's white and I lose my teeth."

The rest of their day in Hong Kong was a blur of shopping, eating, and people-watching. Even the ferry ride between Kowloon and Hong Kong Island, taken for granted by residents, was an adventure to Figgy. Her attention wandered between the flotillas in the harbor and the people jammed together on the ferry's benches. They were munching on unfamiliar foods, many reading newspapers with characters unintelligible to her. But the pictures of celebrities posing in plunging necklines and skimpy skirts were certainly familiar.

The children were the most fun to watch. Running where they could and squeezing through crowded spaces, they were pampered and petted each time they stopped and given sugary treats whenever they asked. Figgy might not know the language but she recognized the wide-eyed entreaties of youngsters holding their families in thrall.

"Little kids here seem to get away with more than they do in the States," Figgy commented as she waited in line with Tessa to leave the ferry and return to their hotel.

Her friend nodded.

"Chinese parents are really indulgent with their young children. I think it's because they know that in a few short years the kids will be off to school, gone from early morning till dusk. Then it's evening tutoring classes to get them into the right schools and universities. At home they study nonstop until bedtime. Students work so hard here that their parents and other adults give them lots of attention and pampering while they're little, before the tough grind begins."

Figgy said, "Maybe American students, given some of that rigid instruction, would complain less about their homework."

"I doubt it," Tessa said as they juggled their packages on the walk back to their hotel. "I knew how hard Asian teenagers worked from my travels with my family, but that never stopped me from griping."

"You were just a bratty adolescent," Figgy said.

"Sometimes I think I still am," Tessa answered.

Figgy groaned. "I can't move another step. I hope that's our hotel and not a mirage. If you hadn't arranged for us to stay there overnight, I swear I'd sleep in the street."

In their hotel room, they added the results of their shopping to their suitcases and, mercifully for Figgy, settled in for the night.

After what felt like minutes, Tessa was shaking her.

"Come on, wake up. We have to get downstairs and catch the shuttle to the airport. Getting through the crowds to our gate won't leave much time to spare."

Figgy mumbled about the need for coffee, but Tessa shook her head.

"Get dressed. We'll grab some tea and moon cakes at the airport."

Moon cakes? What, Figgy wondered, was she talking about? She made a pass at brushing her teeth and fumbled her way into her clothes. Tessa steered her through the lobby and outside, where they handed their luggage to the shuttle driver. She dozed again until they arrived at the airport, where there was more hustling by Tessa.

After cups of tea and some round cookies with a flavor too subtle for Figgy's taste, they were standing in line yet again. Tessa put her arm around the shoulders of her groggy friend.

"I know you feel zonked, with so little sleep and all the rushing since you landed. But I wanted you to enjoy some of Hong

Kong in the short time we had before flying to Taiwan. Sorry if I acted like Elvira Smithson on steroids."

Figgy laughed. Tessa could always lighten her mood.

"I had a great time. It made me want to come back, and not only to shop. I'll be better when we get to Kaoshiung and my body catches up with the time zone."

"You'll have plenty of opportunity for that. I have to go into the office in the morning, so you can sleep late and check out the neighborhood near the hotel. I should be back by midday, to show you around the city and help you get your bearings. I know how directionally challenged you are, Fig, so you can write everything down if it makes you feel better. Then when I have to go to Serenity for a few hours, you'll be fine on your own."

"Going to Serenity sounds great — almost as good as eating a moon cake."

After the brief flight to Kaoshiung and the drudgery of waiting in yet more lines, Figgy felt like a dinghy towed by the yacht named Tessa. She followed in her wake to a cab stand, then into the Majesty Hotel where she'd be living for the next few weeks.

Tessa was greeted like an old friend by each hotel employee they encountered. She

492   9969

introduced Figgy, requested an extra key card for her, shepherded her to the elevator, then along the third floor corridor to her apartment. A teenaged bellhop followed and looked at Tessa adoringly as he maneuvered the cart, overflowing with luggage and Hong Kong purchases, into their rooms.

When their possessions were unloaded Tessa spoke to him in Chinese and gave him a tip. Grinning at them both, he backed out of the door.

"You can do that in any language," Figgy said as her companion moved into the bedroom, took off her shoes, and flung herself on one of the twin beds.

"Do what?" Tessa said, sitting upright again.

"Mesmerize any male you come in contact with, like that boy who brought our luggage. It was the same way in Hong Kong, not to mention at home in Mersdale. What you said to him sounded different than the Chinese in Hong Kong."

"It is. Here and in mainland China the language of choice is Mandarin. In Hong Kong the people speak Cantonese. Clever of you to notice the difference. You were always a quick study."

"Except when it comes to men."

"You just haven't found the right one yet."

51

ORLAND PARK PUBLIC LIBRARY

"I'd settle for some interesting substitutes in the meantime," she said, lifting her suitcase onto the other bed and beginning to sort through its contents.

"That's Ken. He's fun and always ready to find new ways to avoid responsibilities."

"That must irritate his daddy." Figgy looked around for some place to store her clothes.

"The bottom three drawers of that chest are yours. And there's room in the closet for stuff you want to hang up. Most living spaces in this city are tiny — by comparison my apartment is spacious, although there's not much storage room. The management added that chest of drawers as a favor. Most local people have fewer clothes than we do."

"A few extra smiles at that bellboy and he would personally knock down a wall to make more space for you."

Tessa chose to ignore the comment and said, "You're right about Ken annoying his father. Mr. Chu's very proper, even in his dress. He always wears gray or dark blue suits, white shirts, silk ties that are expensive but subdued. When Ken comes into the building in jeans — designer, of course — and a sweater he bought from some high couture shop in Paris, you can see his father's jaw clench. But he never raises his voice, only gives him 'the look' and goes about his business."

"And Ken keeps indulging his expensive tastes?"

"Of course. And takes particular delight in irritating his father. I think it's his motivation coming to work each day. Ken is Mr. Chu's only son. There are two daughters, both married, one to a stockbroker in Manhattan. Ken is the best hope for keeping Serenity Insurance a family business, but as far as I can tell, he doesn't take it as seriously as his father would like."

Finished unpacking, Figgy handed Tessa a package wrapped in shiny blue paper.

"This is something I didn't think you'd find in Taiwan."

Tessa unwrapped her gift and enveloped her diminutive friend in a bear hug.

"Chocolate truffles from the Sweet Shop. Thank you, thank you. I've been thinking about e-mailing Mrs. Finnerty to order some from Mersdale, but like so much else, I've never gotten around to it."

"Mrs. Finnerty sends love and says to come home soon. Her profits are down since you left."

"She's probably not exaggerating. Each time Elvira Smithson got on my case, which was often, I'd stop at the Sweet Shop after work and start devouring the truffles before I got home. Instant nirvana."

"Mmm," Tessa murmured, popping one into her mouth. "Even better than I remember. I'm not offering you any, because you can get them anytime."

She stashed the box in the top drawer of her dresser and looked at her blinking phone.

"Back to the real world." She listened to the messages. "I'll go to the office for just a little while. Usually I teach four English classes each day, then do some individual tutoring. This afternoon I'll just check my work schedule and catch up with my students."

"While you do that, I'll try to wash away my lethargy in the shower."

"Jet lag. Another day and you should feel fine."

When she reemerged, Tessa was gone. Figgy changed into a light cotton skirt and blouse. Odd to feel hot in December, but the apartment was almost warm enough for air-conditioning. She'd try a short walk to explore her surroundings.

Preparing to leave, Figgy realized she was hungry. Tessa — with her typical lack of interest in substantial food — could manage on tea and moon cakes, but she needed something more filling. A quick check of the apartment's tiny refrigerator revealed three bottles of water and a tangerine, its shriveled skin dotted with brown blotches. Visiting the hotel's restaurant seemed an increasingly good idea.

Even at midday the lobby was busy. Clusters of businessmen sat in a circle of couches and chairs, their conversation interspersed with gestures and laughter. Four teenagers wearing checked skirts, white blouses, ties, and knee socks — very much like the school uniforms at Shadyhill — clustered near the restaurant entrance. Chattering, they covered their mouths when they giggled. Figgy felt a pang of homesickness for her own classroom.

Two of the girls turned and responded to her smile with "Ni hao." Figgy knew that meant hello, but there was no possibility of further conversation, other than repeating the greeting. How frustrating, she thought, to be struck mute by her ignorance of the language surrounding her. On her summer trip to Montreal, she managed well with two years of college French, but in Kaoshiung she'd be helpless without Tessa beside her. The students giggled at her "Ni hao" response and were led, still chattering, to a table near the back of the restaurant.

As she waited, a compact young man, slightly taller than Figgy, approached from the kitchen area. Hair styled in a military buzzcut, he wore a beige suit and a crisp blue shirt.

"Miss Newton? Tessa told me to look out for you. She said you are always hungry."

When she laughed and said that sounded like Tessa, he nodded.

"She's very funny lady. Everybody's friend." He held out his hand. "I am called Buddy."

"That doesn't sound very Chinese."

"It's not, but easier to say than real name."

Figgy had read about Chinese speech patterns and the difficulty in pronouncing certain letters, but it would take some getting used to. "I'm called Figgy, but that's not my real name either."

"Yours is hard to pronounce also?"

"I just don't like it. And, since my last name is the same as an American cookie called a Fig Newton, you can guess where the nickname came from."

"That's called nickname?" He laughed. "Sounds Chinese. Cool! Maybe, like Tessa, you'll teach me more good English."

Figgy answered, "Sure." Buddy led her to a small table near a window. Figgy hoped Tessa's lessons were "more good English," not bawdy slang.

"We have fine soup today — chicken with corn, very traditional — and ham sandwiches," he explained, handing her a menu printed in Mandarin and English.

"I can eat ham sandwiches any time. The soup sounds fine. Will you choose something else traditional for me to try?"

"Shrimp and vegetables. Rice. Perfect! I'll tell the chef and Mei-Lei, your waitress, will bring tea. You will not be wanting Lipton's, I think."

Figgy smiled at his infectious grin. "Only Chinese, please."

Mei-Lei was as friendly and determined to please as Buddy, but with more limited English. She brought a pot of tea and a pink cup and saucer painted with blue and yellow flowers. Before Figgy could pour some, Mei-Lei did that for her, then waited while she tasted it.

"Good?"

"Excellent," Figgy answered, "Ding hao," trying out one of the few phrases she'd learned online and hoping she remembered it as meaning "good."

Mei-Lei giggled, covered her mouth, and hurried away, still laughing. Figgy decided she'd better stick to English.

Soon, she was happily spooning up a

creamy concoction of chicken and corn from the wide bowl of a curved ceramic spoon. The rice, shrimp, and vegetables in a spicy brown sauce were tricky to eat with chopsticks, but she managed. Between sips and bites, Figgy looked out at the bustling street from her seat near a window.

Although she'd researched the city on the Internet, Kaoshiung was different than she'd imagined. The storybook versions of Chinese culture she'd read growing up, based on centuries-old images, were nothing like the modern reality. Sidewalks were crowded with people who could be workers in any big city, dressed for the office or the shop. Some female passersby wore the latest fashions, favoring leather and spike-heeled boots. School uniforms prevailed among middle-school-aged students and teens. Boys were apparently required to wear jackets and ties, girls, sensible shoes and skirts at decorous lengths.

A pretty woman in jeans and a T-shirt passed the window, steering a stroller through masses of pedestrians. Its occupant, a toddler in pink ruffles and bonnet hugged a doll in matching pink, clearly enjoying her ride. An older child, a boy, ran ahead. When he collided with a pedestrian, the adult smiled, patted his head, and walked on.

Dipping her last shrimp in the spicy sauce and feeling smug at being able to manage it with her chopsticks, Figgy looked up to see Tessa walking toward the hotel entrance. As always, she moved with the leggy grace and model's stance that colleagues in the teachers' lounge had noted with a mix of admiration and envy. When a comment sounded snide, Tessa would ignore it, choosing to focus her attention and affection on her young students.

Matching Tessa's long strides was a lean Chinese companion, slightly taller, dressed in jeans and a pale-blue cashmere sweater. He was startlingly handsome, the fine bones of his face like sculpture by a master artist. The two, unaware of Figgy's appraisal, disappeared from view as they entered the hotel. Then they were standing near the restaurant entrance, Tessa chatting with Buddy. Her green-eyed gaze followed his gestures until she spotted Figgy, waved, and started toward her table, her companion following.

"Buddy has taken good care of you, I see." She sat down, then gestured at the man with her.

"This is Ken Chu, Figgy. He knows all about you, and you know that he's the boss's son." She looked at him, still standing, and said, "Do sit down Kenny. You needn't practice your fancy school manners with us."

He laughed and folded himself into the remaining chair.

"Are you as candid as your friend? I'm not sure what I appreciate more about Tessa — her teaching skills or her attitude."

"It must be attitude because she doesn't need to work on your English. You're better at it than some of my native-born neighbors."

"I went to school in England before university in California so I had good role models, even before Tessa."

"He's not nearly as modest as he's sounding, so don't be fooled by that innocent demeanor. He's as much a snob as Elvira Smithson."

"Who?" he said, forehead wrinkling in confusion. Figgy noticed it didn't change the drop-dead handsomeness.

"The head mistress at the school where Tessa taught and I still do. Don't ask."

"Okay," he said, frown disappearing. "It's probably best I don't know."

Buddy, overseeing the restaurant, approached their table.

"Tessa, would you like something to eat? Mr. Chu?"

"Nothing for me, Buddy, thank you," Tessa responded, favoring him with her brightest smile.

"Coffee, your strongest brew," Ken said.

When Buddy left, Ken turned to Tessa.

"You shouldn't encourage the hotel help to be so familiar, calling you by your first name. It's okay at the office — the people you teach are professionals. But here — inappropriate."

Tessa's serene expression changed to a scowl, its full force directed at Ken.

"Buddy's my friend, just like the people at Serenity. Your influence on my behavior starts and ends with my job responsibilities."

Uncomfortable in the uneasy silence that followed, Figgy said, "I didn't expect you back so soon. I was just getting ready to explore the streets near the hotel."

"You'll have plenty of time for that, but without me, Fig. That's why I came back with Ken. We have to go to Taipei as soon as I pack a few things for an overnight trip. I'm sorry to do this to you, but the trip is totally unexpected and absolutely necessary. I asked Mr. Chu if you could come along, but he was opposed to the idea. I explained how much I wanted to spend time with you and suggested that he send Ken alone. He vetoed that idea too."

"The truth is that Papa Chu thinks his only son is more playboy than businessman. He didn't say it, but he's fearful that if I get away from Serenity and his supervision, I'll neglect my duties and waste my time in the Taipei clubs. Tessa is chaperoning to make sure I tend to business."

Silent through the explanations, Figgy tried to quell the twist of anxiety in her stomach. Being alone in a strange city where she didn't know the language was not what she'd bargained for on this vacation. Worse, without Tessa as guide, she was nervous about getting lost. That happened often enough in places around Philadelphia, but there she could ask for directions. In Kaoshiung, who would even know what she was saying?

"It's only for a short time," Tessa said, reading the look on her face. "We'll drive to Taipei, meet with the people at the National Museum and leave as quickly as possible. You and I should be together for dinner tomorrow. Meanwhile, you can check out the local department store, visit the shops, or, if you like, go to the Science and Technology Museum. It would be something to tell your students about. Buddy or any of the other staff at the registration desk can help you."

Right, Figgy thought, *and how would they help if I got lost?* Tessa knew she was notoriously bad at finding her way in unfamiliar places. It generated much teasing when they traveled somewhere and Figgy was driving. She couldn't help feeling resentful at this turn of events.

Ken smiled at her, showing perfect teeth. A few strands of dark hair fell on his forehead, producing a disarming look Figgy suspected he knew was attractive.

"So unfair, to have Tessa invite you here and then desert you. Blame my esteemed father. Your friend put up quite an argument, even suggesting that bringing you along to see more of the country so you could tell your students about it would be good for Taiwan's image. He refused, saying it wouldn't be appropriate company policy. Big deal! We're only escorts for a little green horse."

Tessa looked around the room, then glared at Ken.

"You shouldn't be talking like this in public. You never know who might hear you and cause trouble for Serenity."

"And you spend so much time with my father you're beginning to sound like him."

Tessa started to respond, then seemed to

think better of it. "I'm going up to the apartment to pack a few things. Come with me, Figgy?"

"Don't be long," Ken said, signaling to Mei-Lei for more coffee. "The sooner we get this show on the road, the quicker we're back. Then I'll make this up to you, Figgy. We'll go to the best clubs in town. Cool music, great beer. Dance till we drop!"

Tessa grimaced, then started out of the restaurant. Figgy followed.

Waiting for the elevator, she said, "Does he always speak in clichés? He didn't learn that at his fancy schools."

"He watches too much American television. And he belonged to a fraternity at college in California. The brothers worked extra hard at teaching him to be cool."

"Mr. Chu must be delighted with the results of his son's expensive American education," Figgy said.

In the elevator, Tessa sighed.

"He could have been tutored by Albert Einstein and it wouldn't make much difference, except maybe Ken would emulate his hairdo."

Figgy practically ran to keep up as her friend loped down the corridor to her apartment.

"Tessa, you couldn't help this. Please

don't worry about me. I'll be fine, just roaming around town. It's only one night. This has to be important or you wouldn't be going."

After she'd unlocked the door and pulled a small suitcase from her closet, Tessa sat on her bed, signaling Figgy to join her.

"Mr. Chu is insisting I go along because the trip is important to the company, despite Ken's dismissive attitude. One of the most powerful local honchos — a guy involved in shipbuilding among other, more questionable businesses, and with connections to all the important people — started collecting jade miniatures some years ago and has been insuring his very expensive acquisitions with Serenity. Recently, he came into possession of a sculpted jade horse. I've seen it; it's small, exquisitely detailed, very beautiful. The person he bought it from doesn't have a record of its provenance — says he found it at an estate sale in Hong Kong, the property of an old, wealthy family that fell on hard times.

"The seller claimed the family has had it since the eighteenth century. The horse is the color of a green apple and of superior workmanship, according to local experts. The new owner wants it insured for a huge sum but Mr. Chu, without concrete evidence to prove its age and value, is hesitant. He has to be careful because he doesn't want to offend the new owner. So, he's decided to have the horse examined by the jade experts at the National Palace Museum in Taipei."

"Couldn't he bring the experts here to have a look?" Figgy asked.

Tessa shrugged. "Makes sense to me, but Mr. Chu insists on the specialists at the museum evaluating it, using their expertise and the technology in place to aid their judgment. He won't risk damage to the jade by commercial carrier and that's where Ken and I come in. Ken will represent Serenity and I'll be there for subtleties of language and as another set of ears."

"More like a set of brains," Figgy said.

Tossing clothes and make-up into her bag, Tessa looked at Figgy and smiled.

"You weren't bowled over by the charms of Serenity Insurance's heir apparent?"

"The charm was a little too practiced and overdone. The tired American slang didn't help either."

"That's the style in his crowd. They think American pop culture is very cool and cool is what they want to be. They're disdainful of other young professionals, some of them Serenity employees who are motivated to work hard and succeed in their careers."

Tessa zipped her bag shut, changed from office suit into green silk slacks and white blouse, then took a final, self-appraising look in the mirror. She reached into a drawer behind her for a bright green silk scarf to complete her outfit.

"Don't underestimate Ken, Figgy. Beneath that calculated hipness is a shrewd, clever mind. He complains about his father's caution and old-fashioned style, but he's very aware that the business will someday be his and he relishes that status. No one else dare criticize Mr. Chu in his presence, nor question Ken's own status."

"I noticed the condescending behavior with Buddy . . ."

"Yes. Typical. Now, I'd better get going. Again, I'm so sorry about this. We'll make up for it when I get back, I promise. If anything comes up, call the Serenity office. But I can't imagine that you'll need to."

Figgy nodded, hugged her friend, and watched as she raced down the hall to the elevator. What now, she wondered.

Determined not to feel sorry for herself, she went back downstairs to take the exploratory walk she'd thought about before Tessa's arrival. She approached the desk, hoping for suggestions from Buddy, but he wasn't there. Instead a plump, gray-haired woman looked up from her computer, smiled, and parroted "Good Morning, Sir" as she'd been trained. No help there, Figgy thought, nodding and turning away to hide her smile as she made a mental note to tell her students about that exchange.

Outside, Figgy studied the surroundings she'd been too groggy to notice when she arrived. The sidewalks were jammed with people. Motorbikes zigzagged through lines of traffic, speeding around the cars, then braking to noisy stops at red lights. She noticed that some of the bikers, as well as children and adults among the sidewalk crowds, were wearing surgical-like masks.

She knew that in Japanese cities residents with colds often wore masks to prevent the spread of germs. That could be true here too, she thought, but her own nose soon detected another reason. The air smelled foul, a noxious mix of exhaust fumes, industrial smoke, and dirty water from the nearby Ai River. Figgy guessed that the people who lived here were used to it and most didn't notice the polluted environment the way she did.

Some of the trees lining the street looked like giant versions of the rubber plants her grandmother coddled in her Iowa living room. But Gran's house plants had shiny green leaves and these were dust-covered and dull. A few palms also struggled to stay alive, but did little to dispel the grime that co-existed with the bustle and lively activity all around her.

Walking without a plan or destination — except to remember how to return to the hotel — had its charms, Figgy thought. She stopped often to look at shop displays, intrigued by the combinations of traditional and trendy items. Next to a store window filled with ceramic teapots and high-collared scarlet jackets embroidered with fire-breathing golden dragons was another shop displaying mannequins in jeans and knit tops like one she'd bought recently at her suburban mall. The models wore baseball caps sporting American sports team logos.

Figgy's fifth-graders would be delighted, she thought, if she told them she'd bought an Eagles cap in Taiwan.

As she stopped to window shop, a youngster approached with a smile and tentative "Hi" and "Hello" to the Western stranger. The mother, waiting nearby with a mixture of pride and shyness, watched Figgy's reaction, apparently ready to apologize. When Figgy replied with a grin and a handshake, the parent explained in her own limited phrasing that her child was learning some English. Figgy's explanation, equally limited, that she was a teacher and liked meeting children caused both adults and the child to giggle. She was grateful for human contact in a place where she felt nearly invisible.

CHAPTER THREE

Figgy spent the next hours exploring. She browsed in a department store with familiar clothing labels, but price tags much higher than those at home. She paused near a card table set up near a storefront. There, two old men with shiny bald heads and faces of parchment drawn over sharply angled bones confronted each other over a mahjong game. Intent, they paid no attention to the foreigner.

Food stands were everywhere, many of them with tables where people ate family style. Bowls of soup were especially popular, with diners fishing solid contents out of their bowls with chopsticks. Some of the stands featured fish tanks, a few with fierce-looking occupants. Customers could pick their meal by pointing to the swimmer of their choice.

Nearly as popular as the food stands, Figgy noticed, were the bookstores. Almost every block had a store or a street stall crowded with people examining volumes. Some customers looked like students, but there were men and women of all ages checking the displays and commenting to each other about them. Parents leafed through picture books, showing their children the illustrations.

At the harbor, fleets of container ships were anchored, their cargoes stamped with words in many languages. Figgy watched as greasy water sloshed against the vessels, refuse floating on its surface. She wondered again how residents grew accustomed to the pervasive odor of pollution. But, all around her, people moved confidently, purposeful and energetic. And the children, with their fat, rosy cheeks, looked as healthy as they were beautiful.

Without Tessa, Figgy didn't trust herself to travel farther than she could walk. Her friend had suggested a museum visit, but that would involve a cab, complicated currency transactions, and, most daunting, navigating her way through unknown surroundings. Given her propensity for getting lost, the idea was unappealing. Instead, she decided to go back to the hotel, have dinner in the restaurant, and read until she fell asleep.

As she waited to be seated, she looked around at the other diners. Men in suits occupied several large tables, deep in conversation she assumed was about business. Scattered throughout the room were family groups, one with two teenaged daughters dressed in jeans and sweaters. The girls picked at their food while their father, in suit and tie, spoke and their mother, dressed nearly as formally in a gray pants suit and white blouse, listened and occasionally responded. At a table near them, four fashionable women engaged in animated conversation, frequently interrupted by bursts of laughter.

Figgy was envious. She could vanish into the tall potted plants decorating the dining room entry and no one would notice . . . or care, she thought.

She was startled by the voice behind her.

"This is my lucky day. Meeting my travel partner when I didn't expect to see a single familiar face! Hi, Figgy. How are you adjusting to Kaoshiung?"

Figgy turned to encounter the friendly face of Will Bowers and returned his greeting with a broad smile.

"You're a welcome sight, especially when I was wallowing in self-pity."

"You can tell me why when we're

seated . . . unless you're waiting for someone."

"I'm alone and grateful to be rescued from my wallowing."

After they were seated and handed menus, Figgy said, "Why don't you order for both of us? I'm still new at this and the menu doesn't look anything like the one at my take-out place in Mersdale."

When their waiter returned, Will spoke in rapid-fire Mandarin that left Figgy wide-eyed. The waiter nodded, asked a few questions, then left.

"You said you were an engineer, but nothing about being a linguist."

"In college I minored in Asian studies and discovered I liked the language part. It's helped me land overseas assignments."

"You must have zipped right through those long lines in Hong Kong."

"Not really. I'm okay with the Mandarin here, but in Hong Kong, where they speak Cantonese, I'm as out of it as most Americans."

Figgy sighed.

"I thought I did a lot of reading and research to get ready for this trip, but it hasn't helped much."

Will nodded his thanks at the server, who set bowls of steaming soup before them, then said, "It would take years of study to understand even a little of the complexity of this part of the world, so just relax and enjoy it."

"Mmm. Beginning with this soup. What is it?"

"The local version of hot and sour, to be followed by all kinds of good stuff. This is one of my favorite eating places. If I'd known you were staying at the Majesty, I would have mentioned that. How has the visit been so far? I would've thought you'd be out with your friend."

"Me too — and so would she — but there were complications. That's why I was feeling sorry for myself."

Figgy explained about Tessa's unexpected trip to Taipei, omitting details of her visit to the National Museum.

"Too bad you didn't go along. Taipei's a fascinating city, but I prefer Kaoshiung. The pace here is slower."

"Slower? You're joking! Crossing the street today I was tempted to pray, close my eyes, and sprint. The traffic's insane, and those motorbikes carrying whole families and zooming between cars make Fifth Avenue in Manhattan look like slow motion."

"You'll get used to it, although I'd advise against the closed-eyes sprint. When is Tessa coming back?"

"Tomorrow, in time for dinner. I'm on my own until then."

"I'd take the day off to show you around, but we have some bigwigs from Germany visiting tomorrow. It could mean important new business for the company, so I'm involved with them all day. Why don't I give you my phone number, just in case? I won't be able to get away, but at least we can talk if you have a problem. Meanwhile, have some more of these dumplings. They're the best in town."

Her experiences with take-out Chinese dinners at home didn't help much as she chased a dumpling around her plate with her chopsticks, finally deciding to spear it and hope no one noticed. Glancing around, she saw that the other diners were all absorbed in their food and conversation. Will was writing a number on the back of his business card and hadn't noticed.

Figgy decided she needed more practice using chopsticks. At home with take-out orders from her local Chinese restaurant, she usually grabbed a knife and fork and ate while watching a movie rental.

Nibbling on her speared dumpling, she looked across the table at a smiling Will.

"Try peanuts," he said, his gaze moving

from her impaled dumpling to her puzzled look.

"The best way to get better with chopsticks is to practice with peanuts. Once you're comfortable picking them up, you can tackle anything, even the slippery noodles that are our next course. Meanwhile, I'll get a fork for you."

When a bowl of steaming noodles in an aromatic brown sauce was set before them, Will spoke to the server, who nodded, disappeared, then returned with a fork.

"I feel like a failure," Figgy said, "but that won't stop me from eating these noodles."

"Enjoy. Lots of younger Chinese prefer forks, especially the ones who attend universities in the West. Traditions are ignored by Asian kids hooked on Western pop culture."

"Especially the music," Figgy said. "It was blasting from stores I passed on my walk. One displayed all the latest American hit CDs and computer games. And right next to it was a shop with no sign, crammed with shelves. Each held huge jars with contents I couldn't figure out."

"Dried plants," Will said. "Through the ages, the Chinese have believed in the medicinal power of herbs. They still do and Western scientists are finally paying attention and studying their remedies. That shop owner could mix up a combination of herbs for whatever ails you. The guys I work with swear by his medicines and they're modern, highly educated, well-traveled scientists."

"What I need is a quick dose of local-custom savvy. A little help for directional dysfunction would be nice too."

"The herb doctor's good, but no one claims he's a miracle worker," Will said.

"Now you sound like Tessa," she answered, grinning.

The noisy buzz of conversation and laughter was so much a part of the restaurant's atmosphere that Figgy was surprised when it suddenly stopped, replaced by a low hum of whispers.

Will glanced away from her and Figgy followed his gaze. She saw a portly man in an immaculately tailored navy suit standing at the restaurant's entrance. Beside him was a much younger woman, glamorous in the short white sheath hugging her body. Spike-heeled sandals and an outsized jade pendant said expensive. Behind the couple were two crop-haired men whose tailoring didn't conceal the muscles beneath the jackets.

"Our world has been graced by a big-time guest, Figgy. You're looking at one of the town's movers and shakers, Mr. Liang. If you want anything done around here, or if you have a business rival you'd like out of your way, he's the go-to expert."

Figgy stared at the entourage being shown to a table not far from their own. "You mean he's a hitman?" she whispered.

Will, teacup raised to his lips, started to laugh, then choke on the hastily swallowed hot liquid. When he stopped he looked at her, distracting Figgy with the intensity of deep blue eyes.

"You need to get out of your classroom and away from television. Men like Liang never do the dirty work — which doesn't mean he might not when he deems it necessary, arrange for someone else to do it. He's the power broker, connected to the most important people in business and government. Ambitious young men clamber to work for him and every social climber in the community invites him to parties. If you want to see your company prosper, or your son become successful in Kaoshiung, you try to be a friend of Mr. Liang."

Figgy watched as serving people crowded around the newcomers' table. Their center of attention must have felt her stare; he looked up, eyes meeting hers. Liang nodded, a slight upward curve to his lips. Figgy looked away. The half-smile had been benign, but his eyes were chilling.

She sipped some of the strong tea she'd come to expect in her short time here. The bargain-priced tea bags in her own kitchen would have to be replaced.

"So, what do you think?" Will asked. He'd apparently watched her reaction to Mr. Liang.

She couldn't tell him she'd been thinking about throwing out the tea bags in her apartment, but she was stalling, repelled by what she'd seen in the man's eyes.

"In one of the classrooms at my school there's a snake that we use in nature-study lessons. The kids pick him up, stroke his skin, carry him around. He's harmless, of course. They've named him Raymond. But for all his tameness, there's something cold and wild in Raymond's eyes. That's what I saw when Mr. Liang returned my glance."

She picked up her chopsticks to spear another dumpling, then thought better of it and reached for her fork.

"But I was staring and he may have been annoyed by my rudeness."

"I doubt it. He's used to being stared at, toadied to, and waited on. Goes with the territory. And, usually, that territory includes one or two nubile girls in designer dresses and showy jade."

"I noticed the necklace. Pretty spectacular."

"Liang has a particular fondness for jade. He's a big-time collector. One of the supervisors at the plant recently mentioned that Liang's been trolling the international markets for antiques. The older the better."

"But if those pieces are ancient treasures, aren't they protected by law? I thought they belonged to their country of origin. You know, like the big fight between England and Greece over the Elgin Marbles?"

"Something as piddling as international law wouldn't deter him. Don't look now, but he's gobbling up dumplings faster than the waiter can bring them. Liang's even greedy about eating."

"That explains the skinny girlfriend. Nothing is left on the plate for her."

"She'd probably rather have the jade than the dumplings."

"Since I've never had jade with designer clothes thrown in, I'll settle for dumplings. They're really good." After choosing another, she said, "Besides inhaling dumplings, what does Mr. Liang do?"

"He's into all kinds of things besides the activities no one mentions publicly. If you walked down to the docks, you probably noticed what a thriving port city this is. He owns a big portion of the commercial vessels docked there. Serenity insures some of them."

Figgy nodded, only half-listening. Despite Will Bowers' obvious interest, she no longer cared about Mr. Liang, her thoughts returning to Tessa. She hoped her friend would return early tomorrow. Until she came back, Figgy would continue to feel adrift in strange new territory. Will was nice enough, but he'd soon be back at work, and she'd be alone again.

"You said your friend's getting back tomorrow?" Will said, attention returning to her.

"She thought late in the afternoon. I hope so. It'll be a long day until Tessa returns."

"I doubt it. You could roam for hours in Kaoshiung. The park's nice in the morning; the shops are fun and so is the people-watching. But remember to look out for motorbikes. Some of the drivers take sadistic pleasure playing chicken with pedestrians crossing the streets. And resist the food sold at street stalls. It's fine for the locals, but you don't have the right resident microbes to avoid a nasty stomach ache."

"Tessa told me the same thing, but thanks for the reminder."

Looking at her, Will must have seen some

of the uneasiness she tried to hide.

"It'll be okay, Figgy, even with the different language and your concerns about getting lost. Just in case, keep that card with my phone numbers. I need to go back to my apartment now and attack all the work I brought home from the plant. Call me if you need to, but mostly just relax and enjoy yourself."

Easy for him to say, she thought, as they said good-bye at the restaurant entrance and she started toward the elevators. Neither noticed that Mr. Liang watched them go, his glance following Figgy without the hint of a smile.

The next morning, Figgy lingered over breakfast in the hotel dining room, gazing at others drinking tea and reading newspapers in a variety of languages. She supposed she could stay here indefinitely, buying an English version of an international newspaper and drinking yet more tea. But she felt restless, unwilling to wait cloistered in the hotel for Tessa's return.

As she left the restaurant and walked across the lobby, she heard her name. Turning, she saw that it was the day clerk, the friendly young employee who'd asked her to call him Buddy.

"How are you this morning? I hear Tessa

left for Taipei with young Chu. You doing all right without her?"

Grateful for a friendly face, she returned his smile, reminding him to call her Figgy.

"If you don't, I'll feel like I'm back in my classroom. Did you see Tessa before she left?"

"No, but I heard from the doorman. Hotel is like gossip factory. We all know what's going on with our guests and everybody likes Tessa."

"What about Ken Chu?"

Buddy's smile faded. "We only see him when he eats in the restaurant or comes to meet Tessa."

"Your tact should be a great advantage in your career, Buddy."

Figgy saw the beginning of a response. He seemed to change his mind and said, "What are you planning today?"

"Not sure. I want to stay close to the hotel because, to be honest, I'm afraid of getting lost."

"No worries. You could take a cab to a museum. The driver would know to bring you back to Majesty."

"I'd rather wait to see the museums with Tessa. For now, I'll be fine walking around. I might look in the shops for gifts to take home."

"Good idea, but the shops don't open for another hour. Try walking in the park, only a few blocks away if you turn left when you leave the hotel. Nice place, full of little kids and old people, with flowers and benches to wait and watch the people until shops open. But don't buy food, even if street vendors try to sell to you."

"I've been warned, but the food I saw at the stands yesterday looked so good."

"It is. I eat it all the time. Tessa, too, but she's here long enough that our germs like her, think she's one of our own. She even eats stinky tofu."

Figgy thought she hadn't heard right. Buddy grinned at her confused expression and explained. "Very popular with us. Cubes of fried bean curd, smells awful. But so does some fancy French cheese. Stinky tofu much cheaper. Tessa likes it with chili sauce. If you pass a stand with bad smell, that's good stinky tofu. Walk away very fast." He laughed again.

"You really seem to like what you do, Buddy. You're so cheerful."

"Tessa says so too. She thinks I should be called Sunny. Nickname! I like that word you taught me. I am glad to be at Majesty, in the hotel training program. Someday I want to manage a hotel like this. Maybe even own one. That's my big dream."

"Sounds good to me."

Buddy sighed.

"I wish my family thought so. My father believes I shamed him and doesn't want to see me."

Before she could respond, he said, "I must go. Starting work in one-half hour and needing to organize. We'll talk again."

With that he was gone, leaving Figgy to wonder how someone so capable and conscientious could disappoint his family. She trusted her gut feelings about people and was sure Buddy was one of the good ones.

Figgy didn't have the same response to Ken Chu in the short time they were together, but Tessa seemed to think he was all right and spent lots of time with him, so she should know. Funny — Tessa often teased her about her gullibility in trusting people; yet, in the case of the boss's son, Figgy had the sense that her friend might be the more gullible one.

She shrugged, left the hotel, and turned left, planning to ask Tessa about Ken that evening. She passed people dressed in heavy jackets despite what Figgy considered a comfortably warm morning. She paused as an old woman weighed down with bags that bulged with cooking greens and what looked like giant white radishes moved around her. The woman, like many of the others pushing past, was apparently shopping for today's dinner. Despite her wrinkled face and frail frame, she moved briskly. Figgy noticed that most of the people, whatever their ages, were lean and energetic. We Americans could learn from them, she thought.

Crossing the bridge over a turgid river, Figgy looked into the brown water and shuddered, a wave of loneliness engulfing her. With Tessa gone, she felt deprived of speech. She had Will's card in her pocket and a cellphone she wasn't sure would work here. All she needed now was confusion about directions and she'd be lost in every sense of the word.

Past the river, she saw the park entrance. Taking a deep breath, Figgy admitted to herself that her fifth-graders were gutsier than their teacher.

The cement tables near the entrance were occupied by old men absorbed in chess games, looking up only to assess their opponents' expressions. Stopping to watch, Figgy stood a few paces back. She didn't play chess, but the faces above the boards intrigued her. The webbed skin over delicate bones testified to myriad experiences, making old age seem elegant, special. Observing them, she thought of their contrast with the cosmetic masks filling magazines and television screens at home.

Chapter Four

Startled, she turned as a voice near her left shoulder said, "You must be a dedicated chess player."

"No, I don't play," Figgy answered. The lithe man, whose silver hair contrasted with his athletic appearance, spoke English perfectly. Instead of being grateful, she was wary.

"Nor I, but my father is very skilled at the game and comes here for matches with his friends. I've been looking for him, but he's not at the tables this morning. It's disappointing to him that I have no talent at chess."

Figgy smiled, forgetting her hesitation. "My father plays, too, and tried to teach me when I was younger. He finally gave up, deciding I lacked the necessary patience."

The stranger nodded. "The same with me. Fortunately, most of us have compensating skills." He paused, then said, "Do you work here in Kaoshiung?"

"No, I'm visiting a friend."

"I hope you like our city."

"I haven't seen much of it yet, but yes, I do."

"Good. This park is a fine place to relax. With all our industries, we don't have too many quiet spots. Have you seen the people practicing Tai Chi?"

"I was heading in that direction. Do they mind spectators?"

"Like the chess players, they won't even notice. They're focused on clearing their minds and concentrating on the movements."

"I'll check it out then. Thanks."

He smiled and said, "I hope you enjoy your visit," and walked away.

Figgy, her back turned, didn't notice him reaching for the cellphone attached to his belt.

Beside a gravel path, on a stretch of grass furthest from the street and its noises, a group of people looked as if they were rehearsing an intricate ballet. Figgy sat on the grass near them. Fifteen men and women in loose-fitting shirts and trousers followed the movements of a leader standing a few feet apart from the others. Bending, dipping, arms and hands gliding in synchronized patterns, they assumed a series of postures that were deliberate, yet ethereal and dreamlike.

Figgy admired their ease and unity of movement, each Tai Chi practitioner sharing a seamless flow of energy, their expressions serene above the agile limbs.

Their faces were wrinkled and most of the men were bald. The leader, still in possession of a full head of gray hair, must have been eighty. They gracefully defied the American preoccupation with youth, she thought. There wasn't a decrepit oldster in the group!

As she watched, mesmerized, their leader moved from a long, elegant stretch into an upright stance, arms falling to his sides. He stood motionless, as did the others. After a few minutes of silence, the group dispersed, saying a few words Figgy assumed were good-bye. The ballet had ended; now they looked like senior citizens, a few chatting, most going toward the street to blend with other pedestrians.

Figgy left with them, passing the chess players. She noticed that the man who'd been looking for his father was nowhere to be seen.

Wandering through the shops near the

hotel consumed the rest of the afternoon. Figgy chose postcards for her students and a porcelain tea set for her parents in Iowa. She knew they'd enjoy displaying an exotic souvenir on their dining room table. Something for the formidable Dr. Smithson was more of a challenge. Finally, she settled on a container of tea in a scarlet silk box, its fiery red the color of choice everywhere she looked. For herself, there was a long silk robe in the same brilliant color, sleeves adorned with blue and green dragons. Stuffed with popcorn and watching a late-night movie, no one would look sexier than Hazel Newton, she thought, as she watched the salesperson fold the robe in layers of tissue, place it carefully in a box, and tie it with a red ribbon.

Tessa would be back soon, she thought, as she added the box to the packages in her shopping bag. She bought her friend a bouquet of fragrant white flowers from a street stall she passed on her way back to the hotel.

Buddy, behind the registration desk in the lobby, smiled when he saw her approach.

"Only place you got lost was in shops, I guess."

"Your directions were so good, even I didn't go astray."

"Good. Part of my job not to lead guests astray."

Figgy, not sure he understood the implication of his words, thought it best not to try to explain.

"Has Tessa returned?"

"Haven't seen her and she didn't pick up her mail." Seeing Figgy's disappointment, he added, "Traffic on the highway between here and Taipei very awful, so the trip is slow. You maybe should have dinner without her."

"I think I'll wait. If I miss seeing her come in, please tell her I'm in a quiet corner of the lobby, writing messages on postcards."

Buddy nodded, then turned his attention to the businessman behind her who was frowning and tapping his fingers against his briefcase.

Setting her shopping bag on the floor beside her, Figgy sank into a leather armchair nearly big enough to swallow her, in a part of the lobby where she could see the entrance and watch for Tessa. Western men in business suits, Asian families looking around for acquaintances, clusters of women laughing and chatting as they walked to the dining room — all came through the doors as she watched, but not Tessa.

Figgy tried to quiet her jittery nerves, but her uneasiness grew as an hour passed. She was getting to be like her mother, who imagined grotesque disasters when anyone she cared about was late. Annoyed as Figgy would get at that trait, she couldn't quell her own sense of dread.

Reaching for her handbag, she took out her address book and retrieved the postcards from the shopping bag. Writing messages to her students would distract her until Tessa returned.

She'd nearly finished the cards for her class and written one to her parents when she looked up again. People leaving the lobby buttoned coats against the night chill as they walked into the darkness. She noticed a silver-haired man standing near the door, who reminded her of the one she'd spoken to in the park earlier. He glanced her way, showing no sign of recognition, then left. She must have been mistaken.

Checking her watch, Figgy saw that she'd been back at the hotel for nearly three hours, well past the dinnertime return Tessa had promised. Maybe there was a message from her.

At the desk, a new staff member introduced herself.

"I am Daisy, Miss Newton. No one called for you while I am here. You could ask Buddy, in the dining room."

Knowing Buddy would have given her a message, she decided to find him in the dining room anyhow. His friendly face might ease her growing anxiety.

The restaurant was nearly empty when she entered. Most diners had finished and left. Those few still at tables were weary-looking business travelers eating alone, laptops beside them, as solitary and isolated as she felt. Near the back of the room, Buddy was sitting at a table and waving at her.

She joined him, grateful for a familiar face.

"I hoped you would come in and tell me about your day."

She described what she'd seen and done. Buddy nodded approvingly, then poured tea from his pot into the cup before her.

"You look like you could use some of this."

"Tea seems to be the solution to all dilemmas here. Nearly everyone in the shops had a cup close by."

"We Asians believe in the power of tea to cure toothaches, sore feet, itchy nose. So drink up."

The smile he expected was slow in coming.

"More than sore feet bothering you,

Figgy," Buddy said, regarding her.

"I'm worried about Tessa. She expected to be back here by dinner time and there's no sign of her."

"Like I say — said — Taiwan roads very crowded. Maybe her meeting lasted longer than she planned. Other people with them?"

"Only Tessa and Ken Chu. They were meeting others at the National Museum in Taipei."

He nodded, drank more tea.

"Tessa drive company car?" he said.

"Ken was planning to drive."

"Mmm. He likes fast cars. Probably took his new Italian model."

"Tessa didn't say anything about the car, but she likes sporty models and fast driving too."

Neither spoke until Buddy broke the silence.

"Don't worry about the way Ken Chu handles his cars. He likes to speed, but he's expert driver." He drank more tea, then added, "Besides, if something went wrong, you would hear."

"How? No one but Tessa knows about me. And the Chus."

"Most likely, they're just late. Happens all the time. Hard to keep appointments when you're stuck in traffic."

Figgy sighed and sipped her tea. She wasn't reassured.

"Are you working this evening?" she asked.

"Night shift, but not for a few hours. I came back early from seeing my family. I said I had to leave for work, but it was a small lie to save embarrassment."

Figgy could sense Buddy studying her face. If he thought she had reason to worry about Tessa, he wasn't saying so.

"My father and I are in a long fight. I am big disappointment to him and he lets me know. It upsets my mother and sisters so I visit as little as possible and leave early."

"Not to pry, but I can't imagine your father not being proud of you. At your age, your responsibility here at the Majesty is quite an accomplishment."

"Not to him," Buddy answered, resentment creeping into his usual upbeat tone. "An only son is expected to go to university, become an engineer. My examination score was high enough and he thought I was all set."

"Examination score?"

"Our schools are different from yours. When students are in secondary school, they take important tests. Those with best scores get into universities. Others must learn trades or take jobs that do not get them the respect given university graduates."

"But you said you had a high score . . ."

"That was the problem. I didn't want to study engineering or other science. Medicine wasn't for me either. I faint at the sight of blood."

Buddy was pleased to make Figgy smile. He refilled her cup.

"See," he said, "the tea is working."

"Either that or your story. Please, go on."

"I wanted to work with people, make them happy. I decided to learn the hospitality business, maybe own a big hotel someday. Or a whole chain, like your Mr. Hilton. Father very pissed." Buddy looked at Figgy, who was trying not to react to his language choice. "Tessa taught me that word — good one, huh? He said I was disgracing the family, shaming him. He made what you call a big scene. My mother cried, my sisters cried."

"That must have been awful for you," Figgy said.

"Yes and no. I was sorry to cause such pain, but going to university only to please my father would be worse. I couldn't."

"Did your family finally understand?"

"My sisters, yes. They called our father a

tyrant, not to his face, of course. My mother understood, but she wouldn't go against my father. In our tradition, sons honor and obey their fathers. I honored, but couldn't obey. My father refused to understand."

"And you chose to do what you wanted."

"Yes. After more tears from my mother and sisters, I left home and took a job at another hotel in town. I lived with a friend from school who was lucky enough not to pass the examination, so he could train to be a mechanic and fix cars, just like he wanted.

"After much hard work, I was accepted into a hotel training program. Afterward, I took a job here and worked my way up. Soon, I'll be transferred to a bigger hotel, owned by the same company, maybe in Taipei. I hope, later, I'll move to a resort in Hawaii as a manager."

"Sounds terrific. If I were your family, I'd be proud of you."

"My sisters are. They used to sneak out to see me here until my father got tired of my mother's crying and agreed I could come home for dinner a few times a month."

"Does that mean he's forgiven you?"

"No way. The evenings are tense. Nobody acts normal. My sisters and mother smile, but their eyes look scared. My father says almost nothing or is so — so — I'm not sure of the word . . ."

"Sarcastic?"

He nodded. "He makes cruel remarks and pretends they're jokes."

She and Buddy drank more tea in silence. Then he said, "It will be easier when I move from Kaoshiung. Farther from home and with no car, so it's an excuse not to visit."

"Maybe your sisters will come to see you," Figgy said.

"Probably so. They're strong and smart. Our father won't have an easy time ruling them when they get older."

"Would your mother come to see you?"

He shook his head.

"She's smart too, but angering my father is against everything she was taught. My sisters are new generation. They should do well in their exams and be accepted into university. But when my father finds out my younger sister wants to be an actress — woohoo! Glad I'll be away from that explosion!"

Figgy smiled, then looked around and noticed that the dining room was empty. Buddy checked his watch and stood.

"Time to get to work." He looked at Figgy, trying to find a way to cheer her. "It's late and you had a big day in town. You can still order dinner. Kung Pao chicken tonight — very good."

"I'm sure it is, but I'm not really hungry. Mostly, I'm tired and probably still a little jetlagged."

"If you go to the apartment now and rest, Tessa will wake you when she returns."

He walked with her to the elevator, making small talk, but he could do nothing about her sense of dread, like a stone in her chest. Something was wrong with Tessa, the buzz in her head kept repeating, and she didn't have a clue what to do about it. Should she notify the police, she wondered, as the elevator ascended. If she could make herself understood, they'd probably shrug her off as a neurotic tourist. Buddy had dismissed her concern, but she didn't share his optimism.

In Tessa's apartment, she searched through drawers, hoping to find an address book, anything that would help her to contact Tessa's friends, seek some advice. There was nothing.

She tried a warm shower, using the lavender bath lotion Tessa had brought from home. Relax, she told herself, all the while listening for sounds of her friend's return. In bed, mystery novel in hand, she stared at the ceiling and kept turning to look at the bedside clock.

She must have fallen asleep, although she had no memory of putting her book aside or turning off the lamp. Groggy and semi-conscious, she switched on the lamp and looked at the other bed. It was empty. She checked the clock: 4 A.M.

Figgy climbed out of bed, paced, and thought. In a few hours, she would call Will Bowers. In the meantime, there was nothing to do but wait. She tried to read, but the words were drowned in the maelstrom of her thoughts. Another shower helped a little. Then, putting Will's card in her handbag, she went downstairs to an eerily empty lobby. Eating had no appeal but the dining room was open, so she ordered tea and toast, then looked at her watch. Six-thirty. She would wait another half hour, then call Will.

Several tables were occupied, mostly by men in suits and ties, undoubtedly preparing for business appointments. Two Western women and three Asian men sat at one of the tables. For a wild moment, Figgy considered approaching them, explaining her plight to the Westerners and seeking their advice. She shook her head to clear it of the absurdity of the idea, wondering if anyone had noticed the peculiar woman sitting alone, her head swiveling toward the entrance. When the group that included the women passed her table, speaking in rapid French, she smiled at her own foolishness.

Figgy reached into her purse for Will's card, glancing at a silver-haired man who'd just entered the dining room. He looked familiar; she thought she'd seen him before, but then she'd passed many gray-haired men on her walks in the city.

Determined to speak to Will, she left the dining room to use the phone in the lobby.

Reaching him, she told Will only the most essential facts, but her voice must have revealed her alarm.

"Stay at the hotel," he said. "I'll meet you in the lobby as soon as I can get away, and we'll figure out what to do."

"Sorry about taking you away from your work, but I . . ."

"We're wasting time talking. Just sit tight, I'll be there soon."

She ordered another pot of tea, leaving the toast untouched — it wouldn't go past the knot in her throat. As she poured another cup, the man she'd noticed was seated a few tables away. His gaze moved past her, without recognition, but she was certain she'd seen him before. He opened his newspaper and began reading. Then she remembered — he had been in the park, looking for his father and exchanged a few words with her about chess. Apparently he didn't remember the encounter. Her curiosity satisfied, she drank more tea, signed the check, and returned to the lobby. She hoped to see Buddy, but there was someone else, a man she hadn't met, at the desk. Choosing a chair near the door, Figgy sat down to wait for Will.

Seeing him before he spotted her, Figgy was reassured by his steady, self-confident look. She really knew little about Will. She guessed he was five or six years older, but had no idea about his personal life. Yet, here she was, pleading for his help as if her life depended on it. That melodramatic phrase didn't seem so out of place in her present circumstances.

"Let's find a more private spot to talk," Will said after greeting her. He led her to the cocktail lounge, deserted at this time, and ordered coffee from the bartender. Then he guided her to a booth, sat next to her, and said, "Now, start at the beginning and tell me all you know about Tessa's trip and assignment."

His no-nonsense approach was both reassuring and ominous. His tone told Figgy he took her fears seriously.

She inhaled, then released a deep breath. As Will sipped coffee from an incongruously dainty flowered cup, she described the events from the time Tessa appeared unexpectedly at the hotel with Ken Chu, announcing that she had to leave on a business trip. Because Figgy had promised not to reveal details about the jade horse, she told Will only that Serenity needed an appraisal of some art for insurance purposes. Tessa and Ken's assignment was to take it to a museum in Taipei.

"That likely means it was quite valuable," Will said, thinking aloud. "And that Mr. Chu, uncertain about his playboy son's handling of the task, was counting on Tessa as backup."

Silent again, he finished his coffee, set down the cup, and looked at Figgy.

"There's only one thing to do. Talk to Mr. Chu. I'll call and arrange for us to see him."

Before she could answer, he'd taken out his phone, pushed some buttons, and was speaking in Mandarin. Then, as he listened, he took a pen from his jacket pocket and jotted down some numbers on the cocktail napkin next to his coffee cup.

"I spoke to a colleague at the plant whose sister is married to a nephew of Mr. Chu.

He gave me the number of Chu's private line."

Figgy looked puzzled. Will smiled at her, a nice change from his solemn expression, she thought.

"That's how it works here. Family or business ties pave the way for all kinds of transactions. Not so different from the States, but it's a much smaller pond we're swimming in here in Kaoshiung."

Pond? Swimming? She decided her anxiety was making her slow-witted. Then she remembered her father teasing her about choosing to be a little fish when she decided to go to school in the East.

While she'd worked that out, Will used his phone again, mostly listening this time. Finished, he said, "We're in luck. Chu will see us if we get there before his next appointment, so we have to leave right now. Baldy, one of my Taiwanese colleagues, worked it out for me. Using his name was a huge help. Without it, we'd have been turned down flat."

He took her arm and steered her toward the door as she said, "Baldy?"

"Not his real name, of course, but easier for Westerners than his more formal given name. Besides, he likes it; he's vain about his long, thick hair, worn hippie-style.

Unusual for a Taiwanese executive, but he's smart and successful enough to get away with it."

As they left the lobby, the silver-haired man standing near the registration desk watched their departure.

Among the chaos of street traffic, the entry to Serenity Insurance lived up to its name. The building, near one of the busiest intersections in the city, was an oasis of quiet. The security guard near the door granted them passage after Will spoke to him.

Men and women in groups of three or four passed them, their voices barely heard in the high-arched space and their footsteps muted by the thick gray carpet. Golden dragons glittered on a pair of porcelain vases displayed on lighted pedestals. Teak tables etched with carvings held more vases, overflowing with blossoms of crimson and gold.

"Mr. Chu's business must be prospering," Figgy whispered, the only voice level that seemed appropriate.

"No time for sightseeing," Will answered, taking her elbow and steering her toward a bank of elevators. "If we're late, we miss Mr. Chu."

Ornate mirrors in the elevator directed

their images back at them. Will, Figgy thought, looked both handsome and professional in his navy suit. His hair was dark like hers, but better-behaved. She looked, as she often thought when she was with Tessa, unfinished. Tendrils of curls persisted in falling forward, despite her efforts to contain them. Her clothes were okay on her small frame, but without Tessa's flair. It was partly because she was so much shorter than most people, she'd often rationalized. Her head didn't reach Will's shoulder; sometimes she felt the same size as her students.

When the elevator stopped Will took her arm again, hurrying her along the corridor to a glass-walled entry. She was nervous enough by then to ignore the luxurious furnishings.

Behind the sleek wooden desk, its contemporary look in sharp contrast to the traditional teak in the lobby, sat a man of about her age dressed in pin-stripe blue. He looked up from his computer as they entered and rose to shake their hands.

"Mr. Chu is expecting you. Tessa told me you were visiting, Miss Newton. She's my teacher here, just as you teach in the States."

Figgy smiled, but before she could respond, the man said, "Mr. Chu waits. Please, follow me."

They were ushered into a large office dominated by a rosewood desk, its surface bare except for a celadon tea set and small silver vase containing three white orchids. The man behind the desk rose to greet them, so thin he seemed skeletal, like those photos of prisoners of war.

Mr. Chu was impeccable in a gray suit that matched the walls around him. It was his face, Figgy decided, with its hollows and the eyes — something in his eyes — that reminded her of those pictures. He folded her hand in his bony grip.

"I feel I already know you, Miss Newton. Tessa has spoken so enthusiastically about her good friend." Turning to Will, Mr. Chu shook his hand and said, "Your colleagues at Taiwan Mills say many good things about you."

Will looked surprised by the comment, as Mr. Chu motioned them to be seated and returned to his place behind the desk.

"You know how it is in Kaoshiung. Business people in local families know each other, so information about good reputations — and bad ones — easily spreads. Now tell me, to what do I owe the honor of this visit?"

Figgy was certain he already knew, but quickly poured out her concern about Tessa and the delay in her return from her business trip with Ken. She didn't try to hide her worry, explaining that Mr. Bowers was a new friend to whom she'd turned for advice.

Will sat quietly, eyes on Chu. He noticed, but wasn't certain Figgy had, that the man's gaze did not meet hers, looking past her as he hesitated, seeming to gather his thoughts before speaking.

"I understand your concern, but let me reassure you. Tessa and my son are on company business that is taking more time than expected. There have been no traffic accidents or sudden illnesses, so do not worry that Tessa is injured or sick. However, there are unforeseen delays in this delicate transaction."

"But they were only going to see some people in Taipei," Figgy said. "What could be so delicate about that to . . ." Before she could continue, she felt a jab in her leg. Will had signaled her without looking at her or altering his expression.

She changed course.

"Mr. Chu, I'm sorry to sound like an alarmist, but I've been looking forward to this time with Tessa for so long and her unexpected absence is really disturbing."

Mr. Chu nodded.

"I understand and am sorry to be an ogre of a boss." His smile transformed his face. "Tessa taught me that word only a few days ago. I did not expect the opportunity to use it so soon." His face grew solemn again. "You must blame me, not her, for disrupting your plans. When she and Ken return, I will find a way to make it up to you. A party perhaps?"

"Can you tell us when to expect Tessa's return?" Will said, speaking for the first time, although Figgy was aware he'd been studying Mr. Chu during her conversation. She assumed Chu knew that as well.

Serenity's owner smiled again. This time, Figgy noticed, the smile didn't reach his eyes.

"A direct American-style question. We Chinese admire that straightforward approach, although we rarely use it in business. My equally direct answer is that I can't say because I don't yet know. Sorry to be vague, but, as you will understand, Mr. Bowers, it is often so in business dealings. Please, Miss Newton, difficult as it is without Tessa, try to enjoy what my city has to offer. If you like, I can arrange for a staff person to show you around Kaoshiung, or schedule a drive into the countryside?"

"No thanks. I'd rather wait to sightsee

111

with Tessa, as long as you can assure me she's all right."

His gaze shifted before it returned to her face, eyes reminding her again of those photographs. "As I've told you, there have been no accidents or illnesses." He rose from his carved rosewood chair. "I regret that I have an urgent appointment . . ."

She and Will stood, thanked him for his time and, again, Figgy felt the skeletal hand in her own.

As they started down the corridor, Figgy began to speak. Will stopped her with an abrupt, "Later."

Nothing else was said until they left the marble elegance of the Serenity lobby, which was much busier than it had been when they arrived. Several people waited near the elevators, including a silver-haired man who stood off to one side and reached for the cellphone attached to his expensive reptile leather belt.

On the sidewalk Will took her arm. "There's a coffee shop a few blocks away. We'll talk there."

Again, they angled through the usual crush of working people in business suits, young women pushing carriages, and clusters of girls in school uniforms, giggling and chattering near the entrance to the local

McDonald's. Figgy dodged shopping bags and baskets filled with produce for the day's meals until Will led her into a small cafe. Its counter was dominated by a shiny espresso machine with as many knobs and buttons as the ones in her neighborhood.

"Cappucino?" Will said when they'd chosen a small table near the rear of the shop.

"An espresso, double shot," she said. It had been that kind of a morning.

He was soon back at the table, where he placed their coffees and looked around before sitting down.

"Good. No one close enough to eavesdrop."

"Do you think we need to be careful?" Figgy asked, feeling a chill that wasn't helped by the jolt of strong coffee she swallowed.

"I don't know what to think except that Chu was deliberately evasive. I'm beginning to feel uneasy about your friend, Tessa."

"But he said there hadn't been any accidents or sudden illness. Surely he wouldn't lie about that."

"It's what he didn't say that's troubling. Accidents and illness aside, that leaves plenty of room for other hazards."

The dread she'd been suppressing reappeared. Another swig of espresso didn't lessen it.

"You think Tessa's in some kind of danger?"

"Nothing Chu said denied it. And his expression — or lack of one — was even more disturbing."

"His eyes," Figgy said, index finger tracing the outline of her cup. "They didn't go with the rest of his face. They looked . . . bleak."

Will gave her a long, admiring look.

"Under that beguiling ingenuousness lurks a very shrewd mind. Exactly. Something has shaken him, and the Chus of this world aren't easily rattled. Have you told me everything you know about Tessa's trip with Ken?"

She hesitated. Repeating what Tessa had said felt like betraying a confidence. But in her gut, Figgy knew something was wrong; she had to do everything she could to help her friend.

"She and Ken were taking a jade figurine to the National Museum in Taipei. It's a small horse the owner recently acquired and believes is old and extremely valuable. He expects Serenity to insure it, but the jade lacks a provenance and Mr. Chu wasn't comfortable with the value set by local appraisers.

"He arranged for the jade experts at the museum to examine it, using the special techniques they have available at their facility. Mr. Chu wanted to have it shipped to Taipei but the owner objected, insisting it be personally delivered to the museum. Tessa told me that Ken said the owner is temperamental and difficult, but an important client, so they had to oblige him."

"Is he local?"

"I don't know, but that was my impression. Tessa hinted that everyone caters to him."

"Did she mention a name or a company?"

The espresso machine whirred, the perfume of ground coffee beans filling the room with an aroma so familiar she was almost transported to the coffee house a few blocks from her apartment, chatting with her favorite barrista or drinking a velvety Costa Rican brew as she read the Sunday paper. Instead, she was thousands of miles away from home, surrounded by people speaking a language she didn't understand, and growing frantic about her missing friend.

"Figgy?" The intensity of Will's gaze plunged her back into the present.

"I'm trying to remember the details of our conversation. It was brief because she was rushing around, getting her things together for an overnight trip, and Ken was waiting in the lobby. I think she said the client owns a fleet of freighters."

Will's expression changed. He shook his head, as if to clear it.

"I need a refill. How about you?"

"Yes, but not until you tell me what that scowl and headshake mean."

"A passing thought, but no basis in fact, so ignore my reaction."

He reached for her cup, starting to get up, but she held his arm, stopping him.

"Don't patronize me, Will Bowers." Before she could stop herself, she was pouring out pent-up anger she didn't even realize she harbored. "Just because I teach children nearly as tall as I am doesn't mean I exist in a bubble. I understand reality even if I spend most of my time with fifth-graders, so stop treating me like I need to be pro-tected from adult-truths."

"Whoa! I didn't know I was doing that, but if you'll let go of my arm so I can get us more coffee, I'll come back, duly apologetic, and tell you what I was thinking."

116

CHAPTER FIVE

When Will returned and set their coffees on the table, Figgy spoke first.

"Sorry about the outburst, but I do get furious when people assume things about me because I'm short and work in a classroom instead of what they consider the real world." She paused to sip some coffee. "Also, I have a rotten sense of direction, I'm probably still jet-lagged, and I'm worried sick about my best friend. But I'm not naive and I don't need to be spared the truth, however nasty."

Will had been listening, eyes focused on her face. Now a smile played at the corners of his mouth.

"Feel better now that you've gotten that off your chest?"

"Not really, but you don't deserve to be dumped on, so I apologize."

"No need. So far, your exotic vacation hasn't been what you expected and is far from idyllic. You have every reason to be angry. But I wouldn't patronize you, Figgy. I admire your toughness and your insights. Besides, my mother always said good things come in small packages."

She made a face.

"I'll overlook that last part if you tell me what you were thinking earlier."

"These are assumptions without facts to back them up, which is why I hesitated about speaking. But what you've told me about Tessa's conversation with you before she left strengthens my hunch.

"Remember when we were having dinner at the Majesty and a guy came in with a stunning girl hanging on his arm? Backed up by two heavyweights in custom-tailored suits?"

"Sure. It was like a scene from an old Hollywood film. You said he was the big man in town, a business type with underworld connections."

"Good summary, but much more complex than a B-movie. The man is a very powerful local leader, with connections to all the important people in town. And with legitimate credentials in the shipping industry."

Figgy put down her coffee cup and stared at him.

"You think that he's the owner of the jade

horse? That would explain all the deference to his wishes, even from the esteemed Mr. Chu."

"Exactly. Mr. Liang is a client of Serenity Insurance. Anyone who reads the business pages in the local newspaper knows that."

"Suppose you're right. What does that tell us?"

"That the situation may be more complicated than we think. A man like Liang has enemies as well as influential friends. Tessa and Ken could be caught in the middle."

"But you heard Chu say there were no accidents or illness."

"And I told you about my concern with what he didn't say. If the client is Liang, it's easy to understand why Chu was so evasive. But you can be sure he has his people working to find Ken and Tessa. Could be that Liang is searching too."

"Where does that leave us? I don't care about power brokers and big shots with their own agendas. I just want Tessa back."

"Chu and his people will do everything they can. Ken is involved too, and his father would do anything to protect him."

"Not good enough. If I can't get direct cooperation from her employer, then I have to figure out some other way."

"You won't leave this alone while Chu

sorts it out?"

"And wait around twiddling my . . . my . . . chopsticks? No way."

"Since I can't let you do this alone, I guess I'm in on the Tessa search too."

"Suit yourself."

As soon as she'd said it, Figgy realized how sullen that had sounded. She unclenched her jaws.

"Sorry to respond like an ungrateful witch. I appreciate your wanting to help, but what about your work at the plant?"

Will shrugged.

"My colleagues know I'm a pretty independent guy, and since I'm a consultant from my own firm, I don't report to anybody on a daily basis. I'll say I need a few days off, keeping in touch on my laptop. I've done it before when I've been a little stir-crazy and needed free time to travel. Their production won't collapse while I'm gone."

"Are you sure? I don't want to be responsible for a crisis in the world market."

He grimaced.

"Have I sounded that stuffy and self important? I guess I need to spend some time with fifth-graders."

"When I get back to Shadyhill, you have an open invitation. But what do we do now to find Tessa?"

"Go to Taipei and see the experts at the museum. Whatever they tell us about Tessa and Ken's visit may give us a better idea about what to do next."

"If they're willing to tell us anything. There must be issues of confidentiality in their appraisal of the jade horse."

"Undoubtedly. But that shouldn't stop us from trying to find out what we can. How soon will you be ready to go?"

"I'll need to pack a few things. It won't take long."

Will nodded. "Then I'll meet you in the lobby in less than an hour."

As she moved toward the elevator, Figgy noticed that Buddy was working at the registration desk. Finishing with the couple he was registering, he waved her over.

"I hoped to see you. Have you heard from Tessa?"

"No. And I guess she hasn't returned while I was out or called?"

He shook his head.

"Like you, I am starting to worry. Maybe you should call her office, find out if people talked to her or to Ken Chu."

She hesitated, then decided not to mention her interview with Mr. Chu.

"Thanks for the suggestion. I'm working

on a few ideas, one that will take me away overnight."

Buddy's forehead wrinkled, his mouth turned down. He reminded Figgy of an unhappy fifth-grader.

"But you're a stranger! To go hunting in unknown place is not good. Tessa wouldn't like it."

"Don't worry, I have a friend to help me. Someone I met on the plane coming here, who works in Kaoshiung. If Tessa gets back before I return, tell her I'll see her tomorrow."

A happy but unlikely possibility, Figgy thought as she waited for the elevator. When the door opened she entered, so preoccupied she paid scant attention to the man standing near the main desk, his head with its shining white hair bent to his cellphone. But she couldn't shake the feeling that he was around more than seemed coincidental. When she had the opportunity she'd talk to Buddy about him. Maybe he was a hotel guest, but that seemed unlikely because he'd spoken about meeting his father in the park. Of course, that didn't preclude the possibility that he now lived out of town. Right now, though, that conversation with Buddy was not at the top of her priority list.

■ ■ ■ ■

Figgy was grateful for the confident, easy way Will maneuvered his car through Kaoshiung's traffic, heading for the highway that wound north to Taipei. Hours of walking in the city hadn't diminished her fascination with the knots of vehicles and cacophony of sounds: car horns blaring, motorbike engines gunning and roaring, drivers shouting their annoyances in words she didn't understand but whose import was clear. Ignoring it all were the female street cleaners, faces masked with scarves under their wide-brimmed straw hats.

A thick yellow haze and the odor of imperfectly working sewers followed them as Will wove through the traffic leaving the city. Everywhere she looked Figgy saw bamboo scaffolding enclosing new buildings. Along the road poinsettias, leaves coated with highway dust, were in full bloom.

"Amazing," she said to Will. "At home, people buy poinsettias for the holidays, pampering and coddling them. Here, where cars spew their pollution and the air's so bad I've been coughing ever since I arrived, they're as hardy as weeds. These roadside flowers look better than the expensive ones I fuss over at Christmas."

"Tells you something about the comparative values of living in a hot house or learning to adapt to real-life conditions."

"Are you planning to wax philosophical all the way to Taipei?" Figgy asked.

"Only if I get the opportunity," Will answered. "It makes me sound like I'm absorbing some of the wisdom of the East."

"How long have you been working toward that goal?"

"If you're asking how much time I've spent in Asia, the answer is a lot. My junior year in college, so I could practice the Mandarin I was studying, I lived for a year with a family in Taipei, took classes at the university there, and helped their uncle in his jewelry store."

"That must have been fun."

"Not too much. Trying to be polite to rude American tourists wasn't easy. But I learned a little about gold, pearls, and jade."

"That could be helpful during our museum visit."

"I doubt it. Mostly, Uncle tried to make me appreciate the mystique of the stone. He went on about how the mineral jadeite is so rare and valuable because it was subjected to high temperatures and huge pressure uncommon on Earth's crust. Stuff like that. He was disdainful of nephrite, the other mineral in the same family, and explained how all the colors of jade happened because of the pressure on the stone. He told me about other elements too, like iron and manganese. His most repeated lesson was that pale apple or emerald green jadeite, the preferred colors of collectors, is the most superior."

Will turned to glance at Figgy and smiled.

"If you're thinking he sounds like a snob, he was, but only about jade. He loved American baseball and beer and was lots of fun to be with. Before he died three years ago, I used to visit him in Taipei."

"Have you been coming back here since college?"

"No. First there was graduate school. Then I moved to Seattle with my wife to work for an industrial design company."

Figgy hoped her face didn't show her disappointment. Will hadn't mentioned a wife.

"And later the two of you moved to Chicago?"

"Just me. By then Beverly and I had divorced, so when the opportunity came I was glad to leave Seattle. Too many bad memories. The Chicago job involved a lot of international travel, which suited me fine. When the company signed a long-term contract with the Taiwan plant, I became their man in Kaoshiung."

Figgy studied his profile, glad he was unattached.

"I guess you're happy to be working here."

"It feels like my second home, but until I met you it was fairly predictable."

Figgy sighed.

"Believe me, my real life's as far removed from melodrama as you can get — unless you count my school's headmistress. Her inner fascist dictates her administrative style."

Will laughed and listened as Figgy entertained him with stories of Tessa's constant scrapes with Dr. Smithson and her own feeble attempts to mediate.

"When she learned I'd be visiting Tessa she almost denied my request for extra vacation time. She finally agreed, grudgingly, after warning me to beware of the negative influence. The irony is that she admired Tessa's talent, respected her, and regretted her leaving."

Figgy's mind returned to its focus.

"Dr. Smithson would be nearly as frantic as I'm getting to be about her disappearance."

Will reached across to squeeze her hand, a move Figgy found both comforting and disconcerting.

"We'll straighten this out so you and Tessa can have some good times together. Maybe you can both join my Taiwanese friends and me at a club we like. Drink some beer, eat a Korean barbecue dinner, and watch American football."

"Is that a big night out in Kaoshiung?"

"Sometimes we order steaks and watch baseball."

"Sounds about as exciting as my nights out. Except that I cheer for the Pittsburgh Steelers and suffer the glares of all the Philadelphia Eagles fans. Occasionally they yell at me, but no bar brawls so far."

"You could lean down and trip them. All's fair in fan fights."

"No short people jokes allowed. I get enough of those in the States."

"Sorry. But how did an Iowa farm girl become a Steelers fan?"

"It's not so strange. We're everywhere, infiltrating the universe. I bet I could find fans in Taipei, maybe even Kaoshiung. I got hooked on the team because of my dad, who was a fan because of his parents. The family moved to Iowa when his grandfather, who was born in a little town in western

Pennsylvania, decided he didn't want to be a miner like all the other men in his family.

"Every one of my relatives roots for the Steelers; I even converted my high school friends. We formed an after-school Steelers club where we discussed our favorite players and weighed their chances against opposing teams. We collected dues to buy pizza and watched the games at each other's houses. When they weren't telecast in our area we took turns nagging our parents into taking us to a sports bar. We'd drink colas, devour the nuts they put on the tables, and scream our heads off at the TV screen. It was the most fun I had in high school."

Will laughed. Figgy liked the way the sound filled the space around them.

"And you've carried this passion into bars filled with Eagles fans?"

"We had great times before Tessa moved away. She's totally uninterested in football, but she loved mixing it up with the guys at the sports bars. She'd come along just to tease and argue with Eagles fans, even when she had no idea what they were talking about."

Figgy smiled at the memory.

"Now, I mostly watch the games in my apartment. I still drink colas, eat too many nuts, and yell at the opposing teams."

"When I come to Philadelphia I'll call you and we can yell together."

She tried not to sound overly eager at the possibility, pleasing as it was, when she asked if he came to Philadelphia on business.

"Often when I'm in the States. My company has a regional office near the city and they're working on some of the equipment designs I've recommended for the Kaoshiung plant."

"Great. Maybe I can convert you to Steelers fandom."

"Don't even try. My heart belongs to the Bears."

"We'll see. Other than that character flaw, you seem like a good person."

She liked the twitch at the corners of his mouth that was not quite a smile.

When they were quiet Figgy tried to avoid dwelling on her fears. Searching the radio band, she could only find Taiwanese disc jockeys chattering between blasts of American pop music.

"Try the CD," Will said.

When she did, the mellow sound of Miles Davis filled the car.

"Great! That's one of my favorites. I have most of his recordings in my apartment."

"Me too. I always bring some along when

I travel here, mostly to play when I'm driving. They compensate for the car horns and motorbike roars."

He smiled at her before returning his gaze to the road.

"When I visit you, instead of proselytizing for the Steelers you can play some of your Miles Davis collection."

"Glad to, if you promise not to blather about the Chicago Bears. I may even cook my famous pasta with Iowa sausage. It's my specialty."

"Sounds like a rare gourmet treat. What kind of wine should I bring to accompany that?"

"I'd stick with a six-pack if I were you."

Will nodded and a smile played at the corners of his mouth again. As they approached the outskirts of Taipei, his expression changed, focusing on the mass of cars and trucks they soon encountered.

Figgy stared at the scene outside her window. Coming north, they'd passed tiny villages and flooded rice paddies. Once, she'd exclaimed at the sight of a mud-coated water buffalo pulling a plow, guided by a farmer in a conical straw hat. It was like a picture in a child's storybook.

In the city they were swallowed in streams of traffic, brakes squealing as drivers lurched to a stop. Pedestrians swarmed along the sidewalks and the more reckless ones dodged between vehicles.

"I'm grateful you're the driver, Will. By now, I'd have abandoned my car and huddled in the corner of a building."

"This is why I avoid coming to Taipei and take the train when I do. But the train stops in every village and we needed to get here quickly. Until now, this was a great trip."

"That it was," she said, still gaping at their surroundings. "I thought Hong Kong's crowds were formidable, but this is a nightmare."

Will's hands gripped the steering wheel, and Figgy tried to relax. Instead, she found herself staring into the crowds, hoping, although she knew it was foolish, to see Tessa's face.

After what seemed like forever, Will said, "If you look to your right, on that rise above the city, you'll see the National Palace Museum."

She craned her neck and stared.

"Impressive. It looks like a castle."

"In a way it is. A treasure house, holding much of the historical wealth of China. The original museum opened in Beijing in 1925 to house the art and collections of the Imperial dynasties. During the 1930s and 1940s, the treasures were constantly moved and hidden to keep them from the invading Japanese."

"I don't know much about that period. Like some of my countrymen, too self-absorbed, I guess, to learn much about Chinese history. I did read some of it, though, in preparation for this trip. Weren't the treasures brought here to protect them during the civil wars?"

Will glanced at her and smiled. "You have to be careful who you say that to. For mainland Chinese that's a loaded question."

"I would think the people would be grateful to have all those treasures protected."

"Gratitude is questionable. Some would argue there's a fine distinction between protecting and grabbing. Chiang Kai-shek ordered the collections moved from the Forbidden City to Taiwan. To keep them safe, he said."

"Sounds reasonable," Figgy said.

"But art historians in China accuse him of looting, while people here say that if the art hadn't been protected in Taiwan it would have been destroyed in China's cultural revolution."

"The Taiwanese must be grateful to Chiang Kai-shek for bringing the treasures here."

"Not all of them," Will said. "People who support Taiwanese independence complain that the museum symbolizes an unwanted connection with China. And people in the mainland, who have their own palace museum in Beijing, claim that the Taiwan collection, by preserving traditional Chinese culture, represents this country's essential link to their true, legitimate government in China."

Figgy sighed.

"I'll never understand politics. Either here or at home."

"That's one of the reasons I like to travel," Will said. "It keeps me from getting too frustrated with our own politicians while I'm diverted by the antics in other countries. Which brings us to our immediate problem. After we get through this tangle of traffic, we'll find a place to park near the museum. Either that, or I'll try your idea: abandoning this thing and just walking away."

Finally they were out of the car, leaving it with an attendant after a lengthy discussion and significant bribe, and approaching the museum's main gate. It was, Figgy thought, the kind of entrance designed to make humans feel very small. A towering white archway marked the walkway to the building. On either side, columns of pines stood like sentinels, protecting the treasures within.

Figgy and Will passed rows of elaborate plantings and climbed ornate stairways until they reached the main entrance to the building.

Inside, two uniformed guards nodded and, as in American institutions, gestured for Figgy to open her handbag for inspection. Will spoke to one of the men and a flurry of explanation in Mandarin followed. Then he turned to Figgy and said, "We'll wait here until someone comes to meet us."

Responding to her questioning look, Will explained.

"When I asked for directions to the offices of the curators, I was told no one was admitted without appointments or proper authorization. I said it was urgent and important — recognizable bureaucratic terms in any country — and was told someone would come and talk to us."

Standing off to the side, Figgy watched as visitors entered through the massive doors, offered handbags and packages for inspection, then went off to view the collections. Many were Westerners, Europeans mostly, she judged from the languages spoken. One tour group from Japan carried totes decorated with drawings of pagodas and cherry trees. Figgy remembered what Will had said about World War II and the treasures hidden from the Japanese. Now this peaceful group came to see the preserved art. This was an encounter to tell Tessa about and to describe to her students.

That was followed by a more sobering thought: Would she again share her impressions with her friend? She forced the dread from her mind. Of course, they would find Tessa. They had to.

The staccato taps of approaching heels on marble interrupted her thinking. A wand-like woman in black appeared, and extended her hand to Figgy, then Will. Her supple leather boots nearly met the top of a short skirt beneath a long, snug jacket which buttoned into a standup collar.

"I am Nancy Wang, assistant to the jade curator." She spoke in clipped English. "Dr. Wang and I are somewhat confused by the message you sent with the guards."

Wang and Wang, Figgy thought — it sounds like corporate show business. She tried to focus, ashamed of her own reaction and wondering if it unveiled some hidden bias.

As if reading her mind, Ms. Wang said, "Henry Wang is my father, but be sure I am not here because of that. He taught me much, but I have my own credentials in the study of precious stones. And I needed to pass a hard hiring process, like all the other candidates."

Surprised by her defensiveness, Figgy decided the assistant curator must get sardonic looks and petty suspicions — like her own — often enough to feel the need to explain.

"I appreciate your taking the time to see us," Will said, all business. "Could we talk in your office? This is a matter of deep urgency." When he saw her expression, he switched to Mandarin and Figgy noticed her look of relief. Her careful English might suggest she was unsure in the language, despite her formal speech. That could explain her defensiveness in the international world of competing museum professionals and diverse languages.

Ms. Wang and Will continued speaking as they walked across the marble foyer to a corridor lined with offices. Figgy hoped it was only an exchange of pleasantries; she didn't want to miss any details about Tessa's visit to the museum.

Pausing before a doorway, Ms. Wang gestured for Figgy and Will to enter. Figgy looked at the elegant hand with its glossy pink nails and a gold band studded with pale green jade on her middle finger. The sleeve of her jacket was aligned precisely at her wrist where a gold bracelet, set with more jade, rested. Figgy tried to tuck her own rumpled shirt back into her slacks and smoothed down her jacket.

"My father is at a meeting or he would have joined us," she said as she seated herself behind a gray metal desk, much like the ones in Shadyhill classrooms. Its surface was brightened by three yellow chrysanthemums in a blue vase. She saw Figgy looking at them and responded, this time with a real smile.

"They grow in a pot on my apartment balcony. These are early blooms."

"They're lovely," Figgy said. "Flowers grow everywhere here, even poinsettias along the highway. In my apartment, the hardiest plants wither and droop."

Ms. Wang smiled and nodded, but Figgy wasn't sure she understood. It didn't matter, she just wanted to get to the point of their visit.

So did Will. He began to speak in English in order to include Figgy, then in Mandarin.

"We've come from Kaoshiung because my friend, Ms. Newton, who is visiting from the States, came to see her close friend, Tessa Kalen, who, as you may remember, works for Serenity Insurance there. Several days ago, Ms. Kalen and her associate, Kenneth Chu, traveled to Taipei for a business meeting here. They came to the museum for an appraisal of a work of art, an ancient jade horse."

Will continued speaking, but Figgy stopped listening when she saw Nancy Wang's expression change. The openness as she'd listened to Will vanished. Her face shut down: her lips went into a straight line, her eyes studied a point on the wall behind Will's head.

Faint voices echoed from a nearby office. In the silence when Will finished speaking, Figgy noticed the floral scent of the curator's perfume — subtle, like her clothes.

She's composing her thoughts, Figgy guessed, as she decides how to answer. The woman's hesitation intensified her own anxiety. So did the clicks of her nails tapping against her metal desktop.

When she responded, it was in Mandarin. Figgy looked questioningly at Will until he held up his hand, palm out, to Ms. Wang. Then he turned to Figgy, expression nearly as unreadable as the woman behind the desk.

"She says that Tessa and Ken kept the appointment with her and Dr. Wang. They arrived late, apologizing that they'd been delayed by traffic."

The jade expert watched Will's face as he translated. She wants to be sure he gets it right, Figgy thought. He turned back to Ms. Wang, trying to relieve the tension.

"Being late for appointments because of Taipei traffic must be a common occurrence in this town."

She nodded, reminding Figgy of how often she'd responded that way in Kaoshiung while remaining completely clueless about what was said.

Will listened as Ms. Wang spoke again, then translated, "They spent several hours with her and Dr. Wang, waiting as the experts examined the jade horse, then left. The Wangs invited them to stay for lunch and a tour, but they refused, explaining that they needed to start the drive south."

"That's it?" Figgy asked.

Will nodded.

"But what did the curators tell Ken and Tessa? What did they say about the statue?"

Will hesitated, then repeated the question in Mandarin.

Nancy Wang's answer was swift and, judging from her tone, emphatic.

"She says that is privileged information. She and her father sign confidentiality agreements in all such transactions."

"Could she tell us Tessa's reaction? Did she or Ken say what they planned to do?"

"Return to Kaoshiung," Ms. Wang replied directly to her. "That is what they said."

Figgy saw that she was looking at that place on the wall behind them again. If she had more information and chose not to share it, Figgy thought, why would she be secretive? Was it the confidentiality agreement that forced her to be so brusque or something troubling about the whole transaction?

The curator stood, making it clear that the interview was over. There were handshakes again. "Can you find your own way out?" she asked.

When they nodded, she sat back down at her desk and pulled out a file that appeared to require her complete attention. They were dismissed.

Will took her arm as they moved down the corridor to the foyer.

"She could have told us more," he said, "but chose not to."

"I thought so too. Isn't that strange? Would she be violating some ethical code if she'd said something about Tessa and Ken's reaction to the appraisal?"

"Possibly. Let's try some more snooping

around before we leave the grounds of this hallowed institution."

"What's left to snoop?" she asked, hoping she didn't sound too disheartened as she hurried to keep up with Will's long stride. But she was frustrated and stymied by what seemed a wasted trip.

In the driveway before the main gate Will stopped, looked around, and reached for his wallet. Figgy was puzzled — not only had his spurt of energy disappeared, he looked confused. Maybe he was reacting to their frustrating interview, but she didn't think so. Especially when he made a show of checking the contents of his wallet.

"What are you . . ."

"Don't say anything," he muttered. "Just stay close and follow my lead."

A middle-aged man in what looked like a chauffeur's uniform approached with a practiced smile.

"Can I help, sir? You need your car from the valet lot?"

"No car, thanks. Maybe some other help."

Before the man could respond, Will switched from English to Mandarin. The attendant's face reflected his surprise, but that look was soon replaced by one of shrewd attention.

Will kept talking, sometimes punctuating

his words with gestures and, once, laughter. His listener laughed too, then responded with a long passage, Will attending to every word. When he finished, Will pulled some bills from his wallet, uttered the *shai-shai* Figgy knew meant "thanks," and clapped the man on the shoulder.

"I'm going to put my arm around you," he said in a low voice. "We'll walk away like we're heading for a romantic rendezvous. Try to look enthused."

Figgy thought that wouldn't require much acting, but she only nodded, leaning into his body as his arm encircled her. She smiled at the attendant, who positively leered in return.

They didn't separate until they were away from the museum drive, out of the attendant's sight.

"I'll tell you what that was about as soon as we get back to the car," he said. Figgy saw the grim set of his jaw and decided it was wise not to ask questions.

"We'll need to stay here overnight. The drive back is too long to undertake without some rest. And we might as well do it in style."

He angled the car into traffic. Figgy decided to wait with her questions when she saw the pandemonium he was driving through: cars, pedestrians darting between them, mopeds, motorcycles, even hand-pushed carts filled with produce or what looked like building materials. One cart was equipped with cages packed with squawking chickens. Even the fowls were crowded here, she thought, then caught her breath as a crewcut teenager on a moped zoomed across their lane of traffic, cut in front of them, then turned his head to grin as Will leaned on the horn and yelled, "Stupid idiot!"

A few minutes later, a woman on a motorcycle pulled up beside the car. Figgy looked at her: high-heeled black sandals, sheer matching stockings, red skirt brushing her thighs, black leather jacket and red helmet. Feeling Figgy's stare, she turned her head, glared, bent forward astride her bike like a jockey and peeled off into an equally crowded side street.

Thankful she wasn't driving, Figgy leaned back, inhaling a pungent mix of gas fumes, smoke from sidewalk food stalls, and the acid burn of polluted air. After experiencing the rush hour in Taipei, Kaoshiung would seem homey and slow-paced.

"We'll stay at the Grand Hotel," Will said, nosing the car out of the line of traffic and up a hill that seemed to lead away from the busy city center.

"I don't care if it's grand or not, I just want somewhere quiet where I can hear what you learned from that smirking guy at the museum."

Will smiled, a nice change from his grim focus on traffic.

"The hotel's named Grand, and it's an apt title. I know one of the managers, so we should be able to get a last-minute booking."

A name so pretentious would normally put her off the place, but she was hungry and tired, so she kept her grumpy observation to herself.

CHAPTER SIX

The hill they were ascending ended unexpectedly at a curved driveway and an astonishing edifice. Figgy blinked at the mammoth Chinese red structure dominating the site. She glanced up at rows of balconies overlooking the city. Will handed his keys to a crimson-clad attendant, another hurried over to collect their bags, and the two of them walked into a lobby that Figgy gaped at, wide-eyed. Will looked at her and grinned.

"I told you the Grand was grand," he said.

"And I thought that sounded phony and overdone. Now it seems like an understatement."

Dominating the monumental space was a towering staircase, its polished wooden railings incised with carvings and gleaming under the lights of the crystal chandeliers. On the wide landing the symbol of the season, a majestic Christmas tree, was laden with gold and crimson ornaments and ribbons. Gold was the dominant theme in the lobby, Figgy thought. What didn't glitter was either made of marble or shiny wood carved with flowers and animal figures.

At the desk, Will exchanged greetings with a sleek woman who looked like another decorative element of the hotel's design. Her make-up was perfect, her red sheath emphasized a slim figure. A heavy gold chain encircled the smooth skin of her neck.

The woman's smile acknowledged Figgy when Will introduced her and grew much wider when she chatted with him in Mandarin. Figgy waited, conscious yet again of her wrinkled slacks, shirt, and pale-blue sweater. Her clothes looked as rumpled as she felt after the long drive, the frustrating museum visit, and the harrowing traffic.

"Sandra has arranged adjoining rooms for us, even though the hotel's nearly full, with holiday visitors and a big convention in town."

"It pays to have friends in the right places — and she's obviously a good friend."

As soon as she'd spoken, Figgy regretted both her snide implication and tone. Will ignored both. *He's much more civil than I am,* she thought.

"I've known her since college, when I lived

in her house in Taipei. Her uncle owned the jewelry store I told you about. Sandra was a kid then, and her folks were a second family to me."

"She's grown up nicely. Fits in with the grand display," Figgy said, recognizing that her score on the witchiness meter hadn't dropped.

"I'm sure her husband thinks so too. Luckily, their young daughter looks just like her mother."

Subdued, Figgy didn't speak again until they were in the elevator.

"When are you going to tell me about the parking attendant at the museum?"

"As soon as we're settled in our rooms I'll knock on your door, we'll order a room service dinner, and talk."

In her room, her overnight bag had been placed on a luggage rack in the foyer. Figgy stared. Alone, there was no need to feign nonchalance about her surroundings. Her apartment at home, with its two small bedrooms, living room and dining area would seem sumptuous after her stay in the Kaoshiung hotel. But this! This single hotel room could swallow the first floor of her parents' house in Iowa.

Excluding the entry foyer, the main room was enormous, its parquet floor dotted with thick area rugs designed to echo the colors of ceiling tiles painted with gold leaf designs and surrounded by golden borders. A bed the size of her apartment kitchen was covered in blue damask that matched the lamps and fibers in the rugs. A wide desk, carved wooden cabinets, and a dressing table left plenty of room for a sofa and two matching chairs.

An inspection of the bathroom was interrupted by Will's knock, but not before Figgy decided that an entire family could live in that space. Orchids in a rainbow of colors flowed from a blue vase on the marble counter near a bathtub that looked long enough for a pro basketball player. After squeezing into the mini-shower stall in Tessa's hotel apartment, Figgy thought a bath in the Grand Hotel would be the ultimate luxury.

She opened the door for Will, then chose one of the plush armchairs near a sliding glass door to the balcony, with its view of the city below.

"While I sink into luxury, you need to tell me about the guy at the museum."

He chose a chair across from her and sighed.

"Ah, yes, the parking attendant. I told him we'd arranged a little holiday, needing to get away from our own town. I named another place, not Kaoshiung — and our spouses . . ."

"You told him we came here to cheat on our imaginary mates?"

"It made a more convincing story. I said we were looking for a place to stay that another couple we knew, a Taiwanese man and his American girlfriend, had found when he brought her to visit the museum because she's crazy about jade. They'd been there just a few days ago; he was showing off his new Lamborghini. I figured the attendant would remember Ken's car if he was working the day they saw the jade curators."

"Did he?"

"Oh, yes. His shift started after they'd gone inside, but he was the one who brought the Lamborghini from the garage to the driveway afterwards."

"So you verified that they left after the meeting. At least that part of the trip went smoothly."

"I haven't finished," Will said. "From what the attendant told me, their departure was anything but smooth. He said — and he laughed because he thought it was a lovers' quarrel — they were having an argument. Loud, he said, right there on the steps of the museum. He doesn't understand much English, so he missed a lot of what was said. But he did tell me that Ken was swearing, using words I won't try to repeat in English. Very mad, he was, the attendant said. Among other observations about the relationship, he commented there would be no good time for them that night."

"He was swearing at Tessa? Why would he act like such a jerk? No way she would stand there and let him get away with it. She'd be more likely to grab the car keys, drive away and leave Ken there."

"We need to try to figure out what happened to cause that reaction . . . and what to do next."

Figgy said nothing; she stared out at the city below them, seeing nothing but her friend's face.

Will looked at her, then reached out to touch her hand.

"Try to keep your imagination out of the darkest corners. I'll order some food, and we'll work at reconstructing what happened at the museum."

Their food arrived, but Figgy had no interest in the array of dishes the waiter placed before them. The scene described by the parking attendant kept replaying in her mind.

She fingered her chopsticks, used them to sample some of the large prawns covered with a spicy red sauce, followed that with some rice, then pushed her plate aside. Her usually hearty appetite seemed to have disappeared along with her peace of mind.

"What if Ken's anger had nothing to do with Tessa? Maybe he was venting his rage at something said during their meeting."

Will looked at her, sympathy replaced by alertness.

"And the man I spoke to, not understanding much because most of their conversation was in English — aside from the Mandarin expletives from Ken — got the wrong idea. Especially since I steered him in that direction with my story of a romantic escapade with a pretty woman who wasn't Ken's wife."

Figgy nodded.

"And what could the curators say that would so infuriate him? It had to be something about the jade horse that he didn't expect to hear."

Will continued, "If the comments were negative, Ken's reaction may have been shock at first, then anger."

Figgy had been tapping a chopstick against the table as she thought aloud. "He wouldn't be mad at Tessa, they were allies in the plan to have the statue appraised. So who would Ken be cursing? Was the curators' fee so high he was outraged?"

"Not likely. The fee would be recovered in their charges to the statue's owner." He paused. "Would you stop tapping that chopstick, please. It's beginning to have the same effect as squeaky chalk on a classroom board."

"Sorry. I didn't realize I was doing it." She looked at Will. "Ken had to be reacting to something about the quality of the jade."

He nodded.

"My thought as well. I suspect the statue might not be what the owner reported to Serenity Insurance." He was silent, like Figgy, staring into the night. "If Sandra is still at the front desk, she might be able to help us."

He went to the phone, spoke rapidly, then put down the receiver and smiled at her.

"Grab your key card. We'll go downstairs and see what we can learn. Sandra's family inherited her uncle's business but her husband is the real expert and he's due downstairs soon to pick her up. We're going to detain him for a little while."

They arrived in the lobby in time to see a tall, lithe man restraining a toddler who was trying to break free and get closer to the shiny balls on the Christmas tree. When Will and Figgy approached, his harassed expression changed to one of pleasure.

He gripped Will's hand with his free one, then launched into a conversation in Mandarin. Figgy bent down to greet the child with a "Ni hao." To her dismay, the little girl shrieked and hid her face against her father's leg.

The man stopped speaking, looked down at his daughter and then at Figgy's puzzled face. Embarrassed, he said something to Will, who laughed and responded.

"Philip asks me to apologize. His child isn't used to Western ladies at close range and was a little intimidated. I assured him you were used to that reaction, that you frighten the children you teach all the time."

She was about to retort when she saw Will's grin and Philip's extended hand. When she took it, he smiled, showing very white, very straight teeth and attractive crinkles at the corners of his eyes. He and Sandra made a handsome pair, she thought, as she looked down at the toddler peeking at her from the safety of her father's legs.

"Philip is going to take Chichi to her mother, then we'll find a quiet spot to talk."

"Chichi?" Figgy said, catching a shy smile

from the child still clinging to her father's knees.

"A nickname to distinguish the girl from a relative who has the same formal Mandarin name."

Philip said, "Otherwise much confusion at family dinners."

His English, though heavily accented, was clear.

"I know the feeling," she said. "My grandmother and I have the same name, so I was called little Hazel and I hated it."

He nodded, but she wasn't sure he understood. Then he wandered off to find Sandra and turn over their daughter.

"He understands basic English and speaks a little," Will said. "Sandra is trying to teach him more, to help when foreign tourists come into their jewelry shop. But now, he and I will speak in Mandarin. I won't take time to translate because the family has a date with friends at a restaurant several miles away. I'll explain everything he says when we're back upstairs."

When Philip returned, the three of them sat on a red leather sofa in an alcove off the main lobby. Figgy tried to guess some of the substance of the conversation by watching Will's face, but it only reflected intense concentration.

She looked around, studying the crowd — mostly whispering couples in fashionable clothes, hands entwined as they walked towards the hotel restaurant and Asian men in business suits chatting with Western counterparts, similarly attired. She heard some English, smatterings of French and German, and other languages that sounded eastern European but were unrecognizable to her. There wasn't any Russian spoken where she grew up in Iowa, nor much of anything else but midwestern American English.

Seated in the secluded alcove, Figgy could indulge in the people-watching she enjoyed wherever she went. Unseen, she could stare without seeming rude. Now she noticed a man in a business suit, white shirt, and gray-striped tie standing near the registration desk and smiling at Chichi who was hopping on one foot, with Sandra nearby. Probably a grandfather, she thought, admiring his thick white hair. He reminded her of the man she'd seen recently in the Majesty Hotel in Kaoshiung. Then she mentally chastised herself for lumping all gray-haired Asian men together and turned her attention back to Will's face as he listened to Philip.

As both men rose, seemingly finished talking, she saw that Will was frowning and speaking again. Then they shook hands, and Philip turned to her with another dazzling smile, to say good-bye and rejoin his family.

"Do you want anything while we're down here?" Will asked. "Some wine from the bar?"

She shook her head. "I only want to hear what you've learned. The more time that passes without Tessa, the more anxious I get."

He took her hand and squeezed it.

"I know. And what Philip said adds to the puzzle. Let's go back to your room and talk about it."

Figgy liked the warmth of his hand and made no attempt to remove hers from his grasp as they went to the elevator, letting go only when she needed to retrieve her room card from her pocket.

Inside, they sat side by side near the glass balcony doors. The city was enveloped in darkness now. Without the jarring traffic noises far below and the jostling crowds, she could admire the lights glowing like multicolored jewels studding the night.

"I talked to Philip about Ken Chu's re-action when he and Tessa left the museum," Will said. "I didn't tell him Ken's name, of course, and no more than I had to about their visit, but what he said made sense to me. He thought the piece they brought for appraisal was probably valued at far less than they expected it to be."

"But the owner had it appraised earlier by his own experts. Their opinion would have supported the price he expected the horse to be insured for."

"It's not inconceivable that the original owner had bribed the experts to up the ante and to be convincing enough to impress a prospective buyer as greedy as he is wealthy. And even if they were honest, Philip said that there are very sophisticated ways to enhance the appearance of jade. If jadeite is of reasonable quality but stained, for instance, it can be exposed to chemical bleaches and acids, then impregnated with a clear polymer resin. That would make the stone's color and transparency much finer. The only way to test for jade adulterated with polymer is through the use of infrared spectroscopy."

"Does Philip think the earlier appraisers didn't do that?"

"He said it's not likely, especially if the collector is knowledgeable and insistent about his judgment and expertise. If he's rich and influential, Philip said, and hired experts in his own city, they'd be inclined to tell him what he wants to hear, rather than recommending more tests. Additional testing would imply they questioned his ability to recognize quality. And if the owner is Liang, nobody he hired would want to contradict him . . . about anything."

Figgy turned from the cityscape spread out below them to look at Will.

"Supposing Tessa and Ken learned that the statue they believed was valuable turned out to be fake? Ken, furious, calls his father, reveals what they'd been told, then he and Tessa head home with the phony treasure."

"That would seem logical," Will said, voice soft in the lamp-lit room. He didn't look at Figgy, gazing instead into the night. She knew he was not focusing on the view.

"But you don't believe that's what happened," she said, her voice equally soft.

"It was probably their intent," he answered, gaze turning to meet hers.

"What else would they do? They'd want to get back to the Serenity offices, meet with the horse's owner and tell him he'd been cheated. Or assume that Mr. Chu would deal with it, explaining there's no need to insure a pretty ornament."

"A reasonable conclusion." He paused, then spoke again. "But try to think like the owner of that statue when Chu contacts him

— your once-in-a-lifetime find that lets you outsmart every other collector in the world qualifies for nothing more than Aunt Minnie's knick-knack collection."

Despite her worry, Figgy had to smile. She did, indeed, have an elderly aunt — Frances — who collected tiny, garishly painted chickens and kept them on shelves in her bedroom at the nursing home.

Will's next words restored her to the present.

"Imagine how you'd feel if you're rich, powerful, and used to getting your way. What an ego blow! You fancy yourself a connoisseur and you've boasted to other collectors that you now possess the rarest and finest of antique jade statues."

"I'd be raging, just like the parking lot attendant described Ken Chu."

Will sighed.

"I wouldn't want to be in the senior Chu's custom-made Italian shoes when he told the owner he'd been scammed. Nobody relishes facing an important client with news that makes him look like a fool. And to report that to Boss Liang — it's like torching a bonfire!"

"Even if we're right about this, it doesn't explain why Tessa and Ken aren't back in Kaoshiung."

He nodded.

"I don't think there's anything more to be learned here in Taipei. Let's call it a night and leave early in the morning."

Will rose and Figgy stood as well, surprised by the heaviness in her legs. Caught up in the day's emotions, she hadn't realized how exhausted she was. Now, as she staggered a little, Will reached out to steady her, his arm encircling her shoulders.

"You needn't accompany me to the door, like the well-brought-up young woman you are." He bent down, lips brushing her cheek. "Goodnight. Get some rest. You'll get an early wake-up call from me."

After Will closed the door, Figgy raised her hand to her cheek, remembering the touch of his lips. She languidly shed her clothes and climbed into the mammoth bed, her body no more than a minor hillock on its surface. Tucking silken sheets under her chin, she touched her cheek again, smiled, tried to focus on the theories she and Will discussed, and immediately fell asleep.

When the ringing phone woke her, she struggled, half-asleep, to remember where she was. The room was dark, the bed so inviting she wanted only to stay in it. But she couldn't ignore the insistent intrusion. Groping for the phone on the table next to the bed, she grunted a response.

"Time to get moving," Will said, sounding disgustingly alert. "I'll see you in the lobby in about half an hour. If we're lucky, we'll get through the city before the worst of the morning rush."

She nodded, then realized he couldn't see that, muttered an answer, and fumbled her way to the bathroom. Its soft lighting and the vase of orchids reminded her of the planned long soak in the stretch limousine of a bathtub, but she'd been too weary last night. Now, she adjusted the shower spray, mind turning to the reality of a return to Kaoshiung and the fervent wish that Tessa would be there, waiting for her.

When she saw Will in the lobby, he ignored her protestations that she wasn't hungry, insisting she have some breakfast before their drive south. He ordered eggs, toast, and tea, then noticed she was pushing her food around her plate rather than eating it.

Will leaned across the table, putting his hand over hers.

"I know how hard all this is for you. But I think we're getting closer to what's happened and I promise you we'll figure out this mess. So you have to keep your spirits up. And eat."

"But I'm getting so scared, Will. What if

something awful has happened to Tessa?"

"I think your friend knows how to take care of herself. And Mr. Chu assured us there were no accidents or calls from hospitals."

"Maybe he was only trying to make me feel better."

Will, hand still covering hers, shook his head.

"Chu has a reputation as a good man, but he's hardly a touchy-feely kind of guy. If Tessa was hurt, he would have said so."

"That doesn't help much right now."

"Eating some breakfast so we can get out of here would."

Figgy forced down a little of the scrambled eggs, nibbled at a slice of toast, and drank some tea.

"That's the best I can do," she said.

"I'll go check us out," Will said, standing.

"I'll come too, and pay my share."

"This is on me, Figgy. My company pays me far more than I can spend in Kaoshiung and my father was a teacher, so I know about the salaries you dedicated educators make."

Before she could protest, Will said, "No arguments. Besides, I suspect Sandra has arranged a discounted rate for family."

Overnight bag in hand, Figgy waited in

the lobby, trying to concentrate on the luxuriousness of the space. She wanted to describe the fairy-tale Christmas tree to her students at Shadyhill.

At the thought of home, her throat tightened again. So little time left before she had to leave Taiwan. What would she do if Tessa were still missing? She couldn't go without knowing her friend was safe and she hated not knowing what to do next. Thank goodness for Will. She'd feel even more helpless without him.

He returned, to stand beside her and take her bag.

"Sandra isn't working this morning, but she did get a special rate for us as friends of the management. Our rooms were practically a gift. Does that make you feel better?"

She nodded. "Thank her for me the next time you're here."

"I'll arrange for the car. Wait here a little while, then come out to the main drive."

She watched him leave with the long, sure stride she admired and thought how much she liked being with him. If not for this trouble with Tessa, they wouldn't have gotten past the polite acquaintance stage. Exactly what stage were they in now?

Unsure of the answer, she started to cross

the expanse of lobby to the entrance, only to be stopped by a light tap on her shoulder. Startled, she turned and stared into eyes so dark and flat the brightly lit room seemed to dim. From his unnerving gaze, her own moved up to his thatch of white hair, full and luxuriant.

Figgy's stomach constricted before her mind managed the thought: the man with the silver hair, the one she'd encountered in the park in Kaoshiung and saw in the lobby of the Majesty. His presence then, as now, was no accident. She felt a chill unconnected to the hotel's climate control.

"Miss Newton, I have a message for you."

His English, though accented, was clear, his voice low.

"You are to stop prying into the affairs of others. Matters will be taken care of, but you and your American boyfriend must stop meddling. Return to Kaoshiung and finish your visit. Leave things that you do not understand alone or there will be dangerous consequences."

Figgy swallowed her fear enough to ask, "Who are you and what do you know about Tessa Kalen and Ken Chu?"

The midnight eyes bored into her.

"You have been warned."

He turned and walked away. Feeling as if

her icy limbs might shatter, Figgy forced herself to continue walking. When she reached the door and looked back, there was no sign of the man.

Trembling, she hurried out to the driveway just as Will was pulling up. An attendant opened the door and waited as she climbed in. Will stared at her.

"You look like you've met a zombie. What's wrong?"

She sat back, taking deep breaths, while Will's frown turned to dismay. A driver behind them beeped, then waited. As Figgy adjusted her seat belt, he leaned on his horn.

"I'm okay now. I'll explain after we get out of here or we'll be run over by that driver behind us."

They were halfway down the hill when Figgy turned to look back at the hotel's imposing silhouette, its gold and crimson exterior reflecting the sunlight. She'd try not to let the encounter in the lobby spoil her memory of this place.

"Now tell me what frightened you."

Figgy described her encounter with the silver-haired man and the menace in his voice. She repeated his warning and tried to explain the way he'd looked at her, eyes like black pits.

"And he wasn't a stranger. As soon as he

stopped me, I remembered that I'd seen him before. Once in the park in Kaoshuing, where we exchanged a few words; he told me he was looking for his father, who played chess there. And in the lobby of the hotel, on my way to my room."

"Here at the Grand?"

"No, at the Majesty. He looked familiar to me then, but I couldn't place him. With all my walking near the hotel, I thought maybe I'd seen him on the street. It was only when he stopped me this morning that I remembered the time in the park and at the Majesty."

Will's hands gripped the wheel, showing white around his knuckles. They were back in heavy traffic, so she said nothing more. With his mouth set in a grim line, Will stared ahead, waiting for an opening to break away from the jam of people, motor scooters, trucks, and buses.

When they finally reached the outskirts of Taipei and the highway stretched south, Figgy said, "When we get back I'm going to the police."

"I'll come with you to help with language and give you moral support. I want this whole miserable business resolved, especially after that threat at the hotel."

He turned to look at her.

"I wish I'd been with you. You'll need a vacation from your vacation when this is over."

She managed a small smile.

"There are compensations. I never expected to stay in a crimson palace with a bathroom the size of my apartment." She didn't say that the time with him was the biggest compensation.

Attention returning to the highway, Will said, "It sounds selfish, but there are rewards for me too. You've diverted my attention from a lonely work assignment and made me feel useful, in a good way. Without this search we're on, I would never have gotten to know you."

"I was thinking the same thing," she blurted.

"Good. After we find Tessa, maybe we can do something more about that."

When he turned to her again Figgy shook her head.

"I have to leave Taiwan before long, Will. I can't take any more time away from my job. But we need to find Tessa first."

"We will. As it happens, I'll be leaving soon too. My assignment here is nearly complete and then it's back to the States. Before returning to our headquarters in Chicago, I could visit the Philadelphia office and arrange a series of meetings with the staff there. They've been involved, long-distance, in this project too. And it would be a chance for us to get to know each other better."

The weight in her chest was replaced by a stir of pleasure.

"That would be great," she said.

He nodded, returning his attention to the road; they were both quiet, lost in their own thoughts.

Lulled by the Miles Davis CD, Figgy began to doze but was jarred back to wakefulness by the image of black eyes and silver hair, a voice murmuring menace.

"She has to be all right — I can't imagine —" She couldn't finish the thought and Will's tight face told her she didn't need to.

Dusk was settling over the city when Will pulled up in front of the Majesty Hotel. He took Figgy's bag from the trunk and carried it into the lobby.

"I have to go to the plant for a little while. I'll see you as soon as I can get away and we'll go to the police together."

She nodded, then stretched to reach his cheek and brush it with a kiss.

"Thank you," she said.

"I'll hope for a more enthusiastic response another time," he said, folding her in a quick embrace.

"Might be arranged," she answered and walked away.

Starting across the lobby, which felt cozy and intimate after the Grand Hotel, Figgy saw Buddy working at the reception desk. She walked toward it just as he raised his head from the computer screen, spotted her, and smiled.

"Everything okay?" he asked, searching her face.

"Not so great, Buddy. I still haven't heard from Tessa. She didn't come in while I was away, did she?"

He shook his head. "To be truth — is that right — I am getting worried."

"To be truthful, so am I. As soon as I've freshened up, I'm going to the police to report her missing."

Buddy's expression changed from its usual openness to a frown.

"In one-half hour I'll be finished working. Can we talk before you go?"

"I guess. I'm expecting my friend, Will, to meet me here and go with me to the police."

"Mmm. We should talk first."

Convinced by his earnestness, she said, "Okay. By the time I get back downstairs, your shift should be over."

Nodding, Buddy turned back to his computer, but she noticed that his usual benign expression hadn't returned.

The air in Tessa's apartment was stale. The small rooms felt abandoned without her presence, despite her clothes hanging in the closet and her shoes lined up on the floor beneath them, one high-heeled sandal lying on its side. Figgy washed her face with her friend's lilac-scented soap, hoping to restore the feeling of her presence. It was hopeless. Without Tessa, the crowded space was crushing, entombing.

She felt the tears starting and didn't try to stop them, stretching out on the narrow bed next to Tessa's as the sobs erupted. Nothing — not Will, not the compassion and friendship of Buddy, not the knowledge that she would return to the familiar surroundings of home and classroom — could shake the dread, the emptiness she felt now confronting the reality of Tessa's disappearance. And the fear of what might have happened. Her sobs were deep, like convulsions of her soul, and they kept coming.

CHAPTER SEVEN

Empty of tears at last, she rose and changed
into jeans and a soft green T-shirt that felt
familiar and comforting. She washed her
face again, inhaling the fragrance of lavender, found her handbag and key card, and
returned to the lobby.

Buddy was waiting for her near the restaurant entrance.

"It's quiet inside, so we can talk together.
Together? Is that right, Figgy?"

"You don't need to say together; talk is
enough."

"Helpful, like Tessa. First, I'll go to the
kitchen for a special tea brew. My mother's
favorite, insisting to make you healthy."

She forced a smile; it seemed too much
trouble to correct his language.

"It's not my health I'm worried about, it's
Tessa's."

"I know. Be right back."

The familiarity of the empty dining room

made her feel a little better. Buddy soon returned, carrying a teapot and two cups.

"Drink some first. Then we'll talk."

She did as he suggested. Her eyes widened, mouth twisted.

"Wow! That's the strongest tea I've ever tasted."

"Made with herbs and some special roots," Buddy said. "My family drinks it for strength. I keep my canister in the kitchen for necessary times."

Figgy shrugged.

"Whatever works." Her affection for him was clear in her face. "If Will wasn't coming with me to the police, I'd ask you. You've been a good friend, Buddy."

He put down his cup, his expression solemn.

"That's why I tell you going to the police is not such a good idea."

"But that seems the most logical next step."

He hesitated, index finger tracing the rim of his cup as he looked down, avoiding her eyes.

"I don't know how such things are in the States, but here is best to be careful about talking to the police when big, important men are involved. Mr. Chu is very powerful, with much respect."

"I'm not accusing him of anything. All I want is the police to help in finding Tessa."

"Tessa works for Mr. Chu but Ken is his son. Police won't disrespect Mr. Chu, or insult him by going around his behind."

"Behind his back," she corrected, suppressing a smile. "But what you're saying makes no sense — I'm only asking them to do their duty, search for a missing person. They'll include Ken, of course. I want the police to use all their resources to get them both back."

Buddy watched Figgy and waited until she drank more tea.

"What I'm trying to say is the rules are different here from in the States."

"Rules? What rules? Someone goes missing, you call the police. It's that simple."

"You're not listening to me, Figgy. You talk of resources. Police here know that important men have more resources than they do. These big bosses do things in ways police cannot . . . or would not want to if the men are powerful enough. I'm saying to you Mr. Chu is very powerful." He paused. "Other people, also very big, could be involved too."

"Are you telling me that the people who are supposed to be in charge really aren't? Civilians with enough clout can stop the police from doing their jobs? That's like saying the mobs are in charge of running the country."

"No, no. Isn't it true, even in your country, powerful people sometimes can get your government to do what they want? And Mr. Chu is not a mob person — he is honorable, respected."

"All the more reason for him to support my plan to get help from the authorities."

"They may not be willing, at least not before checking with Mr. Chu."

Buddy's voice had been low throughout their conversation, although the restaurant was empty. Now he whispered.

"Figgy, you must believe Chu is doing everything to find them. But his way, privately. He would want you to be private about Tessa also."

"You mean well, I know, but whatever he's doing isn't good enough. She's been gone too long. For all I know, she could be . . . be . . ."

Her hands rose to cover her face.

"Please —"

She shook her head, face still hidden behind her hands. Buddy, helpless to console her, waited.

Will entered the restaurant, approached the table, and looked at the two of them.

Buddy turned to him. "Try, please, to stop her. It will only bring more trouble."

Then he stood, shook his head, and walked away.

Will moved to Figgy's side, gently lowering her hands. The face looking up at him was pale, shadows darkening the skin beneath her eyes. Despite her efforts, tears slipped down. After brushing her cheek with his lips, he wiped them away with his fingertips. Then he sat where Buddy had been and pushed aside the teacups. "Better tell me what Buddy said to upset you so much."

She looked at him, tried another swallow of tea, then repeated Buddy's comments about the police.

Will listened, still silent when she'd finished. Figgy could tell he was weighing Buddy's words.

"He knows how things work around here. This is his town and I think we should pay attention to his warning."

She started to interrupt, but Will held up his hand.

"I know you feel we have no choice except the police, but let's try one more thing. If it doesn't work we'll go to them together."

Figgy waited, listening.

"I think we should go back to Mr. Chu. If

we arrive unannounced, maybe we can catch him with his guard down. We can certainly tell him that our next move is to notify the police."

They left the hotel, moving as quickly as the crowds on the sidewalk allowed, then entered the lobby of the Serenity building and hurried as if they were late for an appointment.

Two security guards chatting near the sign-in desk had their backs turned. As Figgy and Will entered an elevator, the silver-haired man who had followed them came into the building.

In Mr. Chu's outer office, not the young man who'd greeted them earlier, but a composed middle-aged woman looked up from the papers on her desk, prepared to ask polite questions. But the couple brushed past and her composure changed to confusion, then anger, a stream of Mandarin following them as they ignored her and entered her boss's sanctuary.

Mr. Chu was staring at an object on his desk, its contents surrounded by plain brown wrapping paper. He looked up, startled, as Will and Figgy entered, then hastily pulled the paper around the object. But not before Figgy saw it — a small green horse, a child's toy made of plastic. A

176

mutilated plaything with its two front legs missing, only the jagged edges left.

A searing stab in her chest signaled what her mind hesitated to acknowledge — Mr. Chu had gotten a message about the jade horse and was trying to conceal it from his unexpected visitors.

Will, too, had seen the broken toy and wasted no words.

"I think you know why we're here. You can't hide either the message or the situation. Tessa Kalen is missing. So is your son. If that plastic horse is some kind of warning, it's time you quit stonewalling and tell us the truth about what's going on."

The door burst open again. Figgy, with a sharp intake of breath, moved closer to Will. It was the man who had threatened her. He spoke in Mandarin to Mr. Chu.

Will listened, then whispered to Figgy, "He's apologizing for our getting into the office. Blaming the guards in the lobby for laziness and gossiping instead of attending to their duties."

Mr. Chu held up his hands, palms facing the silver-haired man, who was instantly quiet. Then he spoke, in English, weariness as well as caution weighting his words.

"Please, sit down, all of you. You are correct, it's time we talked. Ms. Newton, I understand your worry about Tessa, a concern that sent you and Mr. Bowers to Taipei to make inquiries."

Figgy started to speak but, again, Mr. Chu held up his hand and, like the man who had stalked her, she stopped.

"I asked Mr. Kao, who works for me, to keep me informed of your activities, not to harm you but to protect you. You are in dangerous waters here, young lady. Unfortunately, so are my son and Tessa. I will tell you as much as I think wise about the situation. Then you must not interfere anymore, because your involvement only complicates matters."

"But I can't . . ." Figgy felt a sharp poke in her side and turned to Will. Seeing his tightlipped, unreadable stare as he watched Mr. Chu, she said no more.

"You are aware that Tessa and my son were in Taipei to have an antique jade statue examined by the foremost experts in Taiwan. They, as you probably guessed, determined the piece was not as the owner represented it, but a clever fake, so effectively altered that the man who purchased it was deceived, as were the local experts who examined it."

He paused, pushed aside the wrapping and its content, and steepled his hands, elbows resting on his desk. Mr. Chu was considering his next words before continuing.

"You must understand that the statue's owner had no wish to deceive my company. He is a longtime collector and believed that what he purchased — for a very large sum — was a genuine treasure. He is, of course, deeply disturbed by the treachery."

Figgy could contain herself no longer.

"I'm sorry about the statue, but what about Tessa? You haven't told us a thing about her or Ken."

Despite his solemnity, Mr. Chu managed a small smile.

"You Americans, so impatient. You remind me of Tessa in your . . . your forthrightness. That is part of her charm and yours, but not helpful in our present circumstances."

He paused again.

"Tessa and Ken, after leaving the museum, started their trip back here, but were intercepted. Now their captors tell us that unless we act as if the jade horse is genuine and insure it for its supposed value, they will not return my son and Tessa."

"Are the police searching for them? What are you doing? Have they been hurt?" She turned to Will. "This doesn't make any sense." Before she could speak again, he gripped her hand, squeezing tightly. She lowered her head, trying for calm.

"You ask many questions, most of which I cannot answer. We are working to bring all this to a satisfactory ending. We are assured the young people are not hurt."

Ignoring Will's signal to remain quiet, Figgy blurted, "Then what's the meaning of that toy horse with the broken legs? The one you tried to hide when you saw us?"

The man with the silver hair, who now had a name attached, broke into a stream of Mandarin. Will looked at her and shook his head. Did he mean he didn't understand Mr. Kao, or was this another warning?

"Mr. Kao will see both of you out. Please know we are doing everything possible, but this matter is too delicate to say more. I ask that you return to your hotel. Mr. Kao will inform you of any changes and we hope soon to have good news. Meanwhile, you must speak of this to no one, including your friend at the hotel."

Another hand squeeze from Will. This time she knew its meaning.

"Thank you. It's not necessary for Mr. Kao to accompany us — nor to follow me any longer. I expect to see Tessa very soon, or I'll be forced to take other action."

In the elevator she glared at Will.

"You practically broke my hand in there. Why?"

He shook his head and put his finger to his lips. They exited the elevator in silence, walking through the lobby without speaking. Figgy could feel the sullen resentment of the security guards watching their passage through the lobby and outside.

Figgy looked back, but there was no sign of Mr. Kao.

Weaving in and out of the crowds of pedestrians, they made their way back to the Majesty. Buddy saw them enter and started toward them.

"We can't talk here without snubbing Buddy," Will whispered. "Let's go up to Tessa's rooms."

Figgy waved to him and kept walking. Buddy's wounded look was hard to ignore, but she remembered Mr. Chu's warning.

Upstairs, Will looked around.

"This is as cramped as my apartment at the plant. Living spaces here weren't designed for long-legged Westerners." He smiled at Figgy. "Aren't you glad to be so petite and dainty?"

"If you're trying to distract me, it isn't working."

She began rummaging in a cabinet, her

back to Will, muttering, "I know she keeps it somewhere in here."

"What are you looking for?"

"Tessa's bottle of liqueur. We used to drink it in our apartment when Shadyhill's headmistress was particularly annoying. Tessa always kept some around."

She reached into the back of the cabinet.

"Good. Here it is." From a ceramic tray painted with red poppies, she took two red and gold teacups, pouring some liqueur into each.

"Tessa told me she bought this tea set and the teak chest she keeps it on during one of her trips to Hong Kong. She plans to bring them home with her when she . . ."

She couldn't go on. Will led her to the sofa and sat beside her, gathering her into his arms. His lips whispered against her forehead.

"It's going to be okay. When she comes home the two of you can empty bottles of wine reminiscing about the Taiwan caper."

Figgy made no effort to move from the circle of Will's arms. "You're a good man to have around in a crisis."

"Maybe not bad at other times too, which I hope to demonstrate in the future. Right now, let's figure out what to do next."

She nodded, stood to collect the teacups

and handed one to him. After a few sips, she said, "I'm supposed to fly home soon, but I can't leave until there's news about Tessa. I'll need to notify Dr. Smithson and change my flight plans." Figgy sighed. "Her parting lecture was a warning about Tessa and trouble. I'll hate hearing her smug I-told-you-so, although she'd never want Tessa to be in danger."

"Don't do anything about your schedule yet. I can always arrange a last-minute flight through the plant office. Now we need to think about what Chu told us — and what he didn't."

He looked down at his teacup and frowned.

"This stuff is awful; it must have been stored here, getting thicker and sweeter, the whole time Tessa's been in Kaoshiung. Or do you think she brought it from your apartment this way?"

Figgy, despite her worry, smiled.

"That's the way we like it, sticky and cloying. We rationalize it's like candy with a zing."

"Might as well be sucking a lollypop," he said, putting his cup down. "I'll bring you some good stuff to replace this. Tessa should dump it before it gets toxic."

Figgy's face turned sad again.

"She may be experiencing toxic right now."

"Mr. Chu said they were unharmed. He wouldn't lie about that . . . or much of anything else —"

"But he was deliberately vague about Tessa's captors. Who would be holding them? The dealer who sold the collector the horse? He already has his money, so he wouldn't care about insurance. The collector? Hard to believe he'd resort to kidnapping."

"That depends on who the collector is."

Figgy looked at him, confusion showing on her face.

"Put yourself in his place. You're rich and arrogant, with a huge ego, reveling in your reputation as a savvy collector and the bragging rights that go with it. You want to promote that reputation and you think you've scored an incredible find, an ancient statue of rarest jade. Competing collectors all over the world will envy you and covet your new treasure. Then you learn you've been cheated. Your renown as an art connoisseur — the man of discernment who recognizes the finest and most valuable jade and can afford to own it — could be damaged forever. Other collectors will gloat, happy to exchange envy for ridicule. Not to your face, of course, but you'll know it and feel it. They'll whisper behind your back at dinner parties. Your pride, that ego even bigger than your fortune, couldn't tolerate the blow."

"Kidnapping two innocent people to keep your mistake secret and protect your reputation? That's insane."

"You wouldn't think so if people catered to your every whim, either to curry favor or to save their necks. Not if you're used to getting what you want, by whatever means. And not if you're powerful enough to be completely ruthless without fear of the consequences."

Figgy drained the last of her drink and finished Will's, ignoring his grimace. Then she studied his face, noting his steady gaze, the grim expression that stretched his skin tight across his cheekbones, a look like a clenched fist.

"You think the collector is Liang, don't you?"

"I have no proof," he said, choosing his words carefully. "And the only way to get it could be lethal." He paused, then continued, eyes locked on hers. "You remember how he behaved when we had dinner downstairs? And the strong arm retinue in his wake?"

"As well as the stunning young woman on his arm? The one accessorized in diamonds and jade? Sure. I remember thinking she was so thin all those jewels must weigh her down." She spoke again, tension edging her voice. "You said the man was head of the local crime syndicate."

"Liang is much more than local. His organization stretches north from Kaoshiung, with tentacles as far away as Taipei. Shipping, harbor, and pier control, flunkies in politics — all ruled by that ruthless gangster."

"Why are you so sure he's the one?"

"On one of my first trips here, when I was exploring the city, I wandered into a fancy gallery. There were scroll paintings, elaborately carved ebony tables and chairs from royal dynasties, a few recent landscapes that weren't very good, and some incredible jade. I asked the proprietor to look at one piece — a tiny, antique vase I knew I probably couldn't afford, but just wanted to hold so I could feel its smooth, cool beauty.

"The proprietor explained that none of the jade was for sale. It was part of the Liang collection, on loan to the gallery as part of a city-wide celebration of ancestral art. He was flattered, he said, that his gallery was chosen to display the jade, which was only a small part of the owner's holdings. He would have talked about the jade for hours, but I had to leave for a dinner meeting with one of the plant managers."

Figgy's eyes were intent on Will, waiting for him to go on.

"When I met my colleague and told him about the gallery visit he made a wry face and said he was surprised Liang was sharing part of his plunder with the common folk. Then he changed the subject and, because I didn't know him well at the time, I didn't question him. And, of course, I didn't know who Liang was or anything about him. I'd pretty much forgotten the comment and that gallery visit until this business with Tessa and Ken."

They were silent as Figgy sorted through the jumble of thoughts in her head.

"It figures," she finally said. "Mr. Chu, big-time business man, wouldn't want to offend the even more powerful Liang by refusing to insure his art. But when he learns the jade is fake, he, of course, rejects it."

"Let's not make our insurance king too noble. Chu does plenty of business with the Liang organization, insuring some of his ships and his harbor holdings. He has no qualms about doing legitimate business with the gangster and his associates. There are often pictures of them in the local newspaper shaking hands over a deal," Will said. "But the operative word here is legitimate. Like Liang and other tycoons, Chu has his own oversized ego. To insure a worthless rock at the value placed on precious jade would make him look ridiculous if word got out. A stain on his reputation as a shrewd executive. He wouldn't tolerate that shame besmirching the name of Serenity Insurance."

"But," said Figgy, following Will's logic, "refusing to insure the horse would expose its owner, the collector, to even greater shame for being duped. Paying a fortune for a phony relic when he's supposed to be an expert on the real thing."

"Exactly," said Will. "And it gets worse. Never mind that the guy who sold it to him is probably buried now in some farmer's field. The acceptance Liang covets in the world of art and culture is built on his reputation as a collector who finds and saves national treasures. His phony antique would not only make him a laughing stock in the arcane world of jade, but add to the not-so-subtle disdain he gets from the aristocratic, old-money families he's out to impress. Gossip about Liang's disgrace would enliven fashionable social events from Kaoshiung to Taipei."

"He must have lost a pile of money buying that counterfeit horse," Figgy said.

"Irrelevant. Liang is so rich it amounts to chump change for him. What he couldn't tolerate would be loss of face and the gloating of his enemies if word got out about Serenity's refusal to insure. And word would get out."

"So you think that when Liang learned the antique was fake, he arranged to kidnap Ken — and Tessa, because she was with him — to force Chu into acting as if the horse was real jade."

Will nodded, looking grim.

"We have a contest between two influential, arrogant men, each with as much pride as money. Both have reputations to protect and will go to any lengths to do just that."

"But surely, at least with Chu, not where human lives are concerned — especially when one is his own son. Why doesn't he go to the police and get their help in finding Tessa and Ken?"

Will's grim countenance softened as he looked at her.

"Logical as that seems, it's not the way things work. If the story leaked to the public Liang's revenge would be swift and merciless. People here know his influence pervades every part of the community. Don't

189

you think he has more than a few law officers on his payroll?"

Figgy's response was barely above a whisper.

"That explains why Buddy tried so hard to keep me from going to the police. Do you think he suspects Liang?"

"Everything dirty involves Liang, so it's not much of a stretch for Buddy to be thinking along those lines."

Will reached for Figgy's hand.

"You mustn't say anything to him about this conversation. Involving Buddy would be dangerous for him . . . and could jeopardize Tessa's safety."

"If she is safe."

"Chu won't let anything happen to them. Ken is his only son."

"But what you've said about his obsession with his reputation, his pride . . ."

"In a face-off between him and Liang, it's the mobster who holds all the big cards."

They were silent again, Figgy examining the limited options available in her attempts to help Tessa.

Sensing her despair, Will stood, pulled her up beside him, and folded her in his arms. It felt right . . . safe. If only she could stay there until Tessa came back, she thought.

"We're not beaten by this. I'm going back

190

to the plant, talk to a few good friends there, and see what I can find out."

She moved away to look at him.

"What is there to find out? If Liang is as dangerous as you say, no one will tell you anything. They'll be too scared."

"Depends how I ask. I'll approach it in ways that won't make them suspicious, using my business negotiation skills."

She was doubtful and must have looked that way.

He offered a reassuring smile. "Never underestimate the power of a good negotiator. And please stay up here while I'm gone. Lock the door. Waiting for me in the lobby may no longer be such a good idea. Besides, if Buddy's working, he'd ask too many questions."

After Will left Figgy bolted the door and put on the chain, thinking this would be like a bad movie if not for Tessa's disappearance. Will was the one good part of the whole miserable plot.

Sitting in the only comfortable chair in the apartment, Figgy curled up against the cold leather and looked around. She realized she'd come to hate this space that was Tessa's home. It was small and cramped, but that wasn't the reason. Her friend had covered every available surface with framed photos, fashion magazines, volumes of the Deruda poetry she loved. The clutter was endearing because it was basic Tessa. What was oppressive was the stale, tired feeling in the rooms. Desolate. Emptiness like fog drifting around her, reminding her that without Tessa's energy the apartment felt dead.

To push the morbid thoughts away, Figgy tried to focus on some of the silly, funny episodes that were so consummately Tessa. She remembered the school recess when her friend surprised her young charges by arranging for a pony to be brought to the playground. Her students squealed and giggled, shrieking their delight as they took turns riding around the grounds. There were squeals of another sort when Dr. Smithson, interrupted by the noise during a meeting with one of the school's trustees, looked out of her office window and saw not joyous children, but steaming mounds of manure dotting the play area.

The headmistress rushed outside, murder in her eyes, the trustee close behind. She confronted Tessa, who was grinning at the gleeful student she led on the pony.

The episode had a typical Tessa ending. The trustee's grandson was in the class. When he saw the rapturous faces of the boy and his classmates, Mr. Godfrey congratulated Dr. Smithson on the creativity of the teacher, suggesting that a commendation be added to her file.

Figgy witnessed much of the scene from her classroom windows, along with her envious fifth-graders. She consoled them by explaining that as older, more mature students they were really too big for a miniature pony. But she could hardly tear herself away from watching Dr. Smithson as she listened to Mr. Godfrey and struggled to switch from scarlet-faced fury to bland acknowledgment of Tessa's skills.

Later the headmistress instructed the custodians to distribute the manure in the plant beds surrounding the building. Tessa, hearing about this from a janitor friend, took her class outside to view the fertilized flowers and explain how the pony had helped to make their planet green.

Tessa's magic ruled in another episode Figgy remembered. She and Tessa had gone to a neighborhood bar one Sunday afternoon with their friend, Carol, to watch the Steelers play the Eagles. They drank beer and ate wings at a table near a group of burly men wearing Eagles shirts. When Pittsburgh scored the first touchdown Tessa cheered loudest, ignoring the glares from the next table. Figgy and Carol joined in, then went back to gnawing on the spicy wings. The Steelers were having a great first half, Tessa grew hoarse shouting her pleasure, and the surly stares of the Eagles fans at the next table increased.

As Tessa's enthusiasm grew louder, they muttered, glared, and made audible rude comments. Tessa ignored them, but Carol and Figgy were less comfortable. Their neighbors were big, muscular, and looking ugly.

At half-time, when two of the men approached their table, Figgy and Carol tried to ignore them. But Tessa looked up, gave them one of her dazzling smiles, and said, "Hey, guys, isn't this a great game? So you'll enjoy it even more, I'm asking the bartender to send you all a round of beer and a platter of supersized wings. Think of it as compliments of the Pittsburgh Steelers."

Before they could close their mouths, Tessa rose, deliberately exaggerating the sway of her jeans-clad hips, and went to the bar to order and pay for the drinks and food at the Eagle fans' table. When the game began again, their neighbors raised their mugs to Tessa.

Her friend could turn hardcore misanthropes into friends. But not this time. Tessa was a helpless pawn in a power struggle where her charm made no difference.

The ringing phone startled her out of her reverie. She dashed across the room to answer it.

"I'm waiting outside the hotel. Can you grab what you need and come down? We're going on a little trip."

The sound of Will's voice was reassuring. She knew, if circumstances were different, he could be much more than a helpful accomplice, but there was no time for those thoughts now. She found her handbag and a sweater, picked up her sunglasses, and hurried out.

Although wary in this new world of danger, her old habits of openness prevailed. Moving along the hotel corridor, she didn't look back into the alcove at the end of the hall where a sign in English and Mandarin showed the stairwell exit. And so she didn't see Mr. Kao step out of the shadows and reach for his cellphone.

In the lobby she waved to Buddy, who started out from behind the desk, apparently hoping to speak with her. Sorry to appear to snub him and hurt his feelings, she continued to the door and outside, where Will waited. He took her hand and and hurried her along, not speaking until they got to a side street where he'd parked his car.

"Where are we —"

"Get in, please. I'll tell you on the way."

He was silent as he pulled away from the curb, scanning side and rear mirrors. Used to the dense traffic and foibles of other motorists, he concentrated on his driving until they were clear of the city, heading south. Neither he nor Figgy would have noticed a black sedan several car lengths behind, nor would the driver look familiar. But if they'd seen the man in the passenger seat, they certainly would have known they were being followed again by the silver-haired associate of Mr. Chu.

"Go ahead, Figgy, ask before you explode," Will said, with a side glance and half-smile. "Sorry to be so uncommunicative, but a fender-bender by a foreigner like me causes all kinds of bureaucratic paperwork and major headaches. Our lives are already complicated enough."

"I appreciate the 'our.' You've gotten more than you bargained for, being nice to a stranger on a plane."

His smile broadened. "Best pickup maneuver ever. I had no idea how much more interesting you'd make my life in Kaoshiung."

"Also dangerous. You neglected to mention that."

"Spices things up, like the local cooking."

"I get that you're avoiding explaining where we're going and why."

"I don't have much specific to tell. Just some theories. I talked to people at the plant, trying to find out about possible hideaways for Tessa and Ken. Roundabout conversations, because any hint I might be probing about Liang and his operations and they'd clam up. Nobody, not even privileged plant executives, wants to tangle with that guy."

"So how did you go about your sleuthing, Sherlock?"

They were speeding along the highway, flat farmlands on either side. There wasn't much traffic. Figgy glanced behind her at four or five cars not trying to pass. In a field she saw what looked like like large fish ponds and, beyond them, a farmer plowing with equipment out of an earlier century.

"Amazing, isn't it?" Will was following her gaze. "We've just left a modern, high-tech city, traveled a short distance, and now we're looking at a farmer who belongs in an old novel. But he has concrete pools to raise fish for restaurants in Kaoshiung and Taipei. Sometimes being here feels like I've wandered into a time warp."

She turned to look at him.

"You still haven't told me about your detecting results."

"I used you as an excuse, but I didn't think you'd mind. I said I'd met a woman on the plane whom I was seeing and really wanted to impress. I asked them where the big spenders would take a girl for a weekend out of town if they wanted to — well, an approximation of the Chinese words for hook up."

"But a little more graphic?"

He looked sheepish.

"Guys together, Figgy. A lot of beer and a long lunch away from the plant — with me buying — helped."

"Clever, Mr. Holmes. And what did you learn?"

"About cozy hotels near a big park at the southern tip of the island. Lots of Taiwanese people visit there and some stay in picturesque inns near the ocean. One of the engineers, who talks a lot when he drinks too much beer, said that rumor has it Boss Liang himself has a favorite hideaway near the park. Likes to go there to get away from business — and his wife. One of the other men mentioned that some of Taipei's prettiest women and more than a few of the local girls have had a tour of the park —

and the estate."

"You think that Liang's men may have taken Tessa and Ken there?"

He shrugged.

"I thought we could drive around, sightsee, look like tourists. Maybe find out something useful."

"And then what? Tell the police? From what we know, that wouldn't help."

"I don't have any answers for you. But it's better than doing nothing. If we do stumble onto something, we could try contacting our embassy and learn what they can do."

Her next words stuck in her throat; she had to struggle to get them out. "I hate this, Will, feeling helpless and desperate . . . and scared. Part of me just wants to go home. If — when — we find Tessa I'm going to make her go back to the States with me."

Will moved one hand from the steering wheel to stroke hers.

"From what you've told me, I'm not sure you can make Tessa do anything. But it's okay to be angry and scared. When we get back to town, I'll call an embassy acquaintance. Diplomats here are in a delicate position, with China's insistence on its sovereignty over the island. Our people try to avoid offending either the Chinese or the Taiwanese, so they're very cautious. We don't want to start some kind of diplomatic hassle."

"I don't care about diplomacy, I just want Tessa back."

"We'll do whatever's required to make that happen," Will said. He looked at a sign near an exit from the highway.

"We're near the park I told you about. Let's stop and have a look around. Then I'll consult my map, and we'll check out some of the places my colleagues mentioned. If we pretend to be tourists looking for a romantic inn, we may learn something."

Figgy willed herself to empty her mind, pushing all the horrors back into their dark corners. She studied the countryside around them, surprised anew by the poinsettias, whose hothouse blooms she'd nursed and pampered at home. They were growing along the highway, scarlet and yellow blossoms defying the haze of pollution. Vines of miniature roses trailed through roadside weeds. A few shrubs, sculpted into unnatural shapes by long-gone gardeners, struggled to withstand the wild vegetation threatening their space. *Like me,* Figgy thought.

Will slowed the car as they approached the park entrance. Food and souvenir vendors lined the road. Only a few miles behind them, she'd seen farmers in cone-shaped straw hats, poles with baskets attached at either end slung across their shoulders. They were right out of the old movies she watched late at night when she couldn't sleep. But these vendors were a universal part of any modern tourist trap.

In the distance, mountain peaks disappeared into a veil of mist, like a delicate scroll painting. The road followed the sea, its waves surging across jagged rocks.

When they'd parked, they walked over coral formations that seemed as unreal to Figgy as the plaster her students used for science projects.

Adding to that image were clusters of school children in tidy uniforms photographing the ocean, the coral, each other, and, she soon realized, herself and Will. A few of the braver ones approached them. In a mixture of a few words and varied gestures they asked permission to pose for pictures with the Westerners. Will answered in Mandarin and Figgy soon found herself surrounded by a succession of students, each group posing and grinning as the cameras clicked away.

Will said something else, the youngsters left, and she looked at him questioningly.

"School trips," he explained. "Some of

these kids come from villages where Westerners rarely visit. You and I are a novelty.
The students take photos wherever they go
and today we're the prize tourist attraction."

Figgy smiled, pointing to a statue of
Chiang Kai-shek they were passing.

"So when their parents ask to see shots of
their national hero, they'll see us instead?"

"It's our fifteen minutes of fame. Enjoy
it."

Five teenage girls wandered past them,
grinning and pointing to their cameras. Will
and Figgy obliged yet again. The girls
finished and managed a chorus of good-bye,
although one said hello instead, only to be
corrected, with giggles, by her friends.

"Watch for a lighthouse as a sign we're
heading in the right direction. After we find
it, we'll do some nosing around."

She nodded and they started back, murmuring hellos to other student groups who
waved and shouted greetings until they'd
entered Will's car.

Among the crowds of youngsters and their
chaperones, Figgy glanced at a burly man,
face impassive, who watched as they prepared to drive away. Soon afterward, he
returned to his car and spoke to the silver-
haired man in the passenger seat.

"Will, did you notice the car we just

passed?"

He glanced at her and shook his head. "Too busy trying to squeeze past the procession of school buses and avoid the kids all over the road. Why do you ask?"

Figgy shrugged. "No reason. Just an uneasy feeling. The driver was standing beside his car and I thought he was watching us."

"Probably waiting for his chance to pull out of the lot."

"I guess. There was someone else in the passenger seat but, with the sun in my eyes, I couldn't make out either of their faces." She sighed. "I think I'm getting paranoid, suspecting the motives of people spending an innocent day in the park."

Will turned to smile at her, but didn't respond. A few miles later, he pulled off the road near the lighthouse marked on his map.

"My friend at the plant said this is a must-see."

They looked out at a spectacular view of the water, part of the two straits that surround the island of Taiwan. For a little while, soothed by the splashing of waves, the smell of salt air, and the bounce of spray against her skin, Figgy could forget her fears.

But only for a little while.

"If we're being watched, it's important that we look like tourists," Will said, standing so close she felt his warm breath as he turned to her.

She looked up at him. "Do you think we are?" She tried to keep the tension from returning to her voice.

"I haven't noticed anything unusual, but under the circumstances, it's hard not to be a little paranoid."

She nodded, but said nothing.

"We're going to drive around now and look for lodges and small inns. My map won't be very useful, but I'm hoping to encounter some locals with helpful information."

He looked at her.

"Hungry?"

She shook her head. "Maybe later."

"Sit tight, then. The road will be bumpy."

How true that was of everything that's happened since Tessa's disappearance, she thought. Back in the car, she buckled her seat belt and tried to stay focused.

After what felt like an eternity of rutted roads twisting through forest and farmland they found an inn, its small sign depicting a pan and chopsticks, indicating a restaurant.

"We'll stop here, have something to eat,

and see if someone inside can tell us any-thing."

They entered a small room with dark wooden floors and ceiling supported by matching beams. Will spoke to a tiny old woman behind a desk. She showed a tooth-less grin when she heard his Mandarin, then led them to the dining area. Figgy felt tall following her, a rarity in her life. Will must have seemed a giant to the woman.

"This restaurant's the size of the dining room in my parents' farmhouse," Figgy whispered as they were seated at a small, round table nestled close to three others. They were the only diners.

"Then you should feel at home here," Will answered, struggling to arrange his long legs at the miniscule table. "I probably won't be able to get up on my pretzeled legs."

No menu appeared, no orders were taken, but soon their table was overladen with a succession of fragrant, steaming dishes. A whole fish, head intact and eyes seeming to appraise the diners, glittered on an oval plat-ter nearly as large as the table. Another plate was heaped with huge, pink prawns. Dan-gerously near the table's edge, a bowl of vivid green, leafy vegetable stalks, their sauce rich with garlic and soy, perfumed the room. Their server was a slender male, still in his teens. He placed a tray next to their table, making room for a teapot, cups, and a large bowl of rice.

Will thanked him in English, then switched to Mandarin. Watching the young waiter, Figgy guessed the topic of conversation when he gave her a sidelong glance, then turned to Will and grinned. When he spoke Will listened, nodded, spoke the familiar *shai-shai,* then gestured at the table.

The boy — at least that's what he seemed to Figgy — used a pair of very long chopsticks to divide the fish into portions, separating the head from the body. He picked up the head between the chopsticks, extending it towards Figgy's plate, waiting for her approval. She shook her head so violently that Will, watching, hid his grin with his napkin.

The server turned to Will, offered the head, and smiled his approval when Will nodded. He placed fish, prawns and vegetables on each plate, ladled rice into their bowls, then poured tea for each of them.

As he prepared to leave Will stopped him, spoke briefly, and concentrated on the reply. Then the server left and they began to eat, not speaking until Figgy saw her companion use his chopsticks to pick out some flesh from the fish head.

"Ooh," she said before she could stop herself. "Are you really going to eat that? I thought you were just being polite."

Continuing to spear bits from the head, he said, "Local people will tell you it's the tastiest part of the fish. I decided to find out for myself when I first came to Taiwan and I think they're right. Want a taste?"

She shook her head.

"I couldn't stand to look at those pathetic eyes staring at me."

"They haven't stopped you from digging into the rest of the critter."

"That's because his head isn't on my plate, making me feel guilty."

She ate some vegetables, proud of her increasing ability to grasp them with her chopsticks. "Mmm. Delicious. And no eyes to freak me out."

After tasting her tea, she said, "I'm guessing your conversation with our server wasn't about the cuisine. I caught his ogling look."

"I guess a leer is universal language. I wanted information and the best way was to say I'd brought my date a long way from the city so we could — have a little private time without anyone we worked with finding out. I asked if he had any suggestions for places we could . . ."

"Hook up?"

Will nodded.

"I had a little trouble finding the right phrase in Mandarin, but he got the picture."

"I could tell."

"The look was a compliment. He was approving my taste."

Figgy drank some more tea, hoping the cup hid what felt like the beginning of a blush.

"He told me this inn has a few rooms to rent, but he was sure his mother would disapprove, although Granny at the desk would understand. His mother's an old-fashioned type, he said, who doesn't even like it when he brings female classmates home for study sessions."

"His flirty style might make me suspicious of the homework he planned too. Mama knows her boy."

Will smiled. "And we all know that boys will be boys. Anyhow, he said there were some small inns near Pingting, a place on the Pacific side of the island. He also mentioned a smaller place, Taitieng. And he commented that some of the wealthier families from cities up north built second homes near the ocean, but they're very private. No rooms to rent there."

"Does he know any of the owners?"

"No names were mentioned, but he did

say that sometimes his mother is hired to cater parties at the bigger estates. There's one in particular, where they pay her double what anyone else does. She likes the kitchen there. It's big and well-equipped."

"That could describe any rich family's house."

"How about this? When she started cooking for this man, he sent a driver for her and her equipment, because no strangers' cars are permitted on the grounds. Now he knows her, so she can use the inn's van. Guests are usually picked up somewhere else and chauffeured to his estate for parties. And there are guards to keep intruders away."

"You think that sounds like Liang?"

"It sounds like a man obsessed with privacy . . . or one who has something to hide."

The muscles in Figgy's neck and shoulders felt like guitar strings tuned too tightly. She moved her head in slow circles, then raised and lowered her shoulders.

Will, watching her, said, "I wish I could tell you more, but the best we can do is drive around to some of the places the boy mentioned, maybe ask a few questions."

"Won't that make the innkeepers suspicious?"

"Not if you're with me and I tell them we're planning to get married and looking at some honeymoon possibilities as we make our arrangements."

Figgy looked down at her plate, not wanting to meet his eyes.

"I guess that would work. Shall we get started?"

"Do you want to wait in the car while I take care of the check, maybe get the boy to talk some more?"

She nodded and he handed her the car keys.

"I'll be along soon. Try to relax. We'll get this sorted out."

Will's reassurances helped, Figgy thought as she reached the car.

But her mind shut down when her arms were pinned behind her and a gloved hand choked off her scream. The keys slipped through her fingers. She was half-pushed, half-dragged along the narrow road that led to the inn, then forced into the back seat of a black sedan pulled to the side.

CHAPTER EIGHT

Too shocked to find her voice, Figgy twisted her body to stare into the steely eyes of Mr. Kao.

"You stupid, stupid girl," he growled. "How often do you need to be told to stop meddling in things you can't possibly understand?"

She started to speak, but he cut her off, voice low and ominous.

"No explanations, no excuses. Mr. Chu has been extremely patient with you." His eyes bored into hers. "Much more than I would be. For the last time, I tell you to leave this matter alone."

"Not until Tessa's safe and back in her apartment," Figgy managed, sounding more defiant than she felt.

"Keep interfering, and she'll be lost to you forever. Now, get out of the car and tell your lover to mind his own affairs or risk ruining his career here."

"He's not my —"

Kao opened the door, pushing her so hard she fell onto the gravel of the roadway. The car started up and roared off, scattering more gravel in its wake.

Will found her sitting by the side of the road, knees scraped and bleeding.

"Figgy! What happened? Are you all right?"

Before she could answer, he lifted her and carried her to his car, placing her gently across the back seat.

"When I came out and found the car door open, the keys on the ground, I —"

Will didn't finish the sentence. Instead, he brushed back the hair that had fallen across her face and stroked her cheek.

"Your slacks are torn and your knees are bleeding. Just lie still while I get the first-aid kit from the trunk. I'll clean the scrapes, and put some ointment and a bandage on them."

Figgy nodded, lying back and closing her eyes. She wanted to remember every detail of her encounter with Kao, every word. What she was feeling was no longer fear. It was rage.

"Okay, that's better," Will said after attending to her knees. He raised his head to look at her. "You have a few abrasions from the gravel, but I've cleaned them and they should heal fine. Now, tell me what happened."

She sat up in the back. Will sat beside her with his arm around her shoulders. When she'd finished describing her encounter with Kao and repeated his message, Will's reaction matched hers in fury.

"Who the hell does he think he is, threatening you and hinting he could destroy my career? If he thinks he can intimidate with that kind of mobster crap he's got another think coming."

"His reaction must mean we're getting closer to finding them."

Will nodded, face grim. "Right. Up to a bit more driving?"

"You bet. I think Kao has another think coming too, whatever that means."

"If you're criticizing my clichés you're feeling better. Let's go look for the big house our innkeeper's son mentioned. I should have tried talking to Granny. She probably knows all the local gossip."

Will found a radio station playing American jazz. They were both quiet. Figgy, lulled by the car's motion, tried to think of nothing except the concern in Will's voice and his gentleness as he'd bandaged her knees.

"I think that must be the estate of our 'big

man' as Thomas, the restaurant owner's son, called him. See it up there on the hill, nestled among the trees?"

Figgy looked toward the mountain they were skirting and saw a stone and wood-shingled building blending so perfectly into its forest environment it could easily be missed by passersby. Will slowed the car as they tried to get a better look at the luxurious house.

"Liang's idea of a modest country hideaway?" she said. "Think we can get closer?"

"Not without being spotted," Will said. "If we had binoculars we'd probably see a gatehouse, with guards. If the Lins' employer is Mr. Liang, he'll be very particular about who approaches his estate."

"Do you think that's where he's keeping Tessa and Ken Chu?"

Will shrugged.

"It's isolated and, according to young Lin, always has guards. Nobody can get in or near it without our mob boss knowing about it."

He looked at Figgy.

"I think we should go back to Kaoshiung. We've found out what we wanted to know. Now we need to decide what to do."

Figgy nodded, leaned back and closed her eyes. The next thing she knew, Will was gently shaking her shoulder.

"We're back at the hotel. You've had a well-earned nap."

"Funny. I thought I wouldn't really rest until we found Tessa." She looked at Will, trying to keep her face from crumbling. "Do you think she . . . and Ken . . . are still . . . still . . ."

"Yes. Liang is ruthless and arrogant, but he's no fool. Eliminating the son of one of the most powerful businessmen in the country and an American woman who works for him would, at the least, create ugly notoriety and an investigation by foreign officials. He can't afford to risk his global business enterprises with public attention and a scandal. Men like Liang want to be visible when they're enjoying their celebrity, not when they're committing the crimes that finance it."

Figgy dabbed at her eyes and turned to him. They were still sitting in Will's car, a few feet away from the hotel entrance.

"It's insane, all this menace and furor over a little green horse. It can't matter that much to have been cheated when Liang is so rich. He can buy plenty of other jade antiquities."

"Being reasonable is not what this is about. If other collectors find out that Liang, with all his bragging about being a connoisseur of rare jade, has been deceived, they'll fall all over themselves with glee. Liang is forcing Chu to preserve his reputation by insuring the horse and protecting his secret."

"Since Chu knows how unscrupulous Liang is and the danger to Ken and Tessa, why doesn't he just agree to it?"

"Chu is just as unyielding in this saving-face duel. If he gives in to Liang, he becomes Liang's man. That would be repugnant — and unacceptable — to someone as proud and strong-willed as Chu."

Something that felt like a fireball was building inside Figgy. The fear, the sadness, her desolation without Tessa, all contracted into a single response — outrage. Her hands curled into fists, nails biting into her palms as she pounded them on the metal panel in front of her.

Will stared at her.

"That's it! Enough of this monumental insanity, playing chicken with Tessa's life. It has to stop."

She opened the car door and began pushing through the sidewalk crowds, away from the hotel.

Will, dodging pedestrians to follow her, called, "Wait! Where are you going?"

People on the sidewalk stopped and turned, shaking their heads at the two crazy Americans rushing past them.

"To see Chu. It's time to end this."

When he caught up with her Will tried to slow her down by taking her arm, but she resisted and kept going.

"Figgy, Chu is insulated by an army of secretaries, guards, and lackeys. You saw that last time. You won't get through."

"Just watch me," she said as they approached the building.

As Will had warned, they were stopped nearly as soon as they entered the building. The guard who'd ushered them in when Chu sent for them recognized the Americans.

"You have an appointment, Miss?"

Figgy nodded and the man spoke in Mandarin to Will, who repeated his words sotto voce.

"He says you're not on the list and besides, it's too late for appointments. Mr. Chu will soon leave the building for the day."

She nodded and kept walking toward the elevators. The guard, realizing what she was doing, put down his phone and followed, shouting words she didn't understand but certainly caught the meaning of.

He was too late. Figgy had slipped into an elevator, Will close behind, and the door closed before the guard could stop them.

Inside, Will studied her face.

"I don't know what you think you're doing, but I admire your chutzpah."

"Mmm," she said, stabbing at the button for Chu's floor.

When they emerged from the elevator they were greeted by a large, muscular security guard who took each by the arm, not too gently.

He spoke in Mandarin.

"He's escorting us out of the building," Will explained.

"Not until he gives Mr. Chu my message," Figgy said.

"And that would be?" Will looked at her with a mixture of apprehension and admiration.

"That unless he sees me, I'm contacting CNN to talk to a reporter about a missing American woman and some phony antique that's gotten her kidnapped."

Will repeated his message and the guard whipped out his cellphone, speaking so rapidly that Will's confused look told Figgy he couldn't follow the conversation.

Clipping his phone back on his waist, the guard glared at her, then gestured that she and Will walk in front of him down a corridor. When Figgy hesitated, trying to remember the location of Chu's office, the guard gave her a non-too-gentle push.

Will, scowling, took her arm to urge her along. She moved, muttering, "Tell him that if he touches me again I'll use my knee to stop him in a way he won't soon forget."

Will tried to stifle his grin.

"I'll keep that to myself and run the image in my head."

Figgy permitted herself a small smile, but her face turned grim again as they entered the president's office.

Mr. Chu was seated behind his large, well-polished desk. Kao, every silver hair in place, stood behind him, expression icy and body tense. Like a rattler about to strike, Will thought, but Figgy seemed oblivious, ignoring him. She planted her hands on Chu's immaculate desk and leaned forward, face close to him.

"I'm here to tell you this has to end. I'm sick of these crazy power games. You need to do whatever it takes to convince that crooked mobster you'll insure his fake jade. Then, when Tessa and your son are safe, you can expose him for the fraud he is and preserve the reputation you seem willing to sacrifice your son to maintain. I won't let you sacrifice Tessa too."

Mr. Chu had listened, ramrod straight in his chair, during Figgy's tirade. When she finished his body sagged and the pain on his face revealed his own suffering. Kao started to respond, but his employer held up his hand and silenced him. Kao's face, as he watched Figgy, was a study in hatred.

"You are a foolish young woman if you think this is about an old man's vanity and not a father's anguish. Sit down, please, both of you. What I'm about to tell you must never leave this room. You do understand that?"

Both nodded, then sat in the same elaborately carved chairs Figgy remembered from their last visit. This time all her attention focused on the face across from her. She saw the deep lines that etched his eyes and mouth, the downward-curved lips. Mr. Chu looked much older than she remembered.

"You believe, apparently, that this is all about pride, preserving my reputation when it's threatened by a thug. I've known men like Liang all my life. They never frightened me — until now. I would freely give up my wealth, my company, my life to protect my son and your friend."

"Then why —" Figgy began, but was interrupted.

"Please. I know how impulsive and quick to speak Tessa is and I recognize that you share that trait. But you must listen now and, I implore you, understand."

Figgy nodded, leaning back in the chair, hands clenched in her lap. She could sense Will's tight stillness beside her.

"In your country, prejudices and discrimination against people who are . . . different . . . are, I understand, lessening. You have laws to protect them in their lives and their workplaces. But here, old attitudes prevail. Men who are not like most others are treated with contempt. Family, money, reputation — nothing can protect them from scorn and ugliness. I cannot bear the idea of that happening to my son."

Figgy forced herself to refrain from questions, but her confusion was apparent on her face. Mr. Chu watched her. Figgy saw his chin tremble before he spoke again.

"Ken is a homosexual. I know that increasingly in America such men and women live open, normal lives and are accepted in their communities. That would not be so for my son. Here, he is very careful, very discreet. When he travels to the States or to Europe, he can be much more free. But at home he is entirely correct, never behaving in any way that is . . . suspect."

"But Liang has found out and is threatening to expose him," Will said while Figgy was turning the information over in her mind.

"Does Tessa know?" Figgy asked.

Mr. Chu nodded.

"Ken chose to tell her, knowing his secret was safe with her. They do many things as a couple, go about the city together. Tessa is his closest friend." He stopped to sip some tea from the porcelain cup near his hand. "I believe she helps to keep Ken's secret safe. Because he is free to talk with her about anything, I sometimes think that Tessa keeps him sane too."

"Then why not agree to insure the horse and be done with it?" Figgy asked.

"The problem, child, is that I won't be done with it. Liang has implied this is only the beginning. He would use my firm to insure and support whatever crooked deals he makes in the global market. My reputation becomes the respectable front for evil and corruption. It is horrible to contemplate."

Chu raised his hands to rub his face. Figgy saw how he would look as a very old man.

"What are you going to do?" she asked.

Mr. Kao responded for his employer.

"We've been working on plans to remove

222

them from the place where they're being held. Your interference hasn't helped, as I've tried to show you."

Remembering her scraped knees, Figgy glared and started to speak, but Chu spoke to Kao in their own language. His tone was not gentle.

"Kao means well," he said, looking at Figgy and Will. "But, in his determination, he lacks patience. You must understand, Ms. Newton, that your efforts, admirable as they are, do no good and may harm our cause. You must leave this to us."

"I can't just sit around and do nothing," Figgy said. "I'm expected to go back to my job in Pennsylvania soon and I won't just abandon Tessa."

"I believe you are a sensible young woman and I ask you to use that good judgment now. Keep to the schedule you planned and go home when you are expected to return. When Tessa and my son are safe I promise to give your friend a vacation in the States. You'll be together for a long, happy visit. A peaceful one. But now, until this trouble is settled, there is no peace — or safety — here for you. Do you understand?"

Paling, Figgy nodded.

"And you, Mr. Bowers? You would not want to jeopardize your splendid reputation at the steel plant, nor damage your company's successful growth."

Will said nothing. Only the grim set of his mouth revealed his emotions.

"Then we will say good-bye. Have a safe return to your home, Ms. Newton."

He stood, dismissing them. Kao watched, his frigid gaze locked on their faces, until they left the office. A security guard accompanied them to the elevator; another met them on the first floor and followed them until they left the building.

Walking silently, each seemed lost in thought. As they approached the hotel, Will asked, "What now?"

"I'm not sure yet, but I will not let Tessa's boss push me around, no matter how reasonable he sounds and how sure he is that he can free Tessa. I have to think of a way to avoid him and his goons."

"What about Liang's goons?" Will asked, following her into the lobby.

"Them too," she said. "Let's order some tea. We can talk upstairs."

Will said, "I'll do that and then join you. You look like you need to sit down and take some deep breaths."

"I'm not intimidated anymore, just mad."

As she walked past the desk, she saw that Buddy was working. Figgy waved, but didn't stop, although she could see he wanted to talk to her.

She wasn't ready to answer his questions. She had to think.

When Will arrived with a tray, he found her curled up on the couch, feet tucked under her and a faraway look on her face. He set the tray down on the table near the couch, poured two cups of steaming tea, handed one to her, and then pulled up one of the apartment's chairs close to her.

"I'd ask if you were thinking about the trip home, but I know better."

"There has to be a way to get into that stone castle. If I could get inside, I know I could help Tessa."

"Chu wasn't kidding about the danger. He's under the impression you agreed to stay out of trouble and go home."

"I will stay away from him and his enforcer. But I have no intention of leaving without knowing Tessa's safe."

"What if I go to a government guy I know who's based in Taipei? I'll tell him as much as I can and let our embassy people look for Tessa."

She shook her head.

"By the time they creep through their protocols it might be too late. And unless Chu agrees to Liang's blackmail, the mob boss may get impatient and — and that will be too late too. No, I have to get into Liang's house. And I think I know how."

"Figgy, whatever's in that convoluted mind of yours, it's too dangerous. Liang would think nothing of making you disappear. Just one more crazy tourist who was careless and wandered into the wrong neighborhood. Robbed. Kidnapped. Pity."

"Not if we fool him. Come up with a really good plan."

"He didn't become a crime kingpin by being fooled. I don't think you realize what you're up against here."

Figgy's hand tightened around the cup she was cradling.

"I know that if I don't do something Tessa could die. I can't let that happen."

He took the cup from her hands and held them.

"Don't you think Chu, with all his resources and influence, is better equipped to save her and Ken?"

"Not as long as he thinks he can finesse a deal that will keep his name and Serenity's clean. I know he's trying to protect Ken, but I think his business matters almost as much."

Will put his arms around her. It was a refuge, a place where she could pretend that none of the things that had happened were real. Reluctantly, she withdrew and began to pace. Will watched, resigned to whatever she decided. He waited until she sat back down.

"What I have in mind involves Buddy, Will. Do you think that's a mistake?"

"How can I answer when I don't yet know what you plan to do?"

When she explained, he shook his head.

"It's so outrageous it just might work. But I hate the idea of your putting yourself in that much danger."

"No choice. While Chu ponders about negotiating a deal, Tessa's a prisoner. I know her. She'll get so frustrated, she'll try something extreme and crazy. Those thugs guarding her could do anything if she gets them mad enough."

"You have to be honest with Buddy without telling him too much."

"I know. I'll say that a gang associated with Liang has kidnapped Tessa and Ken. I can tell him they're being held for ransom. That's not exactly lying."

"It would be better to keep him out of it and involve me instead."

"Oh, Will, who would believe you're a culinary expert?"

"Liang's people have seen you. What

makes you think you can deceive them?"

"If I can get past Thomas Lin and his mother, it'll work. Buddy can get me a wig. I'll put on more make-up than I usually wear and pass myself off as an American hoping to be a chef, studying Chinese cooking with Buddy as my mentor."

Figgy saw Will's skepticism and was determined to persuade him — and herself — that it would work.

"I can convince them. Buddy told me he took food preparation classes as part of his hospitality course. He knows how to cook and can convince Mrs. Lin he'd like me to have some catering experience as part of my training."

"He can also slip her some cash to encourage her. Tell her it's extra because you're a rich American and won't object to paying more for the training as a caterer. Something to impress your wealthy friends at home."

"That might work, except that I don't have the spare cash."

"It will be my part of the plan, that, and waiting in the car somewhere nearby to get you all away from Liang's house."

"Thanks. I knew you'd understand. Now, I need to talk with Buddy."

"And I better see what's going on at the plant." Will looked at her. "When all this is over, we need time just for us."

She nodded. "In Philadelphia, after I get back to my job. That is, if I still have one."

"That dragon of a headmistress wouldn't dare lose such a treasure. The kids would rise up in a mutiny. Picket. Storm the building."

Figgy laughed.

"Let's go downstairs before we lose complete touch with reality."

"Wouldn't that be nice?" Will said, arm around her waist as they walked to the elevator.

She watched him leave, then walked to the registration desk. Buddy looked up from the computer to smile at her.

"How you doing? Any news from Tessa?"

"That's what I want to talk to you about. Can you take a break?"

"Sure. Let me find Sherry Chan. New girl in training. Very nice, you would like her." He grinned. "Very pretty. I like her too."

"I'll see you in the dining room."

Figgy went to the restaurant and ordered tea and almond cakes. She leaned back in the chair, rubbing her eyes and trying to ignore the fatigue settling into her bones. *When I get home,* she thought, *I'm going to do nothing but teach and sleep. When I know Tessa is okay.*

"You looking tired, Miss Figgy," Buddy said, sliding into the chair across from her. He knew he could make her smile when he called her that, after she explained about her childhood affection for the long-lashed, winsome television pig.

By the time her order arrived, she'd rehearsed in her mind the way she would present her plan to Buddy. She explained, editing the narrative to keep out the blackmail threats about Ken, emphasizing the kidnapping for ransom by thugs holed up in a house near the ocean. She only mentioned Liang's name in passing, but Buddy wasn't fooled.

"This house where you think Tessa and Ken Chu are — is it the summer mansion of Mr. Liang?"

She hesitated, pretending to be puzzled, remembering Chu's warnings. She hated doing this to Buddy, but she knew she would deceive her own mother if it meant saving Tessa.

"I don't know the owner's name. Thomas Lin just called him 'the big man.' He's not at the house often, but has people staying there all the time. Mrs. Lin only goes there when he's in residence, to cater his parties."

Buddy was silent, considering what she'd told him. He drank some tea, then pushed his cup aside.

"I'm sorry. I can't do what you ask."

"But I don't understand. I thought you liked Tessa and wanted to help."

"I do. And if it didn't involve Liang I would do anything for her. But his men would not do anything without his knowing, even ordering it. And I don't think it's for money. Liang doesn't need Chu's money and wouldn't go against him if it's only about money. Whatever reason, you don't understand the power of this man. I would take the risk if it was only me because I'll soon be leaving Kaoshiung. But my family lives here, Figgy. Liang takes revenge against relatives of those who cross him.

"Everyone in town knows the stories. Houses burned to the ground. Bodies floating in the river. Businesses ruined. I can't put my parents, my sisters, or our cousins in danger. I am sorry."

Figgy felt as if she'd been slapped. She was so sure Buddy would agree to her plan. Now she was out of ideas. The sense of helplessness overwhelmed her. She looked at Buddy, hoping he would understand.

"I don't know what else to do. If I could get into that house and find Tessa and Ken, I could figure out a way for them to escape. Will would be waiting nearby and we'd drive away. Home free. Happily ever after."

She buried her face in her hands. Buddy sat quietly, frown lines creasing his forehead.

His voice brought her back.

"It's not a bad plan. It still could work."

"Not without a way into Liang's house."

"Maybe I know how."

She looked at him, not daring to hope he'd changed his mind.

"Not me, but what if there's someone else to be your cooking teacher? With no family to risk and a real chef."

"I'm not following you, Buddy."

"The hotel cook, Huei-Sheng Tan, came here from Beijing. No family. He lives alone, so Liang couldn't hurt anyone he cares about. He's older but he likes adventure, and I think he might do it. I'd take care of all the advance work. Use his name and call Mrs. Lin, explaining that Will, an American friend, had praised her cooking. I'd say the chef would like to bring his American student to study her catering skill and he'd like working with Mrs. Lin too. No pay involved. If there's a bonus for her to include you and Huei-Sheng when she caters a party, I bet she'd do it."

"Do you really think Mr. Tan would? He doesn't know me or Tessa."

"He knows Tessa. Months ago, she asked

to meet the chef and thank him for something he'd prepared that she really liked. He was pleased, especially when she complimented him in Mandarin. He knows you're her friend. Hotel staff enjoys gossip, like everybody else."

"If only he's willing . . ."

"I'll go talk to him and let you know right away. Will you be in the apartment?"

"No, I'll go crazy up there, pacing while I wait. I'll take a walk, then come back here and wait for you."

Buddy nodded and left the dining room. Figgy tried to drink some tea and eat an almond cake, but her stomach felt full of rocks. She gave up and went outside.

Telling herself not to think about anything, she tried to concentrate on the street sights and sounds. When this is all over, she'd want to remember every detail in order to describe the scenes to her students. She imagined the questions they'd have, then looked around for answers. Because the day was cooler, although still warm by Pennsylvania-winter standards, local children were wearing quilted jackets over their trousers. Male motorbike drivers sported helmets with earflaps, like the pictures of World War II pilots.

As she thought about describing that to

fifth-graders, a female biker whizzed past, but not before Figgy noted her high-slit red skirt, stiletto heels, and net stockings. A leather jacket and helmet with earflaps didn't distract from heavily mascaraed eyes and crimson lipstick. She'd skip that description to the kids.

Further on, near a trash can, a man crouched, knees to chin, in a position that looked natural for local people, but would be clumsy and probably painful if she tried it. He was gutting a raw fish, which he'd soon be cooking and selling at a foodstand a few feet away. Close by another vendor hawked roasted chestnuts, smoke and the burnt smell of charcoal wafting through the air. The hot yams seller was at his stand too. Her students would like that detail, eating yams for a snack on the street.

She walked past one of the many bookstores she'd visited. It was crowded as usual, with lines of people waiting to pay for their purchases. At the start of her visit, Figgy had browsed in this shop and several others, surprised at the abundance of booksellers. She'd bought children's books illustrated in brilliant shades of red, yellow, and green, with captions in graceful calligraphy, to take back to her classroom.

That first day of exploring, waiting for

Tessa to get back from Taipei so they could have fun together, seemed like a lifetime ago. The familiar sick, helpless feeling returned. What if the chef refused? Despite the noise, laughter, tempting food aromas all around her, Figgy felt alienated and alone. Color drained from the surrounding world; for her it became a bleak, desolate place. She walked back to the hotel.

Buddy was waiting for her. Standing with him was a spare, middle-aged man, chef's toque covering most of a balding head. When Buddy said, "This is Chef Tan," the man extended his hand and nodded.

"Does this mean you'll help me?" she blurted and the chef turned to Buddy, who spoke to him in Mandarin. He nodded, smiled, then spoke again to Buddy. Figgy waited, puzzled.

"Huei-Sheng says he'll be glad to help because he likes Tessa. I'm to call Mrs. Lin and make arrangements. He'll go with you to her inn and from there the plan goes into action."

The chef stood by, nodding and listening, then spoke again. In Mandarin. Buddy said a few more words and Chef Tan left.

"He has work to do in his kitchen, but he'll see you soon."

Figgy watched Chef Tan's receding back,

then turned to her friend.

"You neglected to mention Huei-Sheng doesn't speak English."

Buddy looked sheepish. "He understands a few words, but feels more comfortable speaking his own language."

The elation she'd felt when she met him began to fade.

"How can this possibly work? He's supposed to be my teacher and I can't understand a thing he says? No one, Mrs. Lin or the people at the house, will believe us." Her voice was rising, reaching toward semi-hysterical.

Buddy took her hand, leading her to a corner out of the busy center of the lobby and sat with her on one of the leather couches.

"Tessa would say take a deep breath. Come on, in . . . out . . . slowly. Good. For many centuries, Buddhist monks do breathing for calmness."

"This is no time for culture-sharing. I'm not a Buddhist and I'm sure as hell not calm."

He smiled. "Sounds like Tessa. Sometimes she likes to curse — even taught me a few new words in English."

"Buddy, you're stalling. Tell me how this plan has any chance of working when my 'teacher' and I have no idea what the other is saying."

"First, another deep breath. In . . . out . . . slow. Concentrate on movement of chi — life force — through your body."

"Any minute now, I'm going to add to your vocabulary of swear words," she muttered, but did as Buddy told her. Then, quieter, Figgy listened to his explanation.

"First, no other choice. I can't do it and there's no time to find someone who knows cooking and also English." Buddy was using his fingers to count off the points he wanted to make, much like Tessa when she argued — something else he must have learned from her. Figgy didn't know whether to laugh or cry, but she was paying attention.

"Second, it could be a good thing." Buddy held up his hand, palm out, stopping her objections before she could voice them. "Cooking is not about telling, it's about showing. You do what Tan does — follow his moves. If you make a mistake, he can shake his head to correct you and show you the right way."

"This is not reassuring."

"Don't worry. Chef is smart and understands the problem. He says your language ignorance will make the plan more convincing."

"How does he figure that?"

Buddy hesitated. "Don't get mad, but it fits the — what is that word Tessa told me? You know, like thinking what's wrong with some groups of people."

"Stereotype?"

"That's it. Like a rich American wanting to learn Chinese cooking without understanding the language or the culture. She could go to Chinatown in most any city in the States. Instead, silly woman with too much money doing this because she — or Daddy — can pay. It's to brag with her friends."

"I get it. The ugly-American thing."

Buddy nodded, waiting for her reaction.

"So the more mistakes I make, the more convincing I am. Do you think Mrs. Lin will buy it?"

"Sure. No offense, but she sees a few tourists like the one you'll pretend to be. They probably stayed at her inn."

"And she probably made a handy profit, right?"

"Oh, oh, you're getting mad."

"No, I just hate it when a few jerks — of whatever background — give the rest of us a reputation we don't deserve. But, I think you're right about the way I should act with Chef Tan. My nervousness and the fact that

I'm clueless about what's being said should convince Mrs. Lin."

"Okay! Now my job." He was counting on his fingers again. "One, I call her and make arrangements. Two, I find you a wig and more make-up than you wear. You bring any fancy jeans?"

"Are you kidding? On my teacher's salary? I only brought three pairs, my discount store specials."

"Never mind. I know a girl who has plenty, about the same size as you. I'll borrow jeans from her."

"I hope you know her well. She's not likely to lend expensive clothes to a complete stranger."

"No problem. We used to date. She's a good friend, found a richer boyfriend. Maybe she'll lend me some earrings, other stuff too."

"Couldn't we keep the wardrobe simple? Everything else is complicated enough."

"You have to look like a spoiled rich girl. And she has all the right things for that."

Hearing more about Buddy's friend would be interesting, but not now. She returned to the apartment, called Will's cell to tell him the rescue scheme had started, and waited.

CHAPTER NINE

She paced the small rooms, opening drawers to see if she could use some of Tessa's things, then slamming them shut. Was she losing her senses? Her friend was six inches taller. In her clothes, Figgy would look like a child playing dress-up, a game Tessa encouraged among her Shadyhill preschoolers.

Fear beginning to creep in, Figgy sank onto the couch. She couldn't lose it now. She had to stay strong, keep her mind out of dark corners.

Her renewed pacing was interrupted by a knock. Buddy stood there, weighed down with bags and smiling. She took the packages and invited him inside.

"Good news," he said.

"That would be a pleasant change," she sighed, putting down the bags.

"Mrs. Lin has a catering job for the big man tomorrow night. Important business meeting, he told her. Fancy meal, with champagne. She says he only wants champagne when the guests are important men who appreciate the good stuff or party girls. She agreed to Chef Tan's help. She liked the money offer and said you will start in the kitchen at the inn with little jobs. But, mostly, you should watch and stay out of the way in the host's house.

"She wants big pay for this, Figgy. Are you sure you can do it?"

"Will's on his way and will cover the bribery part of the deal."

"Okay, all set then. While we wait, you should try my friend's clothes. She's small, like you, so they'll fit." He hesitated. "I had some trouble finding a wig — only red and blond in the store. I brought one of each, for you to decide."

Figgy took the packages into the bedroom. As Buddy had promised, the jeans were an expensive designer model. She pulled them on, checking the look in the long mirror on the bathroom door. They fit fine. Snug, but feeling good when she moved, demonstrating why the ones she usually wore were sold at a discount.

With the jeans were a black sweater and apple-green blouse. She inspected the sweater, a cashmere so soft she couldn't resist stroking it. No way would she wear this to cook in, no matter how rich she was supposed to be. She returned it to the bag and picked up the blouse, a silk shirt that fit perfectly. Tessa, who adored clothes and shopping, would approve the image in the mirror.

Then she reached into the other bag, pulled out two wigs, and started laughing. The first gave a whole new meaning to the word *red*. It screamed fake, like the rinse-out dyes she and her junior high friends tried on their hair at slumber parties. Where did Buddy find these things, at the local horror-costume shop?

The other wasn't much better — blond, long, and tousled, but, with an effort, she brushed out some of the more extreme ringlets. She tried it on. Whoever said blonds have more fun never contended with a mane like this. Figgy grabbed her comb and brush and set to work, gradually managing to calm the worst of the big-hair look. Then she put on lipstick and blush and returned to the other room where Will was waiting with Buddy. He'd apparently arrived while she was transforming her look.

Both men stared. Then Buddy said, "I'd never tell her, but my friend's clothes look better on you."

Will grinned. "All that hair makes you look taller."

"Will it be enough to fool Mrs. Lin? Her son saw us at their inn. She probably did too. And I have to look different enough to get past Liang's muscle guys who were with him when we were eating dinner downstairs."

"In that outfit, no one would suspect you're a schoolteacher," Will said.

"I don't want to look like a schoolteacher, just survive to be one."

"Maybe a little more make-up?" Buddy advised.

She nodded. "I'll go heavier on the mascara and eyeshadow. And I'll wear some of Tessa's jewelry. I hope all this convinces Mrs. Lin I'm a rich, spoiled American."

"Not much time to get ready," Buddy said. "You leave in a few hours to be at the inn's kitchen early. Lots to prepare, she said. Chef Tan will be in the lobby waiting. He's getting his knives and pans together."

"Won't Mrs. Lin have all the things he needs?"

"Probably, but he's very particular about his knives, won't use somebody else's. Pans too. You need to know that, as cooking student. Chefs are very fussy about equipment. Sometimes bad-tempered too."

"Great! Do I have to worry about Lin and Tan fighting?'

"No, the chef understands how important this is. I never saw him scream or throw things in our kitchen. Of course, he's the boss there and Mrs. Lin is boss at the inn and catering for the party . . ."

"Tell Chef Tan to remind her she's being well-paid to help train his student," Will said. "What is the chef supposed to call you, Figgy?"

She thought for a moment. "My real name, Hazel. That'll keep me alert and annoyed enough to stay in character."

Will looked at her. "I'll remember that. Might come in handy in the future."

She liked the sound of that, but had no time to enjoy the thought.

"I'll need a little longer to work on my make-up. Could Chef Tan find an apron for me? I'd hate to mess up these clothes."

"No worry, she has plenty more. But an apron is good for cooking student. Net, too, for your hair."

"A snood? That should complete the look."

"What is snood?" Buddy asked.

"I'll explain later. You need to watch old Hollywood movies to get the full effect."

"I'll go see the chef, help him to practice

saying *Hazel.*"

"Why does he have to practice?" Will said. "It's an easy name to remember."

Buddy looked at Figgy. She shrugged and said, "Buddy will explain when you go downstairs with him to meet Chef Tan."

By the time she'd finished experimenting with Tessa's make-up, Figgy was satisfied that she'd done a reasonable job of changing her look. The hardest part would be getting comfortable with the wig. It felt heavy and odd over the short casual cut she favored for her brown, flyaway hair. If she had to stuff the long blond tresses into a net, she hoped the whole thing wouldn't dislodge and betray her.

With a last mirror check, she told herself that a slipping wig was the least of her worries. The necklace and earrings she'd chosen bore faint traces of Tessa's perfume. Figgy struggled against the sadness the fragrance evoked as she left the bedroom to wait for Will's return.

The knock at her door came very soon. Will was there, Huei-Sheng beside him. The chef smiled, held out his hand, and said, "Hello, Hazel." He'd been practicing.

"Ni hao, Chef Tan," she answered. What a ludicrous team, she thought, the pupil and the teacher who couldn't understand each other. Judging by his expression she decided Will must be thinking the same thing.

"We'll leave through the back of the hotel," he explained as they walked away from the elevators to the service stairs. "There's a door near the kitchen and I've parked in the back, where the employees keep their bikes. I've rented a car, which seemed smarter than using my own."

"Do you think we're being watched?"

"Hard to say, but Kao is persistent and we certainly don't want him on our tail."

She started to nod, but, aware of the wig, thought better of it.

At the car, Mr. Tan placed a carrier — which must have contained his knives and pans — on the back seat, then sat in the front passenger seat. Exchanging a bemused look with Figgy, Will opened the back door for her.

"Traditional thinking — men discuss important matters while you sit in the back filing your nails and looking pretty."

"How about if I skip the nails and try for a nap?"

"Good idea. In a while, you'll need all your wits about you." He looked at her solemnly. "I wish I could be with you. I hate the idea of you going into that dangerous place on your own." Will leaned into the car, lips brushing her cheek. "I'll be close by and waiting. And take this with you."

He handed her a cellphone. "It's programmed so all you need to do is push this button to get me. It should fit in the pocket of the apron the chef has for you. Use it to call me when you get out of there with Tessa and Ken Chu. I'll be waiting to hear your voice."

Curled up in the back seat, Figgy found the Mandarin chatting of the men in front oddly soothing. She wanted to avoid mental lists of all the things that could go wrong, but her mind persisted in making them: Mrs. Lin, or her son, not being fooled by the hair and make-up, would remember her and spoil the plan; Figgy would be so confused by the chef's wordless instruction the woman would decide she was a disaster and refuse to include her in the catering gig; one of Liang's security squad, suspicious of the new people with Mrs. Lin, would refuse to admit them to the house. And, finally, horribly, the whole scheme would backfire and she'd get them all killed.

Stop it, she almost shrieked aloud. That kind of thinking was toxic. The plan would work. She would make it happen and get Tessa back.

Despite all the internal turmoil, she must

have dozed, because the next thing she was aware of was Will's hand on her shoulder.

"It's time." Will's voice brought her back to the present. "Mrs. Lin's place is just up the road. We've stopped near the spot where Kao confronted you after our dinner because it's too chancy to get closer.

"The chef's story is that a friend from the hotel brought you both out here. Remember, say as little as possible, watch Huei-Sheng, and copy what he does. If Mrs. Lin speaks to you — Buddy says she doesn't know much more English than Huei-Sheng — just smile and follow orders. Don't worry about her recognizing you. Back at the hotel, I almost didn't. And you have that phone I gave you, right?"

"Tucked in my jeans pocket, to be transferred to my apron." She looked at him, fluttering her mascaraed lashes with deliberate exaggeration. "You neglected to reassure me that blonds have more fun."

"I'll save that to demonstrate when all this is over."

"But I'll be a brunet then."

"Trust me, it won't matter. Now go. I'll be close by. Just press the button on your phone."

She nodded, then joined Mr. Tan on the hilly path to the inn. When she turned for a last look, Will was gone.

The inn door opened at once to the chef's knock. Figgy recognized the young man standing there as Mrs. Lin's son, the one who greeted her and Will when they'd arrived for dinner. He looked at her with no sign of recognition, then directed a stream of words at Mr. Tan, who put down his carrying bag and gestured to her to follow. The younger Lin looked in the bag, which Figgy thought was odd, then led them down steep wooden stairs to a cavernous basement room.

It was brightly lit, the air scented with spices and herbs. Figgy saw a huge iron stove, with large woks on two burners, an immense stock pot on another. Mrs. Lin emerged from what appeared to be a walk-in cold storage locker, shook Chef Tan's hand, then turned to give her a thorough, silent appraisal. Finished, she spoke to Mr. Tan and they both chuckled. Figgy was certain that whatever Mrs. Lin had concluded wasn't very flattering. That was probably an advantage. She wouldn't expect much culinary talent from the "student."

Figgy waited while Mr. Tan reached into his pocket and handed Mrs. Lin a bundle of money. She noticed they were American bills, not Taiwanese, and wondered if that had been part of the arrangement. When this was over, she and Tessa would insist on paying Will back. Figgy's only concern was to free her friend. Chu and Kao, his hatchet man, would have to find their own way to save Ken and protect his reputation.

Chef Tan was gesturing to her now. She had to stay alert, keep her mind from drifting and losing concentration. She followed him to a sink in a corner of the room and, as he did, scrubbed and dried her hands. He gave her a long white apron and pulled out his own from the carrier. She was grateful that he didn't offer her a net for her hair. Then he removed a dark, glossy wooden box from his bag, opened it to reveal a collection of lethal-looking knives, and headed back to a long work table in the center of the room.

Figgy followed, then watched as Mrs. Lin returned to the cold storage room with the chef. They reemerged, Mr. Tan carrying a crate full of green vegetables. Mrs. Lin held a tanklike container, its water alive with fish swimming among gliding eels. Throughout she talked to the chef, who said little. Mrs. Lin appeared to be quite the chatterbox, casting sidelong glances at Tan as they returned to the work table. Figgy wondered if she was simply flirting or, instead, gossiping about the Big Man and his dinner party. She felt totally frustrated at her inability to understand.

Mr. Tan dumped the contents of his crate in a mound on the table. "Bok choy," he said, pointing, so that she understood that was the vegetable heaped before her. "Chop-chop," he said, making a cutting gesture whose meaning was unmistakable. Figgy knew his words also meant "hurry" in Mandarin and wondered if that meant she was to be speedy too. Looking at the mountain before her she sighed, thinking this might take all day, and reached for one of the knives in Mr. Tan's box.

Before she could grasp the handle, Chef Tan's hand gripped hers like an iron claw, making her wince. He shook his head and pointed to some knives near Mrs. Lin at the other end of the table. The chef, Figgy learned, was ferocious about his knives.

She moved to the place where the inn-keeper was arranging cutting boards while watching — and smirking at — the knife episode. She directed more words to the chef, who nodded while choosing a large, formidable blade from his own collection. Figgy reached for a less-dangerous looking one from Mrs. Lin's supply and returned to the pile of bok choy.

As she stood beside Chef Tan, he demonstrated the technique for cutting the vegetables into small, uniform sections, his knife flying, fingers nimbly avoiding the blade. Figgy inwardly groaned. No way she could do that without amputating parts of her hand. But when he turned to her, she took up the knife she'd chosen and tried to imitate him.

She could feel Mrs. Lin watching, no doubt still smirking, but she kept chopping. Sometimes the chef stopped her with a light touch on her wrist, to correct a movement or indicate the vegetable stalks should be smaller, the leaves longer, so that they looked like leaves, not merely bits and pieces. After a while she caught on, although she moved carefully, fearful for her fingers. Chef Tan watched, nodded approvingly, and placed a large bowl on the table beside her cutting board. He signaled that she was to put the prepared greens into it, then walked away to join Mrs. Lin. Figgy glanced over long enough to see that they were doing something revolting to the eels they'd fished out of the water tank. She was happy to return her attention to the bok choy.

Her own chopping and scooping of greens into the outsized bowl was punctuated by the chatter and frequent laughter of the two cooks. Either they'd established an instant rapport through their culinary skills or, like some of the other Taiwanese she'd met, they were very sociable. She suspected, too, that Mrs. Lin was flirting with Figgy's supposed teacher.

After what seemed eons, her arms aching, fingers and wrists numb, Figgy had finished the mountain of bok choy, only to discover Mrs. Lin bringing another basket of the vegetable to her workspace. With a barely audible moan, she went back to chopping, trying to ignore the pain in her hands. When this was over she never wanted to see another bok choy, whole or chopped.

At last, she finished the second batch. Sighing her relief, she carried the bowl to the other end of the table, depositing it near Chef Tan. He looked up from the fish he was eviscerating, nodded his approval, then moved to the sink to wash his hands of accumulated slime. Figgy assumed he was preparing to give her another task, one she hoped had nothing to do with fish innards.

Huei-Sheng exchanged a few phrases with Mrs. Lin, then went to the walk-in cooler and emerged with his arms around a sack the size of her parents' obese old cat. That was the way they carried Mortimer too. He approached her end of the table and upended it. Out poured another mountain, this time of a vegetable Figgy recognized. Snow peas, the crisp green pods in the stir-fried meals she often ordered at the Chinese restaurant in her neighborhood.

The chef chose one from the pile and deftly removed the thin, tough strand along each edge. Putting that one into another outsize bowl he'd brought to Figgy, he handed her a snow pea and waited. When she pulled at the stringy part, the pod fractured and the delicate peas inside spilled across the table. Mr. Tan tossed them into a nearby trash container, then handed her another pod, signaling a slower, smoother pulling motion with his fingers.

Figgy tried again. This time the pod remained whole, but the strand came off only partway. Mr. Tan took it from her, finished the job, then handed her another one. He watched and demonstrated through several more attempts, nodding when she finally perfected the technique. Then he returned to his place next to Mrs. Lin and her inevitable comment.

A disparaging one, Figgy was sure. He said nothing, returning to the fish they were now both slicing, shaping, and arranging on trays they periodically returned to the cooler. Figgy was aware of their actions because she had to look up from the heaps of snow peas occasionally or, she was sure, her neck and shoulders would be permanently deformed. The next time she ordered Hunan chicken with vegetables, she'd have a new appreciation of its labor-intensive preparation.

Finally finishing the last of the pods, she glanced at her watch to discover they'd been working in the kitchen for hours. She saw that Chef Tan and Mrs. Lin had begun gathering woks, pans, and other utensils, placing them in large baskets. She joined them, helping to carry baskets to the van parked near the kitchen doors. When they'd finished loading equipment, Thomas Lin climbed into the driver's seat and pulled away. Figgy guessed that things needed for the dinner had to be taken to Liang's estate in shifts.

That meant before too long she'd be joining the two cooks and the younger Lin in the van for the trip that, she prayed, would end with Tessa's freedom. How Figgy would accomplish that once she was in the house, she didn't know, but vowed that at the right time she'd figure it out. The plan had to work. She was Tessa's only hope.

Back in the kitchen, Mr. Tan assigned one last task. He brought her containers of whole pineapples, segmented in their shells, then more trays of varied fruits, some unfamiliar, all cut into decorative shapes. Returning with a stack of platters, he took one, placed a pineapple in its center, then chose fruits from the other trays and arranged them around the pineapple. He finished the artful display by tucking some flowers from another container among the fruits. His gestures told Figgy she was to duplicate the pattern on the other platters. That beat chopping and stringing, she decided, and set to work.

She willed herself to focus on the platters, avoiding thoughts of the challenges ahead. The tasks she'd been given were mindless, well-suited to her state. Her right hand throbbed; her arms and shoulders ached. Yet, when she looked over at them, both Mrs. Lin and Chef Tan were wielding cleavers and knives with rhythmic grace and precision after hours of work. They chatted, seemingly tireless, their conversation sometimes punctuated with laughter. They were ignoring her, which was just as well.

If Chef Tan was uneasy about deceiving Mrs. Lin, it wasn't apparent. As she considered this, Figgy realized that if things got dangerous at Liang's house, the chef had a solid excuse. He could say he was duped by the American. Before he brought her to Mrs. Lin, he had given her cooking lessons, but knew nothing about her except that she was slow and inept! Even if she'd said something suspicious during those sessions, he wouldn't have known since they couldn't understand each other. She reasoned that no matter what happened, the chef would be safe.

Pushing dark thoughts aside, Figgy allowed herself to enjoy the aromas beginning to perfume Mrs. Lin's kitchen. There was the scent of garlic softening in hot oil with the pungent seasoning she recognized as chili peppers. The same fragrance filled her apartment when she rewarmed leftover Hunan chicken. Food being prepared a world away from Mersdale triggered her homesickness.

She was jerked back into the present by a tap on her shoulder. Chef Tan signaled that they were preparing to leave so she needed to hurry with the fruit trays.

Right behind him was Mrs. Lin, inspecting Figgy's work. She nodded, then returned to the stove, removing the lid from the huge soup pot. She reached for a ladle fit for Paul Bunyan and dipped it into the pot. Figgy waited, expecting her to taste the soup; instead, she sniffed it, returned the ladle's contents to the pot, and threw in a handful of seasonings. Mrs. Lin, Figgy noticed, didn't measure ingredients. She cooked by instinct and the clues her nose gave her.

When she was back in her own kitchen, Figgy decided she wouldn't be so compulsive about following cookbook recipes. Her food might turn out better if she improvised. Maybe she would experiment on a dinner for Will. If, that is, this nightmare ever ended, with Tessa safe and her own life back to normal. Better than normal, if Will was part of it . . .

Her musing was interrupted by a jarring noise. Mrs. Lin was clapping her hands, shouting what Figgy assumed were orders to her son, who had arrived back in the kitchen. He came to stand beside Figgy, telling her to cover the trays with plastic wrap. As she finished each, he carried them away to load into the van. When the trays were gone, Figgy helped Mrs. Lin and Chef Tan carry covered metal containers outside to be placed in the van. Last to be loaded were the enormous wok, extra-long chopsticks, wooden paddles, and the biggest electric rice steamer she'd ever seen.

Mrs. Lin then climbed into the seat beside her son and signaled Mr. Tan to join her. Figgy was relegated to a small jump seat behind them, next to the wok and assorted pots and pans. If Thomas Lin stopped suddenly she would be at the bottom of an avalanche of cooking equipment. Death by utensils, she thought, distracting herself from what lay ahead.

The drive was shorter than she'd remembered from her earlier trip with Will. The Lins probably knew a shortcut to the estate.

Their van chugged up a steep driveway, offering Figgy a close-up view of the house. It was even grander than it had looked from the road, a sprawling structure of stone and dark wood, surrounded by thick groves of evergreens. There was a high metal fence that she hadn't seen until they were close to the building. It was the color of the surrounding trees, deliberately designed to blend with them. She wondered if it surrounded the estate or was a gate-like structure across the front. She hoped it was only the front. If the fence surrounded the property, getting away would be much more difficult. Again, she pushed the thought aside. One thing at a time — first, she had to find Tessa and Ken in this rambling mansion.

Mrs. Lin's son stopped the van and honked twice. Then Figgy saw the guards. They too were dressed in green and a few of them looked almost as tall as the surrounding trees. Chef Tan said something to Mrs. Lin, holding up an arm and making a muscle. She laughed and Figgy had no problem figuring out what he was saying. She did believe the chef was now flirting with the caterer! Great, she thought, maybe his attentions would distract Mrs. Lin enough for Figgy to slip out of the kitchen without being noticed. Perhaps he was doing this deliberately but, judging from the silly expression on his face as he looked at Mrs. Lin, she didn't think so.

The security guard responded to the van's arrival by reaching for his cellphone. Soon, two more guards came around the side of the house, their uniforms so green they reminded Figgy of a favorite old movie about Robin Hood's band of merry men. These men didn't look very merry and would probably sneer at Robin's credo of robbing the rich to help the poor.

If the guards could come around to the van without opening the metal gate, Figgy reasoned, the fence didn't enclose the entire perimeter of the building, only the front, where it stretched into the trees. Good, she thought, ignoring the obvious, that other kinds of security and alarms must protect the rest of the estate.

The guards approached the truck and peered inside, exchanging a greeting with Mrs. Lin and her son. The one in charge consulted a clipboard, looked at her and Chef Tan, then again at his papers. He spoke to the chef, received responses he apparently accepted and nodded.

Despite the temperate air of early evening, Figgy shivered as the guard's gaze returned to her. His narrow dark eyes bored into her own, then moved slowly along the rest of her. She tried to remain composed and still, smiling at him. He directed words at her; she shrugged, moving her hands palms-up to show she didn't understand. He spoke again, barking in Mandarin that sounded harsh and threatening. She didn't have to pretend confusion and ignorance as she shook her head. Tan spoke then, waving a hand in her direction.

The guard spat out what she was certain were questions, receiving long responses from the chef. While Huei-Sheng spoke, the man's gaze never left her face — or her body. Figgy tried the tentative smile again, remembering she was supposed to be an empty-headed foreigner with an indulgent family, playing at learning Chinese cooking. Her smile was not returned.

Mr. Tan spoke some more and Mrs. Lin

chimed in. Figgy sat as still as she could, fighting the urge to knot her fingers together or chew on her thumbnail, something she did only when extremely stressed. Tessa, she repeated to herself like a mantra. All this is for Tessa.

Finally, the guard turned away, signaling to the others to open the gate, and the van rolled through. No longer watched, Figgy inhaled gulps of pine-scented country air, her muscles relaxing, if only temporarily.

They drove along the side of the building. Figgy noticed few lights, except for those on what must be the main floor. There were at least two levels above that, in addition to the lowest section of the house. Lights blazed near the back of the first floor — the dining and entertaining areas, Figgy guessed. She doubted that Tessa and Ken would be held near these public spaces. They must be in one of the unlit areas. She had no idea how to get there, but she had to find a way.

Mrs. Lin's son pulled up in front of a wide door on the lowest level. This must be the delivery area and working part of the house. Figgy waited for the others to get out. Mr. Tan turned and signaled her to follow as they entered a long corridor leading past what looked like storage areas and supply cabinets.

When the corridor opened into a large well-lit room, they were met by an older woman, her gray hair pulled back in a tight bun. She greeted Mrs. Lin and her son, shook hands with Chef Tan, then turned her attention to Figgy.

"You are the American student," she said in accented but clear English. "What are you called?"

"Hazel," Figgy answered, surprised at the oddness of her own voice saying her given name.

"These are the rules, Miss Hazel. You obey Mrs. Lin and your teacher. Go only where you are instructed. Other parts of the house are not open to you. Understand?"

Figgy nodded.

"Good. Then help young Lin to unload the truck. I will show Chef Tan where things are kept and Mrs. Lin will start to work. My employer and his visitors soon will be hungry, so no time to waste." A sudden, sharp clap of her hands startled Figgy; this was a no-nonsense woman. "Go, now."

Figgy raced out to the van. The last thing she needed was to offend this woman she assumed was Liang's housekeeper. Knowing some English would increase her usefulness to him. The woman hadn't introduced herself, but she heard the caterer call her Mrs. Jia.

Thomas Lin had opened the back of the van and began handing out cooking utensils. Figgy took as many as she could carry and started back inside, but felt the younger Lin's hand on her shoulder. He gestured that she should wait for him. So she wasn't even permitted to walk through the servants' area on her own? Maybe he thought she might get confused by all the corridors leading to the kitchen. At least, she hoped that was the reason.

He stacked some boxes on the ground, then picked up several and headed inside. Figgy followed with other containers.

Pretending the boxes were more of a burden than they felt, she moved slowly, trying to see down the corridors branching off the main hall as they made their way back to the kitchen. When they passed an especially long one, dimly lighted but with what looked like rooms along it, she paused, trying to see more. Young Lin, not hearing footsteps behind him, turned, an annoyed expression replacing his usual bland one. Figgy pointed to her "burden," making a face and complaining that she was getting tired and needed to rest.

He shook his head in disgust, took the top

container from her, then waved her along. But not before she'd noted at least three doors that might suggest rooms — or only large, enclosed storage spaces. The doors looked sturdy and she thought she saw what looked like locks on them. She reminded herself that Liang might keep his expensive porcelain, silverware, and linens under lock and key. She'd try to watch Mrs. Lin to see where she went to get what was needed for the table upstairs.

In the kitchen, she put down the containers she'd carried and waited while Thomas apparently complained about her slowness. He gestured at her, then spoke to his mother before she followed him back to the van for more supplies.

This time she didn't slow down at the corridor with the doors, but, by counting, memorized where it branched off from the main hall and how far it was to the first door. When they reached the kitchen again, young Lin had no reason to complain about Hazel.

CHAPTER TEN

Liang's kitchen began to fill with tantalizing smells as Chef Tan put the roast duck in the oven to warm while Mrs. Lin tended to her cauldron of soup. She stirred, sniffed, added spices, stirred, and sniffed some more. Meanwhile, the younger Lin hoisted the biggest of the woks onto the stove, gesturing to Figgy to bring the containers of chopped vegetables, fish, and sliced beef and pork they'd carried from the van to the table near the stove.

Nearly staggering under the loads, she decided to make more trips and carry fewer containers. Urging her to move faster, Thomas slapped his hands together, but he wasn't nearly as intimidating as his mother. Figgy had a fleeting image of herself at the front of her classroom, clapping her hands to get her students' attention. She'd never do that again when she returned to Shadyhill — if she returned.

While she hauled containers of food to the worktable, the pace in the kitchen quickened. Chef Tan poured oil into the wok on the stove and turned the flame beneath it so high Figgy half expected it to set off smoke alarms, all the time exchanging comments with Mrs. Lin. Her son momentarily disappeared. When he returned he was transformed from van driver to sleek server in crisp white jacket, black trousers, and black bow tie. Hair brushed back, shoes buffed to a high shine, Thomas looked much as she remembered from her dinner at the inn with Will. A short time ago, yet it felt like the distant past. So did her life in the States. Only the urgency of the present and this place where Tessa could be hidden felt real.

Young Lin was expected to serve Liang and his guests, probably under the supervision of the housekeeper. Chef Tan and Mrs. Lin would be fully occupied here in the kitchen. Figgy assumed she was expected to stand by, doing whatever fetching and carrying they needed. She would have to find an opportunity to slip away, return to the corridor where she saw the doors, and try to learn what was behind them.

Her thoughts were interrupted by a loud exclamation, followed by a stream of words, their meaning unknown but tone universal. Huei-Sheng, standing near the stove, was bellowing his outrage. It was easy to see why: reaching for some seafood in a container filled with fish, ice shavings, and water, he'd bumped it. The contents were strewn across the floor. Figgy hurried to help him, trying not to notice that some of the prawns were wriggling. The chef was pointing and shouting, making it clear he wanted her to scoop up all the slimy creatures and return them to the container.

She did the best she could, throwing prawns and scallops, slippery eels and chunks of fish back into the container and trying to avoid the melting ice that made the floor treacherous. Under other circumstances, wrestling with the sea creatures would strike her as funny but, considering the monumental frown of the chef, she didn't dare laugh. When she'd finally retrieved them all, she handed the container to Mr. Tan, who took it to the big stainless steel sink equipped with a hose spray and began rinsing each specimen of marine life.

Figgy held her red, smelly hands away from her body, wanting to wash them, but Chef Tan was busy at the large sink and Mrs. Lin stood next to the other one skimming fat from her soup cauldron, which she'd finally removed from the stove.

This might be her chance, Figgy realized. Gesturing to the chef that she needed to wash her hands, she was out of the kitchen before Mrs. Lin could protest. The caterer would think Figgy was looking for a bathroom, a place to clean up. She probably would have objected, but she was working with boiling soup, a skimmer, and a ladle, so she had no hands free to signal or point her in the right direction.

Hurrying down the hallway, making a show of looking for the bathroom should anyone try to stop her, she found the corridor branching off the main hall. Figgy stopped, looked around, saw no one, and turned that way. She'd thought there might be other doors along the space, but saw only three.

She paused before the first and listened. She heard nothing. She scratched at the door. No response. Repeating her action at the next one, she had the same result. As she approached the last, the furthest from the main corridor, she noticed a faint light showing beneath the door. She stopped there and listened.

Thinking she heard a shuffling, the sound of movement, she scratched on the door as she had the other two. The shuffling stopped. She scratched again and waited. Then she heard it, the whisper of Mandarin. But the voice was Tessa's, she was certain of it.

Figgy wanted to shout her relief, but she had to be careful.

As she was about to reply, she heard footsteps in the corridor. They were loud and heavy, the sound of boots.

Figgy sprinted away from the door and stopped in front of the first one, pretending to fumble with the handle.

A security guard, a giant in green, grabbed her arm and began to yell, an unintelligible screech of sound. She waved her hands in front of him, gratified that he took a step backwards at the overwhelming fishy stench. But he kept yelling, gripping her arm tightly. Figgy realized this was a chance to let Tessa know she was nearby, so she began to yell back.

"I can't understand you. I'm working with the caterers and have fish smell all over my hands. I need to wash them."

The guard spoke again. Figgy raised her voice still more.

"Stinky hands. I need to find a bathroom. I was looking for a place to wash my hands."

He shook his head, fingers digging deeper into her arm. She was afraid, but desperate to make him understand and to allay his suspicions. Finally, she looked at him and shrieked, "Pee-pee."

"Uh," he grunted. Still keeping his vise-like grip, he pulled her further down the hall to another locked door she hadn't noticed. He took a chain of keys from his pocket and held them close to his face as he pushed a few aside to find the one he wanted. As he bent to see the lock, Figgy figured he must be nearsighted but rejected glasses because they'd alter his tough guy image. Wrong time to psychoanalyze, she told herself.

The room the guard unlocked contained only the barest essentials: toilet, sink, paper towels, and a wooden stool, presumably to be used by an exhausted worker for the briefest of rests. Mr. Liang lived large upstairs, but his domestic staff apparently didn't share in the luxury.

Figgy studied the stool, then lifted it, carrying it to the wall opposite the door where there was a small window midway to the ceiling. She removed her shoes, climbed up on the stool, and peered out. All she saw was some grassy space and more of the towering evergreens; no fence, wall or security people were visible. She stepped down and replaced the stool as the guard shouted and banged on the door.

Figgy flushed the toilet, letting the water run in the sink after she washed away the fish smell. She felt along the wall shared by the adjoining locked room. There were no breaks or openings that she could find. When she scratched, then lightly knocked, there was no response. The room must be empty. Where were they keeping Ken? She turned off the water, then opened the door, smiling in a way she hoped conveyed gratitude and a bit of flirtatiousness. His face remained impassive. She hoped it was his myopia, not her lack of feminine wiles.

Ushered back to the kitchen, she came face-to-face with the housekeeper, Mrs. Jia. Mrs. Lin, working, ignored them, but Figgy saw Chef Tan stealing nervous glances.

"Do you not understand you are to stay in this room and not wander?" she asked.

"But I had to go to the bathroom."

"Then you ask to do so."

"How? No one understands English here except Mrs. Lin's son and he wasn't around. If I tried sign language, it could get embarrassing."

"No need to be rude. Han-Guang knew what you wanted," she answered.

"Only after I got a little graphic with my language. You people should wise up and learn to speak like everybody else." She was really good at this ugly American act. Hazel sounded like the brat she was assumed to be.

The housekeeper muttered some words in Mandarin which Figgy supposed were the equivalent of taking a deep breath. "You chose to intrude into my world. Try to show some of the manners I hope your parents attempted to teach you."

"You don't get that I really had to go to the bathroom and I was desperate. Think how I'd embarrass Chef Tan if I lost it right in the middle of the kitchen."

The other woman made a disgusted face, rolling her eyes in a way that reminded Figgy of Dr. Smithson's responses to Tessa. She tried to keep looking sulky and resentful.

"Stay in the kitchen unless Mrs. Lin or some other staff tells you differently. Understand? That should be clear in any language."

"Yes, ma'am," she said through her pout, loading the phrase with sarcasm.

When the housekeeper was gone, Mr. Tan hurried over with a pan of dumplings and one of the lidded bamboo baskets she recognized from Asian restaurants at home. Signaling her to watch, he showed her how to arrange the dumplings in the basket for steaming. When she'd placed a few to his satisfaction, he nodded and returned to the stove, leaving her to her work.

As she repeated the process, filling the other baskets, her mind circled around what she'd learned in the corridor. She knew where Tessa was being kept now. If that room was like the utility room in size and design, there was probably a window there too, possibly big enough for Tessa to slip through if it were opened or broken from the outside. Her door was locked, with a key kept by a guard with weak eyes but big muscles. Ken's whereabouts were unknown.

It was unlikely — probably impossible — for Figgy to get her hands on the keys. She'd have to find some other way. Meanwhile, all she could do was pretend to be working in the kitchen and keep her eyes open.

The dumplings were all placed in the baskets now and she carried the steamers, two at a time, to the table near the stove. On the table, neatly arranged despite the pressures of speed and efficiency, was an array of utensils and an assortment of knives and cleavers. Off to the side, as if it had been used and was no longer needed, was a small knife with a wooden handle and pointed blade, much like the paring knife her mother used every autumn to peel apples for sauce.

Figgy looked around. Both Mrs. Lin and Chef Tan were working near the stove, their backs to her. She reached for the knife, slipped it into her apron pocket, then slid some of the bamboo baskets over the place on the table where it had been. She thought its point might fit in a keyhole; she could twist and work it to open the lock. Figgy had nothing else and it was worth a try. With luck, the cooks wouldn't notice that a small, unimportant-looking knife was missing.

When she looked up she saw that Chef Tan had turned and was watching her. She felt her hands tremble involuntarily, then reminded herself he was on her side. Mr. Tan winked, then slid his palm across the table toward her. When he took it away she saw that it had covered another small implement, what looked like a thin metal pick.

Figgy had no idea how it was used in the kitchen, but thought it might fit a keyhole better than the knife she'd stolen. She put her hand over it, as the chef had done, slid it to the end of the table and into her pocket. Then she gave the chef a thumbs up sign that brought a smile before he turned back to the stove, giving his task all his attention.

Soon after she carried the last two dumpling steamers to the table near the stove, Mrs. Lin's son came into the kitchen with a tray full of glasses of various sizes and small empty plates. He unloaded them near the sink. Figgy saw some amber-colored liquid near the bottom of a few glasses and assumed that the cocktail hour was over and the main meal about to begin.

She'd learned during her time in Taiwan that, unlike Western meals, all the dishes of a Chinese feast were usually presented, if not together, then in close order and she assumed Thomas would be very busy carrying all the trays of food upstairs, then serving Liang and his guests. What about Mrs. Lin? Would she be preoccupied as well? If so, maybe Figgy could sneak off to the corridor where Tessa was imprisoned and see if the tools she'd hidden might work on the lock.

She was calculating her moves as the younger Lin swept past her, pushing a cart laden with platters and heaping bowls of rice. As she moved out of his way, she felt a tug at her apron. It was Mrs. Lin, gesturing that she was to remove it. She did as she was told, folding it carefully, with the tools concealed deep inside the ample pocket. Now Mrs. Lin was holding out a black skirt and vest and a white shirt. There was also a bow tie.

More hand signals — she was to change into these? What was going on? Figgy glanced at Mr. Tan, who shrugged to show he was puzzled too. Mrs. Lin led her to a corner of the kitchen, behind a tall cabinet, and gestured she was to put on the clothes she'd been given. Still puzzled, Figgy obeyed. The skirt was short and tight. She tucked in the blouse, then buttoned the vest, which fit snugly across her chest. Mrs. Lin had even provided black tights and shoes that reminded her of the ballet slippers she'd worn as a five-year-old in her weekly ballet class. Obviously, the caterer had planned this in advance — the American cooking apprentice transformed into a modified Playboy Bunny! Figgy folded her own clothes into a neat pile, making certain her jeans, Will's phone inside the pocket, were tucked in the center.

When she came out of her improvised dressing room carrying her own clothes, Mrs. Lin nodded approvingly, adjusting the bow tie beneath the stiff shirt collar. Then she led Figgy to the worktable where plates of dumplings and steaming green vegetables waited, directing her to place them on another cart.

Figgy picked up her apron, putting it over her new clothing to avoid any spills. She reached into her pocket, found the knife and pick, and tried to think where in the skimpy outfit she could hide them. There were narrow slits of pockets on each side of the vest, near her waist. The pick fit in one, the small knife barely slid into the other. She glanced down to see if they made bulges in the vest, but it looked okay.

Mrs. Lin directed her to load the cart and to remove her apron, then led her down another corridor ending in a wide door. The caterer pressed a button near the door to reveal a service elevator. She directed Figgy to wheel the cart inside. The door closed behind her and when it opened again the housekeeper was waiting.

"Mrs. Lin chose your uniform well. Now smooth your hair to look neater."

Figgy obeyed, trying not to react to the unfamiliar texture of the wig.

"Follow me to complete your task, Miss Hazel. You are to remove the dishes from the cart and place them on the table. Remember to smile at the guests, but do nothing else to attract attention. If there are used plates, remove them carefully and place them on the cart, then go back to the kitchen for more food and return. Understand?"

"Yes." *No way would I try to attract attention,* she thought.

The housekeeper nodded and led the way through what must have been the study. It was furnished like a room in a BBC television drama, complete with high-backed chairs and a marble fireplace. On the mantel above were tall ceramic vases, their painted flowers outlined in gold.

Figgy was unaware she'd slowed down until the housekeeper gave her a sharp nudge.

"No time to stare. Move along. My employer and his guests are waiting for their food."

The woman led Figgy into a high-ceilinged room paneled in mahogany. Turned away from her as she entered, five men were seated in tall chairs of polished wood, the panels carved with lotus flowers and dragons. A tiered crystal chandelier threw muted light over the table, already covered with dishes the younger Lin had served.

Figgy pushed the cart closer, angling it to parallel the table. The housekeeper whispered a few words to one of the men, who looked up — or, rather, up and down as his gaze roamed over Figgy. She'd only seen him once, the first time she'd had dinner with Will, but there was no mistaking that arrogant appraisal. This was Mr. Liang, Mrs. Lin's Big Man. He exchanged a few words with the man on his left, who also eyed her. Then they both leered.

No need to understand the language, the essence of their remarks was clear from their laughter, the same kind she used to hear from drunken fraternity boys at college parties. She smiled as instructed and began to remove plates from the table to the lower shelf of her cart, concentrating on her task. She hadn't noticed Mrs. Lin's son, standing to the side, until he came to help her place the fresh platters of food on the table.

Figgy glanced at the men sitting opposite Liang and his two companions and nearly dropped the plate she was transferring. She struggled to control her trembling hands, hoping the diners couldn't see how she was shaking. The other two were Mr. Chu and his own enforcer, Kao, the silver-headed man! She was terrified they would recognize her, but they barely glanced her way. Mr. Chu was speaking while Kao sat quietly, using his chopsticks to place some dumplings on his plate.

Liang was apparently listening, but he

continued to ogle her in a way that made her skin itch. Had Tessa been manhandled by this odious creep? She knew her friend would never willingly let Liang victimize her, but she was his prisoner. She was also a bargaining chip, Figgy reminded herself, not one as big as Ken, but important to Mr. Chu. She couldn't imagine why he was sitting at Liang's table, sharing a meal, acting civilized and ordinary. If this was accepted behavior, confronting kidnappers over dumplings and whiskey, it was not only foreign but entirely bizarre.

CHAPTER ELEVEN

Figgy finished serving from the cart, Mrs. Lin's son helping her, then stacked the last of the empty platters for a return trip to the kitchen. Thomas gestured for her to leave and she turned back the way she'd come, feeling Liang and his cronies eyeing her. She hated this! Whatever Chu was up to, she had to get Tessa away from this horror show.

Chu and Kao must be here to negotiate with Liang. What if they could only make a deal for Ken? He was, after all, the scion of the Chu family, so his safety — and his reputation — would be their first priority. Liang might decide to kill Tessa to keep her from talking about the fiasco of the fake jade. The dealer who sold him the little green horse had probably already paid the price for deceiving the notorious Mr. Liang.

Mrs. Jia waited at the elevator for Figgy, pushing the button to open the door.

"Return to the kitchen for more food. When you come back, repeat what you did. My employer may ask you to pour some drinks. If so, smile and do as you're told, then clear more dishes and leave. When all the food has been brought from the kitchen you will not come back here again. Help Mrs. Lin and your chef to pack up the supplies and prepare to leave the estate."

"Yes, ma'am." Figgy hoped she injected just enough sarcasm into her tone to reinforce her role as the spoiled, put-upon foreigner.

In the elevator her heart thumped as she tried to think of what to do; there was so little time left to get to Tessa. Where were the guards? Were they all outside patrolling the grounds or, instead, were most of them upstairs protecting their boss? Instead of returning directly to the kitchen, she'd try going to the room where Tessa was kept and work on the lock.

When the elevator door opened on the bottom floor she rolled her cart, dirty dishes rattling, along the main corridor, looking around but seeing no one. She'd have to leave the noisy cart somewhere and return for it after going to Tessa. She had no plan, except to open that door.

She pushed the cart to the side of the

main hallway, positioning it so it wasn't under one of the overhead lights placed at intervals along the ceiling. Then she scurried down the side corridor to the room where Tessa was kept.

Looking around again to be certain no one was near, she thumped the palm of her hand against the door and whispered her friend's name.

"Figgy?" came an answering whisper. Tessa had heard her earlier shouts. Relief washed over her.

"Is it really you? Or am I hallucinating? How did you find me?"

"No time to explain. If she sees me, Mrs. Dracula the housekeeper will take me to Liang. I have a small knife and pick. I'll try to force the lock."

"If you can push them through, I'll grab them from this side."

Figgy tried the point of the knife. No luck, it just hit against metal. She put it aside and inserted the pick, shaped like a small chopstick but with a sharper point. It struck against metal, as the knife had. She moved it around until, in one spot near the center of the lock, the pick moved inward.

"Tessa? Can you see the pick?"

"Not yet; keep working it."

She pushed harder. The pick moved, then

its length disappeared inside the lock.

"Can you see it now? I'm not holding it any longer."

"No. What about the knife?"

"I'll try to use it to push the pick through."

She gripped the handle and forced the point into the place where the pick had been. Pushing, she hoped the blade's end was forcing the pick further into the lock. She tried the door's handle, but it didn't move.

"Ahieeh!"

Figgy nearly jumped out of her skin. The sound was directly behind her and the knife in her hand clattered to the floor. She turned, expecting to face the muzzle of a gun. Instead, it was Chef Tan who bent to retrieve the knife, grabbed her arm, and hustled her away from the door to the main corridor. He pushed her and the cart the rest of the way to the kitchen.

When they arrived, both Lins were waiting. Whatever the chef told them seemed to work and Mrs. Lin signaled to Figgy that she was to help her son load the cart for the trip back upstairs.

Figgy's hands shook as she placed platters of steaming greens and others of whole fish, heads included, and bowls of soup on the cart. The chef had covered for her, but she'd failed in her botched attempt to free Tessa. And she didn't know if she'd get another chance.

Like a robot, she followed the younger Lin through the corridor and waited while he pushed the laden cart into the elevator, then sent it back down for her. As it returned to the lower floor, she felt numb. She couldn't think of anything but her own ineptitude and she had no idea what to do now.

At the dining table the men were eating and talking. At least, Liang was talking. Mr. Chu looked grim and Kao, beside him, was picking at the roast duck on his plate. When she approached the table, Liang studied her and said something to the man beside him, who nodded and left the room.

He was soon back with Mrs. Jia. She said, "My employer would like you to stay, to pour the drinks and do the serving. Mr. Lin will bring the rest of the banquet."

Figgy nodded, pasted a smile on her face, and placed the platters on the table. As she leaned closer to rearrange some dishes, she could feel Liang's gaze following her every move. Is groping next? she wondered, but kept the smile and moved away to place more serving platters. The host's eyes never left her but he didn't touch her.

As she moved to the other side of the

table, she felt another man's stare. This one wasn't predatory, but intense and searching. It was Kao, the eyes below his silver hair studying her face. He didn't speak, but she wondered if he'd seen through her disguise. If so, she didn't think he'd give her away.

The housekeeper noticed his interest.

"The waitress is an American studying our cuisine. She's apprenticed to one of the chefs and is learning proper serving."

Mrs. Jia then turned to Liang and spoke; Figgy assumed she was repeating her explanation in Mandarin so her employer wouldn't suspect some kind of disloyalty. Liang responded with something that made the woman smile, then turned back to his food.

Figgy, not sure what to do when she'd placed all the dishes on the table and removed the empty ones, moved away, preparing to push the cart to the elevator. The housekeeper stopped her, motioning to Mrs. Lin's son, who waited outside, to take it away.

"You stay here. If my employer signals, pour more drinks. Or he may want tea. You pour that too. And be careful not to spill. He likes things tidy."

Trying to be as unobtrusive as possible,

Figgy chose a spot near a small, decorative table behind Liang and his henchmen, facing Chu and Kao. She noticed that Mr. Chu was eating little, only enough to be polite. On his plate was a small serving of the vegetable dish Chef Tan had created, including snow peas from the mountain of them she'd prepared. There they were with rice noodles, black mushrooms, water chestnuts, and the bok choy she'd chopped, everything lavishly dotted with chile peppers. The ingredients glistened with the soy and sesame oil she'd watched Mr. Tan pour into his wok. Under Liang's chandeliers the food looked iridescent.

Mr. Wang, who owned the Asian Garden in her neighborhood, once told her the Chinese liked greens in their meals because green is the color of life. She remembered that Tessa, before leaving for Taipei, had draped a vivid green scarf over her shoulders. Figgy hoped that was a good omen.

She was jarred from that thought by a loud handclap. Liang was gesturing to her and to the silver teapot behind her. Trying to control her trembling, she carried it to the table and began filling the teacups, starting with the host. Then she moved to the other side, filling Mr. Chu's before she felt the hot stare of the mob boss. His look was anything but erotic; it was appraising and suspicious. Figgy realized she'd blundered. Instead of proceeding from the host to the men beside him, she'd moved to the other person she thought of as the most important in the room — Mr. Chu. Liang would wonder how she knew that, since she was supposed to be a clueless American student working for the chef in the kitchen.

Trying to cover her mistake, Figgy glanced at the others, deciding to act as if she were moving from the host to the oldest of the guests, showing respect for their age. If she was lucky, Liang would buy it. She poured Kao's tea next, then back to his two thugs, choosing the one with the thinning hair first, then the younger one, whose muscles bulged against his suit jacket.

Finished, she looked at Liang. He was still watching her, so she smiled, but noticed he no longer had that look of suspicion that alarmed her earlier. As she leaned across him to refill an empty cup, his hand brushed her hip. She ignored it, reassured he was back in his usual mode, suspicions sur-rendered to lust.

Retrieving plates from the table, including Mr. Chu's barely touched one, she placed them on the cart, then returned with the trays of fruit and small cakes filled with sweet bean paste.

When she'd pushed the carts into the hall, she came back to stand near the small table and looked at the urn next to it, filled with sprays of pale green orchids. Liang, his world dominated by violence, surrounded himself with green symbols of life. That might explain his passion for jade, she thought. She remembered the green plastic horse with its broken legs, the chilling message she saw on Chu's desk.

Figgy replenished the teacups twice, each time to the accompaniment of a pat or squeeze from the loathsome host. She hoped the housekeeper would soon send her back to the kitchen, but Mrs. Lin's son had taken the cart away and not returned.

She dreaded what would happen when Chu and Kao rose to leave. Was she expected to stand here until Liang dismissed her. What if he didn't? What if he had other plans for her? Ignoring the weakness in her legs, she forced her attention back to the men at the table. They were choosing tidbits from the tray. She watched Mr. Chu peeling rind from the fruit Americans called a clementine, so she hoped she'd be safe for a while longer.

He appeared so silently that Figgy didn't notice the uniformed security guard until he was leaning over Liang, speaking into his ear. His boss barked a loud word she was sure was profane when she saw the startled looks on the faces of the other men. They stared as he rose so abruptly he knocked over his chair. The men beside him leaped up to follow as he sped from the room.

Kao looked at Mr. Chu, who nodded. They, too, rose, seemingly uncertain about what to do, and left the room. Whatever had happened, Figgy was sure it was unexpected and disturbing to Liang. She needed to get back downstairs, pretend to return to the kitchen, and see what she could do to get Tessa away.

She hurried to the elevator and pushed the button. No one was in sight, including the housekeeper. After waiting for what seemed like forever, Figgy decided she had to find another way downstairs.

She ran along the carpeted hallway, pushing open doors that revealed only plush, elaborately decorated rooms. One open door was the entry to an office, a row of computers lining a wall. Reaching the end of the corridor, Figgy faced a wall with a tall window overlooking the side of the house. When she looked down she saw three security guards, guns in hand, moving toward the front of the building. As she started to turn away, something green near the curving driveway caught her attention. She pressed close to the window, hoping for a better view. It looked like fabric, part of it caught on the branch of a pine tree, the rest trailing down to the ground, billowing as the breeze caught it.

She couldn't be certain, but it looked like the scarf Tessa wore when she left the hotel! Figgy had to get a better look. This could mean Tessa had used the pick in the lock to open the door. It would explain the words whispered in Liang's ear, his cursing and abrupt departure from the dining table. What if she'd gotten free and they were looking for her? Figgy had to make her way back to the kitchen and the phone in her apron, find Tessa, and take her to the place where Will waited.

As she turned, she was stopped by an iron grip on her arm. One of the hulking guards held her. The housekeeper stood beside him and they pushed and prodded her back toward the dining room.

"I believe you lied to us, Miss Hazel. My employer will be most unhappy. Now you will tell me the truth."

She nodded to the guard, whose hand squeezed her arm harder, forcing a gasp.

The housekeeper spoke to the guard, her

gaze moving past Figgy's face to focus on her hair. The guard tugged at her wig, yanking it off along with some of her own hair. Then Mrs. Jia studied her and pulled a photo from her pocket.

"One of my employer's people took this photo of you at the hotel in Kaoshiung, so do not try lying to me. You're not a cooking student. You deceived Mrs. Lin and Chef Tan with your ridiculous act so they would bring you here. Now you will tell me what you're doing in this house."

Mr. Chu, Kao beside him, had returned to the dining room. Figgy saw that the two cronies of Liang's were back and seated across from them. None of the men spoke or looked in her direction as Mrs. Jia questioned her near the entrance.

Figgy's mind spun, unable to settle on any credible answer. All she could think was that even Liang wouldn't be so reckless as to kill Mr. Chu. She had to use that idea.

"Speak, young lady. You are not stupid. You must understand how much trouble you are in."

"I'll only talk to Mr. Chu."

"So, you are a friend of Chu's. You must also know his associate, Mr. Kao. You will explain your connection to them."

"You have my picture, you know I'm not

a culinary student. If you're so clever, you must know everything else too."

The housekeeper nodded to the guard, who released her arm. Before she could feel relieved, a staggering blow to her cheek sent her reeling. She reached out to the wall to keep from falling, then raised her other arm to fend off any more slaps. Her face burned, then throbbed. The red before her eyes was more rage than pain. She'd be damned if she let this witch intimidate her.

"Insolence will not help you."

"I don't need help. I'm an American citizen visiting in Taiwan. I came here today to work in the kitchen, to learn from Mrs. Lin and Chef Tan. I've done nothing wrong. By abusing me this way, you're the one breaking the law."

"And what law might that be, Miss Hazel? My employer has his own laws and you violated them by lying your way into his home."

"I didn't sneak in. I was invited to work here, and that's what I've been doing. You should know. You've been ordering me around ever since I arrived. And I've followed your orders."

The housekeeper nodded to the guard, who pulled her arm away from her side, twisting it in his beefy grip. Figgy gasped at the pain, then clamped her lips shut.

"I'm waiting for an explanation. My employer is not a patient man."

"Then you need to tell him what I told you." Figgy hesitated before deciding to speak again. "I was staying at the hotel visiting a friend. She had to go out of town, I was bored and thought it might be fun to learn about Chinese cooking. Something to tell the gang back home. I hired Mr. Tan, the hotel chef, for some lessons and asked to come along when he worked the dinner party here."

"That does not explain why you were wandering in the corridor. Or how you know Mr. Chu and Mr. Kao."

"I wasn't wandering; I was lost. I have a terrible sense of direction and this place is a maze. I didn't see anyone to point me the right way and, even if I did, no one speaks English."

"All very tidy, your story. You have not yet explained about the men who are my employer's guests."

"The friend I'm visiting works for Mr. Chu. Mr. Kao came to see me at the hotel when I inquired about my friend's schedule and when she would be returning."

"Didn't this friend tell you herself?"

"Yes, but her plans changed. She was

delayed on her business trip and I wanted to know about her return because I'm expected back in the States very soon."

"You too, may be delayed, indefinitely, if you are not telling the truth," the housekeeper said.

Figgy's heart pounded so loudly she was sure the others could hear it.

"I want to speak to Mr. Chu and Mr. Kao," she said.

"Did they send you here?"

"Don't be ridiculous. I had no idea they were the dinner guests. Neither did Mrs. Lin or Mr. Tan. We were hired to cater a dinner party and we were cooking — or, rather, they were. I was chopping, stacking, and lugging heavy containers."

Figgy, in her peripheral vision, saw the slightest hint of a smile cross Mr. Chu's impassive face. "Nobody told me I was supposed to look and behave like a tart so your boss could ogle and grope me."

Another nod from the housekeeper and another wrenching twist of her arm. Figgy bit her lip, refusing to give them the satisfaction of reacting to the pain.

"For a thin little person in a dangerous situation you are far too stubborn and insolent for your own good," the housekeeper retorted, her face a mask of anger.

"Trying to intimidate me is a big mistake. If I'm hurt, you'll be the one in trouble."

The woman made a sound that apparently was meant as ridicule. Figgy astonished herself at the words coming unplanned from her lips. She was terrified, with no notion whether Tessa had gotten away or if Will had found her. Could he know that she was now the one in real danger? If he spotted the Lins' van leaving and could see she wasn't with them, he might be able to do something. Otherwise, he would only find out from Mr. Tan. By then, it might be too late.

Despite Kao's effort to stop him, Mr. Chu spoke for the first time. Instead of responding, the housekeeper turned to her arm-twisting enforcer and both he and Kao were ushered toward the door. Mr. Chu seemed to be objecting but he was ignored and, with a backward glance at Figgy, left the room. Her body sagged, part of her bravado going with him. She had clung to the belief that, with the men in the room, no real harm would come to her.

But she couldn't let her fears paralyze her. She had to keep her wits about her and get away from the housekeeper and her henchman. Just keep thinking of the woman as a parody from a Dracula movie and maybe her legs would stop shaking.

"Why do you wish to talk to Chu and Kao?"

"Because my friend works for them — I told you that — and they're aware of who I am and that I'm harmless. They know I've been waiting for Tessa's return, even suggested I find something interesting to do until she gets back. They can get Mr. Tan to vouch for me."

"Chef Tan is no longer here. He, Mrs. Lin, and her son have left."

Figgy was afraid she might be sick, the churning in her stomach threatening to reach her throat.

"I was supposed to go with them! Didn't you speak to the chef? Why are you keeping me here?"

"Because I do not believe you. Neither will my employer. Now we must decide what to do with you."

"Take me to Mr. Chu. I can leave with him."

"He said nothing about recognizing you earlier."

"That's because I was wearing a wig. He only saw me in Kaoshuing for a very brief time."

"Why the wig?"

"A lark. I told you I was bored waiting

around for Tessa, so I decided to take cooking lessons and play with the way I looked. I thought it would be cool to tell Tessa I'd been waiting for her so long my appearance changed."

The housekeeper studied her. Figgy felt her eyes boring into her brain. She forced herself to be still under the hostile examination.

"You are either an inventive liar or a complete fool. We'll soon learn which is the real Miss Hazel."

She nodded to the guard who pushed her ahead of him, out of the dining area and along the corridor to another room. A man with his back to her was seated inside. When he turned at her arrival, Figgy was startled to see Ken Chu. She'd only met him once, but couldn't forget that extraordinarily handsome face.

He stared at her. Figgy thought he was trying to remember why she looked familiar. Ken's face was drawn, with dark circles beneath his eyes, as if he hadn't been sleeping much. His hair, which she remembered as immaculately groomed, was tousled, stray strands falling onto his forehead.

As she stood there with the guard gripping her arm, others entered the room. Liang appeared, Mr. Chu and Kao behind him. When Ken saw his father, his look of love and relief made Figgy like him much more than she had the first time they met. The older man and his companion nodded at him, but said nothing. Figgy looked at Mr. Chu and saw that his eyes conveyed feelings he didn't need to express. Ken's shoulders relaxed, his body no longer rigid as he waited in his chair.

As she stood there, Liang studied her, but this time there was no leering. Instead, he barked some words at Mr. Chu. Kao answered instead. As he spoke Ken's expression changed from confusion to recognition as he stared at her.

"What are you doing here?" he asked. "Have you seen Tessa? Where is she?"

Before she could think of an answer — Ken's words revealed what she'd hoped, that Tessa was gone from the house — Mr. Kao answered.

"Ms. Newton, Ken is as confused as we are by your presence. We've assured our host that we knew nothing about it. He is not inclined to believe us. Now we are all waiting for your explanation."

Figgy took a deep breath, hoping her voice would sound normal and her trembling wouldn't give her away. She repeated the story she'd told the housekeeper, reminding

them that with Tessa away, she was looking
for something to keep her occupied. That
her cooking lessons with Mr. Tan had
brought her here to work with the caterers.
It was all a coincidence.

Liang uttered a loud sound that Figgy
guessed was crude. Ken's face grew paler,
Mr. Chu sat like a stone sculpture. When
the mobster finished, Kao answered in a
voice that sounded pacifying and reasonable to Figgy. She hated feeling so helpless,
unable to understand a language when her
life probably depended on it.

Liang spoke again. The stone figure that
was Mr. Chu shook his head, not looking at
his son. Ken stared at him, eyes pleading,
but said nothing.

Figgy could stand it no longer.

"Mr. Kao? You have to tell me what's going on. I deserve to know."

Kao looked at her as if inspecting a specimen on a slide, then shook his head.

"I wish I knew how much of this is your
doing. We came here, at Mr. Liang's invitation, to work out our mutual problems and
to find a way to free Ken and your friend.
We had not seen them but we knew they
were here. Then, in the middle of our meal,
we learned that Tessa was missing from the
room where she was being kept. You were

serving us when the news was brought to Mr. Liang."

"Oh! Is that what caused the uproar?"

Kao stared at her, suspicion clear on his face. At his news, Figgy felt a rush of relief that made her almost giddy.

"Did you recognize me, Mr. Kao? I think my wig was very flattering. Changed my whole look, don't you think?"

"You are an extremely brash young woman. I suppose that's why Tessa values your friendship."

Ignoring the criticism, Figgy took his words as a compliment. If he only knew how often Tessa teased her about being timid and cautious, urging her to be more impulsive, to take chances. She'd certainly come through on that, if she could only live to brag to Tessa about it. And if Tessa lived to hear it.

Ken looked at her. When he spoke, the vulnerability in his voice was far different from the arrogance he'd displayed at their meeting.

"Tessa's gotten out of the room where they were keeping her. Now they're searching for her and threatening me and my father. You've got to tell Liang what you know."

"Ken, you are to say nothing more. Kao

and I will handle this."

Mr. Chu's voice was like a blade cutting off his son's words. Ken's mouth clamped shut. Figgy saw the skin tighten over his cheekbones. The elegant snob Tessa introduced to her friend had vanished, replaced by a shadow who held himself as if he might disappear at any moment.

Liang spoke again, Kao answering him in another exchange whose meaning Figgy could only guess at. Liang looked at Ken, then jerked his head in her direction. The guard with the beefy hands reached for her. Figgy jerked her arm away.

"Wait a minute. This is stupid and pointless. Don't you see there's a sensible way to work this out?"

Mr. Chu and Kao looked at her. Ken stared, doubting his own hearing, and Liang muttered to the man beside him. To her astonishment, the man spoke to her.

"Mr. Liang wants to know what you have to say."

Surprised that the mobster had included an interpreter of his own, Figgy swallowed, then continued. If she could behave as if she were explaining a lesson to her fifth-graders in the simplest, most direct way, she could get through this.

"Each of you has something you want

from the other; both you and Mr. Chu have a lot to lose if you don't get it. There's a way that each gets what he wants without anyone getting hurt."

Liang's man spoke in rapid Mandarin to his boss.

"Mr. Liang says you are to continue."

"Everyone recognizes Mr. Liang's expertise in ancient jade. He has a reputation to protect. But he also should know that even the most prestigious of international art specialists get fooled. Think of the Rembrandts that famous museums bought, only to find they weren't authentic."

She was dragging out her words, hoping that Tessa had enough time to get away if what she was doing didn't work.

"Those museums announced to the public that they'd been fooled and no experts thought the worse of them. The best authorities acknowledge that occasionally they're deceived. What if Mr. Chu, on his word and reputation — which you know to be impeccable — swears not to reveal that the jade horse is a fake? Even though he doesn't insure it, no one outside this room will ever know you were cheated. Then, at some later time — of your own choosing — you decide to tell other collectors that, upon reexamining your jade, you noticed some tiny anomalies that made you suspicious. To your great disappointment you determined the horse was not of the early period you'd assumed, but you've chosen to keep it anyway because of its beauty. Or, as a reminder that even the most astute collector can, rarely, be as mistaken as world-renowned museums.

"And if Mr. Chu should — impossible to imagine — threaten to break his promise, well, there's always Ken's lifestyle for you to expose."

Figgy had no idea how they would do that, but Liang was too shrewd to make empty threats. No matter how discreet Ken had been, there were probably pictures from some clubs in Hong Kong, or film from vacation resorts where Liang's men had followed him. Whatever the proof, it had to be destroyed.

Figgy waited as Liang's interpreter repeated her words in Mandarin.

Mr. Chu was looking at her, his expression a mixture of incredulity and respect. Kao too was staring, as Liang's man continued explaining what she'd said. When he finished, Liang spoke and his interpreter said, "Mr. Liang wants you to go on."

Figgy was beginning to feel better. The guard hadn't grabbed her, the housekeeper hadn't come for her, and she seemed to have the attention of the men in the room. Keep focused, she told herself, the way you do in the classroom. When grown men act like stubborn children, you need to get them to start behaving like grown-ups.

"In return, you agree to release Ken, respect his privacy, and stop trying to blackmail Mr. Chu. Work out whatever business deals you want, without threats. If you both agree, no one gets hurt and everybody's reputation —" she looked at Liang and struggled for diplomacy — "everybody's reputation stays the way it's always been."

There! She'd said it and no bolt of lightning had struck. Her arms and legs were shaking, but no one was looking at her anymore. Liang's interpreter finished his translation of what she'd said. Kao, Ken, and Mr. Chu were concentrating on his words and watching Liang's reaction.

The mobster's glare moved from the men sitting across from him to the young woman in the ridiculous serving uniform. He stared at Figgy. Swallowed by the intensity in his eyes, she could neither read them nor the expression on his face.

A wall of silence settled over the room, smothering Figgy with its weight. Had she really dared to tell these powerful, arrogant men what to do? She must be out of her mind! Somehow, she managed to remain still, forbidding herself to look away or fail to meet Liang's eyes.

At last, his mouth opened in a snarl, directing words at the guard waiting behind her. As he'd done earlier, the man grabbed her arm. She winced as he pulled her to the door, pushed her out, and slammed it behind her.

Now her shaking was uncontrollable. Figgy stood in a corridor that was silent and empty, waiting for whatever was to happen next. Another guard, or the Dracula house-keeper, was probably on the way to put her in some dark room where she'd molder away in this mausoleum. She was too tired to keep fighting, she thought, still standing there, shuddering. Waiting.

The hall remained empty and silent. Her body changed from trembling to rubbery as she forced her legs to move. She crept toward the elevator, staying close to the wall, trying to be quiet. She looked around. No one. She kept moving until she reached the elevator and pressed the button. The corridor was empty still; this time she could hear the creak of the elevator ascending.

When the door opened she entered, trying to clear her head and ignore the torpor of mind and body. She huddled against the back wall, expecting that, at any moment, the elevator would jerk to a stop and security guards would appear and grab her.

It didn't happen. The door opened on the bottom floor and the passageway leading to the kitchen. Hugging the wall again, she moved toward it and the door that opened to the delivery driveway. With each cautious step, she expected to be stopped, caught. But there was only silence.

The kitchen was empty, completely cleared of Mrs. Lin's cooking equipment. She was afraid to turn on lights that might bring in the guards. In the semi-darkness she thought she saw the long apron she'd worn earlier, left in a corner with her clothes. Mr. Tan must have put them there when he expected her to return from her serving duties. She forced leaden legs toward the clothing, then pushed her hand down into her jeans' pocket.

The cellphone Will had given her was still there, buried deep where she'd hidden it. She clutched the phone, moving from the kitchen to the door and out into the emptiness where the van had been parked.

Outside, she was enveloped in darkness and had no idea which way to go. All Figgy knew was that she was near the back of the house, among the thick pine trees, and that if she moved toward the entrance there would be guards and the security fence.

She found a break in the row of trees, slipped through, and loosened her grip on the cell so that she could use it. Will had said she needed to press only one button to reach him. She sat down on the ground, did as he'd instructed, and waited to hear his voice.

CHAPTER TWELVE

Nothing. There was no response. She was in a place where the signal didn't work. Pine needles on the ground beneath her felt cool and yielding, tempting her to lie down and rest. She was so tired. Maybe she could stay here until daybreak, then try to make her way to the road. Away from the trees, the phone might work.

No. She was too close to the house. The guards could practically look out the windows and see her. She'd have to keep going but she had no idea which way.

When Tessa was at Shadyhill she'd teased about lending Figgy her kindergarten students to lead her to the playground. Free now, Tessa would know how to get away.

Figgy forced herself to stand. Gripping the phone, she plunged deeper into the forest, away from the estate, feeling rather than seeing her way. She placed her feet by reaching out to the pine trunks, then moving forward. Sometimes she collided with trees or branches, but by inching along, except for a thump on face or shoulders, she was okay.

Sporadically, when the moon emerged from clouds, the light helped her to move faster. But move toward what? All she could see were more trees, an occasional small clearing, but no sign of either the road or a clear path.

She probably wouldn't hear pursuers because of the soft, spongy earth, so she looked back periodically, half-expecting the pounce and painful grip of the guard again. Trudging between the trees, she struggled to stay alert. The forest that earlier seemed silent was filled with small noises: twitters of birds she couldn't see; low thrumming that she hoped was the sound of harmless bugs; an occasional snap of twigs that made her heart fly into her throat. At first, she was afraid Liang's men were coming. Then, paradoxically, that it might be better if humans, rather than some unknown animal, were making the sounds. In a bizarre flashback, she remembered how frightened she'd been as a child when she first heard the story of Hansel and Gretel, lost in the woods. She'd vowed never to tell that story to her own children.

The scent from the trees was so pervasive Figgy thought she could taste pine pitch. Her mouth was dry, her throat itched.

Extending one foot and feeling for some clear space with it, she pushed on, trying not to trip and become even more disoriented.

Deeper in the forest, the night was alive with sounds. Some were familiar, like the cooing of doves that sometimes awakened her at home in Iowa. Clicks and whistling noises near her head announced the presence of a host of insects. Remembering stories about poisonous snakes thriving in the vegetation of warm, humid climates, Figgy shuddered. She couldn't see where she was stepping — for all she knew, she could disturb a reptile's den and be bitten, with no one to help.

There was no choice. She had to go on. Periodically, she tried the cellphone — dead.

Weary of suppressing her frustration and fear, Figgy sank to the forest floor and let the tears come. When weeping turned to dry gasps she pulled herself up and started moving again.

After what felt like forever, she saw lights through the trees and heard a dog barking. Not daring to hope for much, Figgy thought she might find a house and make the people there understand she needed help. Inside, Will's cellphone might work. She moved toward the lights, stumbling over roots and rocks, growing more careless of hazards underfoot in her rush to reach the house.

Closer, she peered through a stand of trees growing close together. And she froze, sure her heart would stop. The lights were coming from the second floor of Liang's mansion. She'd traveled in a circle, doubling back to the estate where the barking of a guard's dog grew louder.

"Stupid, stupid," the voice in her head screamed. It had happened again; she'd been betrayed by her chronic failure to find her way.

In her panic to get away from the house, she nearly fell when her foot caught in a tree root. She had no idea which way to run, no plan. She only knew she had to go in another direction as she stumbled back into the forest.

The moon emerged again. In its light Figgy saw an opening in the dense pines and moved toward it before the cloud cover hid the moon again. Beneath her feet, the ground felt smoother, as if she'd happened on some kind of path. She moved faster, nearly running. With no idea where she was going, she told herself that at least she was leaving Liang's house behind her. Eventually, she might find a road or the highway the Lins' van had traveled a lifetime ago.

She forced her mind to focus on walking. If thoughts intruded and she considered her options she pushed them away, along with her fears of being bitten or caught or injured. She kept going, past low-hanging boughs, hoping for more light from a moon that stayed stubbornly hidden.

Her legs ached. They were heavy weights, slowing her down. Her feet no longer hurt. Instead, they were numb, as if they weren't attached to the rest of her. Keep going, she told herself, but it was like slogging through sand dunes. Figgy knew she should stop to rest, but she was too afraid. All she could do was keep pushing ahead. Her sense of time was gone, direction obliterated, her only thought to keep moving.

She heard nothing but night sounds, so the hands reaching out to grab her shoulders shocked her into a scream. Her body sagged, but arms held her up and a voice spoke in Mandarin, a long stream of words. They didn't sound threatening or angry, but she couldn't control the trembling that seized her body.

Figgy struggled against the grip, pulling away, kicking and striking out with her hands. Her fists beat against her captor, who wasn't fighting back, only holding on to her. She tried to keep resisting, but she was so tired. Her legs betrayed her, too heavy to move, too weak to get away. Her arms shook with fatigue, as if she'd been hauling boulders. She couldn't fight anymore.

"Shh, shh," were the sounds from her captor, then more Mandarin. She had no choice but to go along as he half-carried, half-led her along the path she'd apparently stumbled on to, and toward another clear space in the forest.

At last the moon emerged from the clouds. In its rays, Chef Tan looked down at her, smiling, nodding his head, patting her shoulders.

Speechless, Figgy hugged him. His embrace was the last thing she remembered until she awoke again, stretched out on the back seat of Will Bower's car. When she opened her eyes, Will was looking down at her, face tense, until she smiled and the muscles in his jaw relaxed.

"Thank God. You're all right."

She tried to sit up.

"Take it easy. You're dehydrated and exhausted. You've been walking for hours and need to rest."

She shook her head to clear it, looked

around, and saw Chef Tan standing near Will, looking at her and grinning. She tried to smile back, but even that was an effort. She fell back on the seat.

Will closed the car door, the chef slid into the passenger seat beside him, and they drove through the darkness. Figgy had so many questions, but she was too tired to ask them. She closed her eyes. Will's voice and the chef's, speaking softly, lulled her into a deep sleep.

Later, when the car's movement awakened her, Figgy sat up and stared into the night, trying to remember where she was. Her eyes accommodating to the darkness, she saw that they were in a place she recognized — the road near the inn. She shuddered, memories threatening to overwhelm her.

"Why are we here?" she said to the back of Will's head.

He turned to smile at her. "Sorry to wake you, Sleeping Beauty. We have a pickup to make, then we'll be on our way back to Kaoshiung."

"What about Tessa? We have to find Tessa."

"We will, I promise. Just sit tight and rest until we come back. Then I'll answer all the questions you're bursting to ask."

Too tired to argue, she leaned back and closed her eyes. She hadn't realized she was asleep again until a voice said, "You could show a little more enthusiasm about seeing me after all this time."

Her eyes popped open.

"Tessa!" she screamed as the two fell into each other's arms. "Where did you come from? Are you all right? How did you get here?"

"I can only answer one question at a time, Fig."

Figgy disentangled herself from her friend, sat up, and stared at her. Tessa was pale, purplish shadows beneath her eyes. Her long blond hair was stringy and unkempt, face smudged with dirt. The slacks she wore were wrinkled, her blouse rumpled and hanging loose above her trousers. But, as far as Figgy could tell, she was unhurt and sounding like herself.

Now Will and chef Tan returned and climbed into the car.

"Everybody okay back there?" Will asked, looking from one woman to the other. Both nodded, he gave them a thumbs up, and started the car.

Fatigue forgotten, Figgy peppered her friend with questions until Tessa said, "Whoa! Why don't I just describe what happened after I heard you in Liang's house? Then it'll be your turn okay?"

Figgy nodded. Up front, all was quiet. The men were listening. She had no idea how much they knew of the events. She waited, head turned to Tessa, eyes intent on her face.

"I had no idea how you'd managed to get into the estate. When I heard your voice I was beginning to feel really desperate. I knew Liang wouldn't kill Ken, he was too important in the scheme to force Mr. Chu to do what he wanted. But I'd begun to think what happened to me wouldn't matter much to Liang. Mr. Chu would try to free me, I knew that, but I figured I was further down on his list of priorities.

"The room where they held me was tiny; I think it was some kind of storage space. There was a small window way up high, near the ceiling. Even if I'd been able to climb up there, I couldn't squeeze through it to escape. I'd tried to trick and seduce the guy who brought me food, so I could slip past him, but nothing worked. I'd run out of ideas and, pretty much, hope when, incredibly, I heard you in the corridor sounding like the person you spoke to was deaf. At first, I thought I was hallucinating. Then I figured you were loud so I'd know you were nearby. You'd somehow managed to find out where Liang was keeping me."

Figgy nodded but said nothing.

"I didn't know where you'd gotten the pick I used on the lock until later, when I was hiding in the shrubs near Liang's driveway. I heard the caterer cursing her American kitchen help and the chef who'd brought her. That was the first laugh I'd had in days. My roommate, whose culinary attempts were usually inedible, and who scorched frozen pizza, studying to become a chef!"

Figgy ignored the chuckle from Will as well as the Mandarin explanation that followed, along with Mr. Tan's laughter.

Tessa leaned over to hug her.

"I don't care if you never learn to be a good cook. You can have a brilliant second career as Indiana Jones."

"Very funny. Could you just get on with the story?"

"When I managed to reach the pick you'd left in the lock, I started working it from my side of the door. It took a while, but apparently Liang's thugs were involved elsewhere, so I had time to get the door open."

Figgy said, "The guards were preoccupied with Mr. Chu and Kao in the dining room. Even the vampire Mrs. Jia was there, hovering over me."

"She's not so bad. She went from being

one of Liang's mistresses to his house-keeper. I'd call that a promotion."

"Tessa?"

"Oh, right. On with the story. I opened the door and slithered along the corridor, toward the lights in the kitchen. The caterer and the chef didn't notice, so I got down on hands and knees, ducking behind tables, until I reached the open door, leading out to the place where the van was parked near some shrubbery. I ran for it. Soon, Tom came out and opened the door on the driver's side . . ."

"Who?"

"The caterer's son. I figured he was my chance to get away. I made up some story about being one of the boss's friends, but that he hadn't liked me much and I didn't want to hang around and see if I could change his mind. Tom looked me over, saw that I was a little the worse for wear, and bought the explanation of my career in a fancy escort service. He told me later that he'd met other Americans — you and Will — when you dined at the inn. I'm surprised he didn't recognize you when you came back."

"I was wearing a horrendous blond wig that Buddy found somewhere and about six layers of make-up. And tight jeans under a long apron. You wouldn't have recognized me either."

"What you're wearing now isn't exactly you either. It's hideous, Figgy. Where did you find it?"

"Your friend, the housekeeper, had me put it on at Liang's request. I was surprised there wasn't a bunny tail to complete the outfit, but I wasn't about to argue. Liang didn't seem like he took kindly to contradiction."

"What a pig. Mr. Chu must have been revolted by the whole business."

"I couldn't tell. He was expressionless the whole time I was serving the men. You know that old movie cliché about inscrutable Asians? Well, Mr. Chu pulled it off. Kao looked at me with a calculating eye a few times. I thought he might have recognized me, but if he did, before I lost my disguise and started teaching, he didn't show it."

"What do you mean, before you started teaching?"

"Later. Finish your part of the story."

She nodded. "The van was waiting there, with Tom beside it. I hoped he had more work inside, thinking I could sneak to the back of the truck, get in and hunker down among whatever was stored there so I could get away from the house. Then I'd figure

321

out how to help Ken, who was still inside. Maybe the caterer's son would think I'd walked down to the road to hitchhike my way home."

"Ken's father and Kao were still in Liang's house too."

"I couldn't know that. They must have been negotiating for our release."

"Over a sumptuous dinner."

"Tom said their employer had guests. He didn't know their names, but they were eating the most expensive meal his mother and the chef working with her could prepare."

Figgy stared at her friend.

"How did you and Mrs. Lin's son get on a cozy first name basis?"

"Haven't you noticed how friendly we are here in Taiwan? You and Will are a perfect example."

Figgy felt her face redden.

"Don't try to change the subject."

"Only making my point. So there I was, waiting for my chance, when Mrs. Lin did call from the kitchen. Tom started there, I headed for the back of the van, but then he turned and saw me."

"Oh, great!"

"He came up with some interesting words, and I was sure I'd blown any chance I had to get away. Mrs. Lin called from the kitchen again, asking why he was cursing. He looked at me, pointed to the back of the truck, and waited until I'd climbed inside. Then he answered his mother, saying he'd twisted his ankle when he slipped on some gravel.

"He soon came back out with some huge pots, arranged them around me, then covered me with some kind of tarp he had in the back. He whispered that Liang treated him like trash when he helped his mother at the estate. He hated the way the man looked down on Mrs. Lin too, but the money was good and nobody refused to do what Liang asked. He said he understood why I wanted to get away from such a lowlife, but he was taking a big chance and was very nervous about it.

"I asked him to find some excuse for stopping at the bottom of the road near his inn. I'd get out there, so he wouldn't get in trouble when the van was unloaded."

"And that's when you left the van?"

"Right. He told his mother something was rattling around in the back and he'd better secure it, so he stopped. That's when Huei-Sheng said he'd get out too, and call the friend who brought him to come get him. While he and Mrs. Lin were settling their business, I slipped out and hid behind some trees near the road. The van pulled away and the chef started walking like he had somewhere particular to go. I followed him, finally running to catch up when I realized the chef was my friend from the hotel."

Will spoke then.

"Huei-Sheng and I had arranged a meeting place, one that Figgy knew about. He brought Tessa to the car, then left, saying only that he had something more he needed to do. Later, after he'd found you, he told me he didn't want both of us crashing around in the forest, possibly alerting Liang's guards. He knew that if he told me where he was going I would've insisted on joining him, no matter how much he objected. And someone needed to stay at the car and look after Tessa."

"I didn't think I needed looking after," Tessa said, "but I had no idea whether you'd gotten away from Liang's estate. I also didn't know how much you'd figured out about my disappearance. Will filled me in with the details. Then we both waited, wringing our hands, until Will's cell rang, with a message from Huei-Sheng. Will told me to wait out of sight to avoid Liang's men, started the car and rushed off."

"You've never wrung your hands in your life."

"But you should have seen Will. He wanted to storm the castle to rescue you from the lair of the evil mobster."

Will said, "That describes it more colorfully than I would, but I was crazed about your safety. When the Lins' van passed where I was waiting and I couldn't see you inside I didn't know what to think. Tessa told Huei-Sheng and me about your way of letting her know you were there and how you took a knife and a seafood pick from him to use on the lock. I'd decided to go to his estate and confront Liang, demanding that you leave with me or I'd have the whole American State Department land on him."

Tessa said, "I was trying to get him to wait a little longer, thinking you'd get away on your own without threats from Will. Liang doesn't respond well to them and I worried that Will wouldn't get out of there alive. Then the chef called to say he'd found you. Will didn't know what to expect and insisted I wait here, where I'd be safe. We were afraid you were hurt, but you just have some superficial cuts and bruises from the branches. You were exhausted and couldn't stand."

"You'd be tired too, from going around in circles for hours. I got out of the house, but then I had to depend on my sense of direction — no help there. I couldn't find the path out of the pine forest to get back to the road. But after what felt like a walking marathon, I did manage to make my way back to Liang's house."

Tessa clucked sympathetically.

"Before your next adventure I'll buy you a GPS that you can carry twenty-four seven."

"No more adventures. I'm going back to my classroom, one of the few places I know my way around."

Figgy could feel herself growing drowsy again. Her limbs were heavy, eyelids drooping. She tried to concentrate on getting out the phrases she needed to say.

". . . go back to town. See if Ken . . ."

She didn't finish the sentence. The last words she heard before falling into a deep sleep were Tessa's: "She didn't tell us what she said to Liang or how she got away. Should I nudge her awake?"

"Don't you dare," Will answered.

Figgy smiled and slept.

CHAPTER THIRTEEN

The next time she opened her eyes she was in the hotel lobby, sitting on one of the leather sofas and surrounded by faces. Tessa, Will, Chef Tan, and Buddy were all watching her, beaming when they saw she was awake.

"She needs to eat to get her strength back," Will said. "You too, Tessa. Food will be sent up to your apartment. And Figgy looks like she could sleep some more." He spoke to the chef, who nodded and started toward the kitchen.

"No bok choy," Figgy muttered.

"What?" Buddy said. "What did you say?"

"No bok choy. And skip the snow peas."

Tessa looked at Will. "Do you know what she's talking about?"

Will shook his head. Chef Tan had come back when he heard Figgy's voice. Buddy spoke to him, apparently explaining what she'd said.

Chef Tan started to laugh. Buddy tried to say something, but the chef only laughed harder. Figgy saw that two of his lower teeth were missing, something she hadn't noticed before. But, then, she'd never seen him laughing until tears flowed down his cheeks.

The others stared at him. Finally, he calmed down enough to speak, punctuating his words with chopping motions. The others listened, then grinned.

"So you didn't like being the cook's apprentice?" Tessa said. "At least, you kept all your fingers. I hope you'll set a good example for your students and learn to enjoy your veggies again."

"Not amusing," Figgy mumbled as she shuffled to the elevator. When Will reached out to assist her, she resisted. "Help Tessa. She's the one who was kidnapped."

In the apartment, she showered and replaced the torn and dirty skimpy uniform with jeans and a T-shirt. She dried and combed her hair, applied some lipstick and rejoined the others. When she reemerged, Tessa went to her and hugged her.

"Now that you're back in the world, I get to thank you for what you did. And you have to tell us how you did it."

"Mmm," she murmured, looking past her at Will who stood beside the food-laden table.

"Chef Tan said to tell you he prepared all this without including your least favorite greens." He took her hand and led her to a chair. "Everything's intended to restore your energy, he said. Rice noodles, dumplings, lots of ginger, and some chilies with the beef to rebuild your chi."

"Chi? As in Tai Chi?"

Tessa nodded. "Your life force, your energy."

"As I see it," Will said, "she already has a splendid life force. But the chef worried you depleted it with vigorous chopping and the hike in the woods."

"I lost more than my chi blundering around in the pine trees behind Liang's estate. I couldn't believe I managed to get away from that house of horrors only to circle back to it. Do you think scientists could implant the GPS device Tessa mentioned in my forehead?"

"Then you'd be perfect, and we couldn't stand you," Tessa said. The grin left her face. "I don't know how you did it, but you saved my life, Fig. Liang didn't care about me. I was collateral damage in his scheme to blackmail my boss. Ken was the prize and I still don't know what happened to him, but Liang wouldn't hurt him. He's too valuable a pawn."

"I think he's all right. I'll explain after I renew my chi."

They opened the wine Buddy sent with their meal and devoured the feast the chef had prepared for them. When they were finished Figgy curled up on the couch, Will next to her, holding her hand. Tessa sat in the other chair, facing her.

"Now you have to tell us how you got away, especially when Liang suspected you were responsible for my escape."

Figgy took a long sip from her wine glass, then launched into her story. She described her shock and attempt to conceal it when she entered the dining room and saw Mr. Chu and Kao with Liang and his cohorts. "I thought Kao recognized me. I caught him staring a few times, but his expression didn't change."

"He was probably mesmerized by your golden hair and the mini-outfit," Will said.

"Save the compliments until she tells all," Tessa interjected.

Figgy continued. When she got to the part about losing her temper and yelling at them, offering what seemed the reasonable way to fix the mess they'd created, Will and Tessa's expressions, incredulous, changed to astonishment.

"You said that? To one of the most danger-ous mob bosses in the country? Did you have any idea of the risk you were taking?" Will said, staring at her.

"I didn't think about it because they really annoyed me. I'd had it with their behavior, both Chu's and Liang's. All I could see were two grown men acting like the most im-mature boys on the playground, double-daring each other to land the first punch. Playing their stupid game of chicken. They needed to be separated and given a time out, made to stand in a corner."

Tessa began laughing, nearly as hard as Chef Tan had earlier.

"You are too much, Hazel Newton. Treat-ing two of the biggest power brokers in Taiwan like they were fifth-graders. And when did you ever make one of your kids stand in a corner?"

"Never. But those two were being ridicu-lous and someone needed to say so. I was so sick of the whole idiotic business I couldn't keep quiet any longer. I reacted like I was in a classroom, explaining in simple terms to a couple of slow learners."

"Amazing!" Will said, still staring at her in disbelief. "And they bought it?"

She shrugged. "Who knows? Did I men-tion the thugs brought Ken Chu into the room too? When I'd finished speaking my piece I didn't know what would happen next. Nobody spoke. I hoped they were thinking over what I'd said. I was pushed out of the room, the door slammed behind me.

"When I edged into the hall, I saw that nobody was there. I crept along to the elevator, looking around for the guards or Mrs. Dracula. I guess they were all searching for you, Tessa, because the corridor was empty. I went down to the lower level and along the passage to the kitchen. It was empty too, the Lins and Huei-Sheng gone in the van. So I walked out the door, and promptly got lost. After all the stumbling through the forest, when I saw that I was back at the house, I nearly gave up. That's when the chef found me."

Tessa smiled.

"Remember that day we went shopping at Macy's to buy some towels? You wandered off, got lost, and ended up in the employees' lounge?" She turned to Will. "One of the stock clerks — he must have been all of eighteen — led her back to the linens department."

"Tessa, you can repay me for rescuing you by promising never to tell any more of my 'lost' stories."

"They're endearing, Figgy," Will said, squeezing her hand, "suggesting that someone to look after you — directionally speaking, that is — could be a welcome addition to your life."

She was beginning to blush again, another embarrassing trait, but his words were certainly beneficial to her chi.

"The right direction for me now is to the airport. I need to get home or I won't have a job any longer."

"You could always stay here and teach English to adults," Tessa said.

"No, thanks. If Chu and Liang are examples, I prefer the maturity of my fifth-graders. Tessa, will you help me make travel arrangements?"

"I'll do that," Will said. "Tessa needs to see Mr. Chu, find out about Ken, and decide if she wants to go to the police about her kidnapping."

Tessa nodded, but said nothing. Figgy guessed she'd already decided not to involve the police. Her loyalty to Mr. Chu and her affection for life in Kaoshuing would stop her.

"I'll call the plant agent who makes travel arrangements," Will said, "as soon as I get back to my apartment. Can we meet for breakfast?" He forced his gaze away from

Figgy. "You too, Tessa, if you'd like to join us."

She looked from his face to Figgy's.

"No, thanks. You two would probably like some time together and I want to get to the Serenity office first thing and learn what's happened."

Figgy frowned. "Shouldn't you have a guard, or someone to go with you? You can't be sure you're safe until you know what Liang and Mr. Chu decided. Maybe I should come along?"

"I don't think so. If Mr. Chu sees you coming into his office he may duck out the back door. You're pretty formidable, you know."

"And you're pretty silly. Having said that, I need to be sure you're okay, Tessa. After you tell me how you kept from going berserk in that cell Liang kept you in, I'm planning to collapse. It's been a busy day."

"Yeah, all that aimless roaming through the piney gloaming."

Figgy picked up the pillow she'd been leaning against and threw it at Tessa, who caught it and tossed it back.

"I've heard about those lethal pillow fights in girls' dorms. Time for me to clear out." Will leaned over to plant a kiss on Figgy's cheek.

"Get a good rest. You've earned it. I'll be waiting downstairs in the morning."

Tessa stood, waving good-bye to Will as she headed for the bedroom.

Figgy nodded and rose to follow, planning to talk with Tessa as she began packing for her trip home. Then she decided she'd rest a bit before starting that chore.

When Figgy opened her eyes the sun was streaming into the bedroom window. Confused — she'd been dreaming about Mrs. Jia chasing her down endless corridors — she looked around, saw that Tessa's bed was neatly made, with a note on her pillow, and that her own clothes were folded in the open suitcases near the doorway.

Tessa knew how much Figgy wanted to return to Mersdale and her life there and had accomplished what she'd been too exhausted to manage. How her friend could be so energetic after her imprisonment Figgy couldn't imagine, but it was typical Tessa.

She read the note: "I want to see Mr. Chu first thing this morning; I'll fill you in on everything when I return. IF I return! Just kidding. See you soon, that is if you can take your eyes off Will long enough to notice your dearest friend." She'd drawn little hearts across the bottom.

Will was waiting for her downstairs. She liked the way his face changed when he saw her, skin around his eyes crinkling and the smile spreading from his eyes to his mouth. He came over, took her hand, and they started for the restaurant.

"Figgy, wait!"

Buddy came out from behind the registration desk.

"I am so glad to see you looking better. Chef Tan has been asking too." He nodded to Will. "I saw Tessa as I was coming in to work. She was in a hurry, so we didn't talk much." He looked at Will, then back at her. "You are amazing."

"Thanks. You're not so bad yourself. Without your help, I don't know what would have happened."

"You took crazy chances with Mr. Boss." Before she could say anything, he raised his hand. "Don't tell me any more about your adventure. It's best for my family I don't know."

"How are things with your father?"

"Better, now that I'm leaving."

Figgy looked at him, waiting for an explanation.

"While you were studying Chinese cooking, I was getting ready for my own big adventure at the company's hotel in Hawaii. I will be assistant manager in Honolulu."

"Buddy, that's terrific." She reached up to hug him. Some of the hotel guests waiting in the lobby watched. A few smiled. Buddy looked both flattered and flustered. Then Figgy had a sudden, disturbing thought.

"I just remembered something awful. Your friend's expensive jeans and beautiful silk blouse. I left them in the kitchen at the estate. I'm so sorry. Find out the cost and I'll send her a check."

Buddy shook his head. "No worries. Her closet's so stuffed she'll be glad of the extra space. Excuse to shop more. Maybe I'll invite her and the rich boyfriend to my Hawaii hotel and give them a special rate, to say thanks. Too bad, though, you don't still have the clothes. They looked better on you."

Will extended his hand.

"Congratulations, Buddy. Soon, you'll be waxing your board and catching waves. Not to mention presenting orchid leis to pretty women."

Looking puzzled, he thanked Will and turned to go.

"Buddy, wait. I may not see you again before I leave because I hope to fly back to the States today. Thank you for being such a good friend. Maybe I'll take my next vacation in Hawaii . . . but only if you promise sun and sand. No cooking lessons."

He made chopping gestures with his hand, then took both of hers in his.

"It was an adventure knowing you, Miss Hazel Newton."

"When I come to your hotel that name must never cross your lips."

He laughed and walked away.

As Figgy watched him go, Will put his arm around her shoulders and they turned to the dining room.

"You've made more than one conquest in your time here."

She decided not to pursue that intriguing line, happy enough to be with him now.

When they were seated, Will slid an envelope across the table.

"That's the ticket for your flight home. Your plane leaves in a few hours. I used your original ticket for a trade-in. Unless you'd like to stay in Kaoshiung longer? I know you have some vacation days left."

"No. Tessa and I talked about that and she understands why I want to go home. Besides, she'll be so busy working through everything that's happened to her, there wouldn't be much time for hanging out with me."

She looked at the envelope Will had given her.

"How did you convince the airline?"

"Not a problem. The travel specialist at the plant has lots of friends in powerful places. He had no trouble arranging for two seats in business class."

"Business class? Two seats? I must still be groggy because I don't understand what you're saying."

"I've scheduled meetings with the Philadelphia branch of my company, so it seemed logical for us to fly back together. One of my perks, although I don't always request it, is traveling business class. I upgraded your seat as well. I hope you don't mind the company."

"I guess I can stand it," she said, reaching across the table to place her hand over his.

"Good. That way, I can be sure you won't get lost in one of the airport terminals."

"Now you're sounding like Tessa. Could we order breakfast? I'm starving."

Figgy, absorbed with Will, hadn't seen Tessa enter the restaurant with Ken Chu. She and Will were talking about the trip to the States.

"I'm planning to spend several weeks at our office in Philadelphia. When you've settled back into your teaching schedule, we'll have time together without the distractions of kidnappings and a mob boss."

"If you meet my headmistress at Shadyhill, you won't be so confident about avoiding mob bosses." She was happy to see his responding grin, even happier at the prospect of their time together in the weeks ahead.

"Figgy? Sorry to interrupt but Tessa said you would be leaving Kaoshiung and I didn't want to miss seeing you."

They looked up to see Ken and Tessa. Will stood, gesturing to the empty chairs at their table.

"Thank you, but I can't stay," Ken said. Figgy saw the hollows in his cheeks, the shadows beneath his eyes. He looked different than she remembered, more serious.

"You must be Will. You were a huge help to Figgy, I know, and so to Tessa and me as well. I am very grateful. If you should ever need my assistance — or my father's — during your work in Taiwan, we would be honored to be asked."

While he spoke, Tessa sat down beside Figgy, gave her a quick hug, but said nothing.

"I appreciate that, but I expect to be away from Kaoshiung for a while. I'm flying to Philadelphia today to consult with colleagues there."

Figgy tried to suppress a smile as Tessa shot her a significant glance. She knew that if she showed her reaction to Will's plans, she wouldn't be able to stop smiling.

"But I will be coming back to Kaoshiung, so perhaps we'll see each other then."

"I hope you can persuade Figgy to return for a visit as well. I'd like an opportunity to show her our city without any . . . uh . . . disruptions."

"I'd like to come back, especially if Tessa is here."

"Mr. Chu has convinced me to stay at the Kaoshiung office for another year. That will give Ken time to establish a branch of Serenity in Hong Kong. He'll be in charge of the family's business there, and I'll be assisting him."

Ken smiled. "And we'll both study Cantonese," he said.

"First you'll learn it, Tessa, then teach English to Cantonese speakers? That should be a challenge," Figgy said.

"I'll find many more English speakers in Hong Kong than here in Kaoshiung," Tessa said.

"Especially in the shops," Figgy added.

"I expect my boss, the younger Mr. Chu, to pay me a salary commensurate with my shopping habit."

"I see some tough negotiating ahead," Ken answered. Then he reached into his pocket to extract a small box wrapped in gold paper and tied with a red ribbon.

"My father sent this for you, Figgy, with his thanks and good wishes for a safe trip home. And he asked that I tell you that if your employer in America causes trouble because of your extended stay here, he'll be pleased to offer you employment in Kaoshiung as his chief negotiator."

Figgy stood to shake Ken's hand. "Thank him for me and explain that I know my way around a classroom better than I do a corporate office."

"That is so true," Tessa said. "Any building taller than two stories and we'd need a search and rescue team."

Will laughed, but Ken looked puzzled.

"Never mind, Ken. Sometimes, when Tessa speaks English and thinks she's being amusing, it's not worth explaining," Figgy said. "Please thank your father. And good luck with your move to Hong Kong."

He nodded and left.

"Now it's your turn, Tessa, to fill us in on what happened."

"Okay, but aren't you going to open your present?"

"Not until you tell us."

"Well, to everyone's amazement, your advice in dealing with the impasse worked. Mr. Chu agreed not to reveal the truth about the jade horse and to let Liang hint to the other collectors that it's so fragile he's decided not to display it, but to keep it safely stored where it won't be damaged. If he decides to admit that the horse is fake sometime in the future, we'll all be surprised, but that choice is his. Serenity will be the insurer of Liang's growing fleet, but only those ships that are legally registered and with the proper documentation. In return, nothing about Ken's private life will be made public, either in Kaoshiung or anywhere else.

"Sending Ken to Hong Kong, a much bigger and more sophisticated city, will make him happier and get him away from his father's iron grip. In return, Ken has had to promise that he will do nothing to damage the family's reputation. Hong Kong is a very cosmopolitan place, where Ken, if he's discreet — and he knows how to be — can live as he chooses. I think Mr. Chu believes that my presence will be supportive; he knows Ken can depend on my friendship."

"How do you feel about the location change?" Will asked.

"Happy. You know how vibrant it is. I love Hong Kong — and for reasons besides the shopping," she said with a sidelong glance at Figgy. "I have friends who live there, including an old prep school boyfriend who's become a big-time electronics entrepreneur. We hadn't been in touch for years, but I called him on one of my Hong Kong visits. Now we e-mail and talk on the phone fairly regularly."

"You didn't tell me a thing about him!" Figgy interrupted.

"There wasn't much time for girl talk in Hong Kong. I thought of whispering about him from behind the storage room door when you were playing sous chef, but I didn't think I'd have your full attention."

Figgy and Will laughed, her momentary annoyance at her friend gone.

"Now, would you open that present? I can't wait to see what Mr. Chu sent you."

She and Will watched while Figgy unwrapped the ribbon and carefully removed the box's lid. The three of them saw the plastic horse with its broken legs. Dangling from its neck was a jade necklace, each bead a luminous green. At its center was a prancing golden horse. Both Figgy and Tessa oohed with pleasure. Will rose, removed the necklace from its box and, standing behind

Figgy, placed it around her neck.

"It's magnificent," Tessa said. "What a memento of your visit here!"

"Please tell Mr. Chu that it's exquisite. I'll write to thank him when I get home." She paused, then added, "Tell him too that I intend to keep the plastic horse where I can look at it each day, to remind me to face up to challenges."

"Oh, no. I sense a lesson plan coming on," Tessa said.

"How would you use a broken plastic horse and some chopped bok choy as teaching tools?" Will asked.

"It's a challenge I'll think about on the trip home. And I'll get back to both of you on that."

Will and Tessa exchanged amused glances as they left the dining room.

ABOUT THE AUTHOR

Anne G. Faigen is the author of three historical novels for young people. She has taught American and English literature to high school and college students and has contributed columns and book reviews to a variety of publications. She also leads book discussion groups and works with student writers. Anne lives with her husband in Pittsburgh, Pennsylvania.

You can visit her Web site at:
www.annefaigenbooks.com

The employees of Thorndike Press hope you have enjoyed this Large Print book. All our Thorndike, Wheeler, and Kennebec Large Print titles are designed for easy reading, and all our books are made to last. Other Thorndike Press Large Print books are available at your library, through selected bookstores, or directly from us.

For information about titles, please call:
(800) 223-1244

or visit our Web site at:
http://gale.cengage.com/thorndike

To share your comments, please write:
Publisher
Thorndike Press
295 Kennedy Memorial Drive
Waterville, ME 04901

ORLAND PARK PUBLIC LIBRARY